A Worthy Woman

The Montford Cousins: Book 3

By

L.L. Diamond

A Worthy Woman
By L.L. Diamond
Published by L.L. Diamond
Copyright ©2023 L.L. Diamond

Cover and internal design © 2023 L.L. Diamond
Cover design by L.L. Diamond/Diamondback Covers
Cover photos: Red-haired girl in a ball gown with a fan in her hands on a sofa in a bright room by Evgeniya Fedorova Dramas courtesy of Shutterstock.

ISBN-13: 9781960057044

Facebook: https://www.facebook.com/LLDiamond
Instagram: @l.l.diamond
Twitter: @LLDiamond2
Blog: http://lldiamondwrites.com/
Austen Variations: http://austenvariations.com/

*"Is not general incivility the very essence of love? – **Pride and Prejudice**, Jane Austen*

Chapter 1

February 1813

With a heavy sigh, Nicholas Montford stared out across the Marquess of Ormonde's ballroom. The grand room boasted of glittering chandeliers, gilded plasterwork, and rich draperies bespeaking of the marquess's wealth. Every year, the Montfords attended the Ormonde's ball to commence the Season, but as the guests milled about the room, seeing and being seen by all and sundry, he bit back a groan. Why was he here once again? Nothing had changed.

Well, a great deal had changed to own the truth. His cousin Lizzy had married and in January, had given birth to a son, Alexander Hugh Nicholas Darcy, the heir to Pemberley. His sister, Amelia, had borne Sir Anthony a daughter, Isabella, who had besotted her father at the moment of her birth, if Nicholas's grandmother was to be believed.

His dissatisfaction this evening, and at every event of late, arose from the scene before him that played out over and over, Season after Season. The same daughters of the same peers vying for his notice, though none could compare to the lady he had once wanted—the lady who had crept into his heart at the impressionable age of thirteen. How she had managed it, he knew not since after the death of his parents, he had not sought those emotions but had been more likely to avoid any hint of an attachment.

"Good evening, Lord Hatton." He snapped from his reverie to Lady Ormonde standing at his side.

"Forgive me," he said. "I seem to have been wool-gathering."

"Think nothing of it, sir. I only wished to enquire of your sister. I had a short letter from her in early January, after her confinement, but nothing since. I assume she has been quite busy with the new baby and seeing to Dereham." Amelia had mentioned a budding friendship with the marchioness, but he had yet to see them together, particularly since the Greenes opted to forgo the Season this year.

"I have had but two letters since Isabella's birth, so you are likely correct in your assumption. The last, a fortnight ago, indicated she and Sir Anthony were very well as was the babe. Amelia claims Sir Anthony even holds his sleeping daughter while he attends to the business of the estate. Can you imagine?" What Nicholas would not give to witness that spectacle!

"How wonderful," said Lady Ormonde. "I am pleased for them both. I must say naming the baby after your mother was a lovely tribute. Bella was a beautiful lady with a disposition to match. I have never met one who equalled her in kindness."

Nicholas frowned. "I was unaware you were acquainted with my mother."

The lady smiled, yet it did not reach her eyes. "I am not surprised. You were young when your father and mother died, so you probably do not recall my visits, though I was present with your grandmother on the day of your birth. My husband and I are also your godparents. We oft times joined your mother and father for dinner on yours and later, your sister's birthdays. The two of you brought Bella and your father a great deal of joy. They were doting parents. I imagine much like your sister and her husband will be."

He had only a few remaining memories of his parents. So much had faded with time. To have Lady Ormonde speak so of their feelings upon his birth, made his throat close and his eyes burn, forcing him to blink and swallow hard.

"I am grateful to you for sharing your memories, my lady. I wish I could remember more of them." He cleared his throat.

"As I said, you were young, no more than five or six, when they died. I am certain your grandparents provided a home full of love, just as Bella and your father would have wanted. Should you ever want to speak of them, I would be pleased to do so. I have a few sketches and small paintings your mother gave me when we were in school together. Now that I consider it, you and Amelia should have some of them. I keep all but two packed in a trunk with my journals and other keepsakes."

"We would be honoured to have them. Thank you."

The marchioness gave a nod with a soft smile. "If you call on Monday, I shall have them ready for you. Now, if you will excuse me. I must return to my husband. I am grateful for your assurances of Amelia's and her family's good health."

"Of course, my lady."

The marchioness crossed the ballroom and leaned to whisper to her husband upon reaching the marquess's side. When Nicholas's gaze lit upon the couple to whom they spoke, his insides flipped and twisted in an unmerciful manner—the Duke and Duchess of Clarence. His gaze flitted from the duke to the duchess, who rested her hand in the crook of her husband's elbow. She could have been on Nicholas's arm, married to him, yet she had chosen the duke. His jaw clenched, and his teeth ground. She was bound to another man for the rest of her life. He gulped back the bile that had risen into his throat and turned his back on the sight of her.

He wove his way through the crush to where his grandparents stood near the doors to the terrace, watching his cousin Jane Montford stand up with...He peered into those dancing in the middle of the ballroom. Nicholas cringed. She stood up with the Earl of Portland. The earl was pleasant enough, though closer in age to his grandfather than to Janey. As much as he loved to tease his sister and cousins, he would never tease Janey about this particular gentleman. The poor man was searching out his third wife, after losing the first two to childbirth. Janey could not believe Portland worth her consideration, could she?

"Nicholas, I have yet to see you dance," said his grandfather, Lord Richmond.

"None of the ladies shoved before me have inspired me to do so."

"Nicholas," said his grandmother in a chiding tone. "Be charitable."

"Forgive me, Gran. I have merely grown weary of the Season and the campaigns waged by eligible ladies to ensnare a gentleman of means. The only worthy ladies to grace the Season in the last few years have been my sister and my two cousins, and I think of Janey as more of a sister than a cousin. I could never—" He shuddered.

His grandmother patted him on the arm. "You seek a lady of substance and education. Few are taught the importance of intelligence and are called bluestockings if they seek to be more. We cannot fault you for your feelings. They are just, and we would be overjoyed if you found a match based on respect and affection, but you must give some lady the opportunity to win your heart."

He gave one last perusal of the ballroom. "Forgive me, Gran, but I desire some air."

Grandpapa frowned. "Where will you go? Do not forget the freezing rain that was falling when we arrived."

"I am certain some room is free and empty of guests. Hopefully, the marquess will not mind me taking a moment for myself in one of them."

Once again, he wended his way through the guests, past the entrance to the card room, and down a corridor. When he opened the first door, a darkened library beckoned him to enter. With a sizeable exhale, he closed the door behind him and stepped over to the sofa before the glowing fire, sitting and resting his head in his hands. The blessed silence washed over him. What he would not do to leave the Season and this ridiculousness behind!

"How are you, Nicholas?"

His head shot up to Rebecca, who stood before him—nay, the Duchess of Clarence who stood before him. When had she entered? "Did you follow me?"

"When I had the first opportunity, yes." She was as beautiful as ever, with long flaxen tresses that, at one time, had reached her waist and had slipped like silk through his fingers.

He shook himself and stood. "For what purpose, may I ask? You were quite clear you were severing any ties between us when you wed the duke."

"You know I had no choice," she said, her eyes pleading.

"You had a choice. I begged you to elope with me, remember? You refused."

She stepped towards him. "The situation was impossible—as you are well aware. The contract was signed, and word had spread in London of the betrothal. The duke could have taken legal action

7

against you or my parents. My father's estate could not afford to pay the duke for the breach."

"I would have helped him. I told you as much."

Rebecca's hands fidgeted before her. "Can we not leave those arguments in the past? We can be together now. I have missed you. Have you not longed for me as well?"

Nicholas gave a bark. "You have missed *me*? And what role am I to play in your life now since I cannot play that of a husband? Friend? Acquaintance? Oh, wait, you said we could be together. You wish me to be your lover—awaiting your beck and call like a desperate schoolboy. Where should we have our assignations? Hatton House is let, so am I to lease a house in Mayfair or Belgravia for nothing more than a stolen hour here and there when we can meet." The venom never left his voice. He would keep his tone so, for he wished her nothing but away.

The duchess lunged forward and took his face in her palms, but Nicholas flinched from her and hastened back until he was near the fireplace. "Do not touch me, madam. You forfeited any right to do so when you wed your husband—nay, when you chose him over what we shared."

With glistening eyes, Rebecca's hands pressed together as she stepped forward. "Pray, why must matters between us be so—"

"Terse? Unfriendly?"

"Hostile," she said. "We loved each other."

"Yes, *loved*. You turned your back on those feelings three years ago and have not spoken to me in the time since. You have borne the duke's heir, and now, you are seeking me out? What conclusion would you have me draw from such behaviour? If you desire me as a lover, then you should find another to fulfil those needs; I shall not be taken in by you again."

"Nicholas—"

"No," he said, his voice tense and firm. "You will not address me so informally. You are not the girl who once promised she would never love another."

"I have held to that promise!" Rebecca stifled a sob. "I still love none but you while you stare at me across the ballroom as though you would prefer to see me dead. I gave you up to help my parents, though my father's habits prevented me from doing much. Why should we not be together now that we can—now that my husband has his own diversions? Do you not love me?"

He shook his head. "I am sorry if you do still hold such affections, but I shall not trifle with another man's wife."

"You had no qualms with taking my maidenhood."

A brittle laugh escaped before he could stop it. "Yes, well, I was young and stupid. I had not considered how succumbing would complicate matters. Not to mention, I had held fast to my hope you would journey with me to Scotland. Now that I know what you are about, your bed is a trap I shall avoid, even if I must chew off a limb in the process. I have no intention of failing my family or my grandfather. I must eventually marry and have my own heir. If I fall victim to your charms, I disappoint them all."

As the duchess stepped towards him once again, the door opened. "If you will pardon my interruption." Janey stood in the opening with her hands clasped in front of her. "Your Grace, I believe your husband is seeking you out."

Rebecca glanced at him. "Nicholas," she said weakly.

"Go." He ensured his voice gave no reprieve.

No sooner had the lady departed, than Janey rushed to him, swinging the door closed behind her. "What were you thinking?" she hissed. "How could you be alone with the Duchess of Clarence?"

"What do you mean?" He attempted to behave as if he were at ease, yet he was anything but. The muscles in his shoulders were so taut, they would surely snap if pulled tighter.

"After her confinement, Amelia asked me to keep a watchful eye on you and the duchess. She had her suspicions, rightly so it seems, that you still hold a tendre for the former Lady Rebecca."

He squeezed his eyes closed. Patience! He required patience! Amelia had his best interests at heart as did Janey. It would not do to become intemperate with his sensitive cousin. "Any affection I may have carried for the duchess died with her marriage to another. You and Amelia need not worry. Her Grace sought me out, and I intended to disabuse her of any notion of more. Since she wed, I have sought to purge her from my heart—"

"Which is often easier said than done," said Janey.

"I agree, yet it is done and done for the best."

"Is your heart truly rid of her, Cousin? Since Amelia requested I watch you, I have seen the way you look at her."

He squeezed his hand into a fist. "Janey, I am aware of my obligations. Those duties and roles I was born to assume prevent me from behaving in any way to shame this family. Again, you need not worry about me or what I may do. You must understand that the duchess returned to town last Season after the birth of her son. I had not seen her since a month before she wed. You and Amelia must give me time. I am still becoming accustomed to her presence."

"You are certain 'tis nothing more." Janey's eyebrows were high on her forehead and her pitch higher than was its wont.

"You have my word, Janey. Nothing will occur between the duchess and myself. I shall not allow it."

His cousin pressed her lips together with a nod. "I suppose that must do for now. Have you considered separating yourself from those events where you may be thrown into company together? Perhaps finding occupation away from the Season will be of aid."

"What am I supposed to do?" he asked in a growl. "Grandmamma is intent I should find a wife."

"Will you do so with Her Grace at every ball and rout? I believe her presence will accomplish the opposite. She will distract you. Seeing her so frequently will maintain that hold she has on part of your heart—that part you must free. Does one of the Richmond properties require your supervision or merely a visit? You would be free of the Season and Her Grace, and you may just gain some much-needed perspective."

Was there some way to relieve himself of these obligations? Janey was correct that he would not find any peace while Rebecca was seeking him out, regardless of her purpose.

"Nicholas?"

"I heard you." He scrubbed his face with his hands. "I had escaped to gather my wits and gain some equanimity before returning to the ball. It seems my efforts were in vain."

"I was wondering where you two had disappeared," said Gran as she entered, startling them. "The supper set is about to begin, and your partner is awaiting you with your grandfather, Janey." After one last glance at him, Janey hastened to return while his grandmother turned a knowing gaze in his direction. "Is aught amiss?"

"No, I am well, though I do believe I shall take the carriage back to Richmond House. I find I am fatigued, and my head is beginning to ache." After leaning down to kiss her cheek, he cleared his throat. "I shall send the carriage back for you, Grandpapa, and Janey."

As soon as he had seen his grandmother safely on the arm of his grandfather, Nicholas found the Richmond equipage down by the corner and after informing the driver of his plans, jumped inside and settled into the squabs.

He was fleeing, but he had no choice. Though he did not love Rebecca anymore—he could not love Rebecca—his anger towards her was as consuming as the tender feelings that once filled his heart. He had to distance himself. His life and his future depended upon it. He had no choice—no choice whatsoever.

Chapter 2

"Ireland!" Grandpapa's fork and knife clattered against his plate. "Are you mad? What would possess you to even consider a journey to Ireland at this time of year? Crossing the Irish Sea would be treacherous indeed."

"The viscountcy holds a property in County Antrim—"

"I know the Hatton holdings well, Nicholas, and if you feel seeing to the property in person is necessary, you can delay your trip until the weather warms." His grandfather spoke with an uncommon growl while Janey and his grandmother glanced back and forth between them.

"Certainly nothing could be of such importance that it cannot wait a few months," said Grandmamma.

Nicholas exhaled and gripped his utensils firmly, his hands had long since fallen so his wrists rested against the edge of the table. "Grandfather, I will go—"

"Perhaps you misunderstood my meaning, Nicholas. You will not go." Janey's head continued to turn back and forth as each person spoke, watching the entire scene unfold.

At his grandfather's edict, Nicholas stiffened. "You forbid me?" His grandparents had not forbidden him anything since he came of age. Why could they not trust his judgement?

His grandmother closed her eyes with a sigh. "If you would both—"

"You may be a grown man, son, but I am still head of this family and must act in a way I deem best for the survival of the earldom and our properties. Too many people rely on us for their livelihoods. We will not let them down."

"You believe I have not thought this through?" Did his grandfather believe him to be capricious?

"No, Nicholas, I do not. You have become increasingly intemperate these past few years, during the Season in particular, and now you desire to attempt a crossing to Ireland in the winter. A crossing is dangerous at any time, but to go now would be insupportable. I shall not pretend to understand your decision or your reasoning behind it. You will remain in England. If you must, return to Richmond Castle or hell, go to Mablethorpe." His grandmother and cousin gasped at his grandfather's uncharacteristic swear. "Go to the Hatton holding in Scotland or the Richmond holding in Wales. I care not which, but you *will not* journey to Ireland."

Nicholas clenched his knife and fork and prayed for patience. "I went through every Richmond and Hatton property, and Moydrum has had no one from the family attend it since my father visited when I was young. I would not expect you to make such a journey, and since I am able—"

Grandpapa levelled a steady gaze on Nicholas. "I would not object if it were late spring or summer when the seas are calmer. The crossing would be an easier journey and put you less at risk. We will not lose you too," said his grandfather weakly.

"Should I stay or should I go, you cannot control whether I live or die."

"You *will not* go." The definitive command of the Earl of Richmond brooked no opposition, and with the presence of the servants for dinner, Nicholas would challenge him no further. Not that he agreed with his grandfather's demand but arguing would serve no purpose here and now.

"I saw you speaking to the Marchioness of Ormonde," said Janey with a cheerful note to her voice. "I have spoken to her briefly during calls at Amelia's. She seems a genial lady once she relaxes."

Gran swallowed a sip of her wine. "Her sister did her no favours with society. The poor dear was considered tainted by the scandal of her sister, Lady Lincoln. When that lady appeared again last Season, I was concerned for Lady Ormonde—she was a great friend of Nicholas's mother as well as your mother, you know—but Lady Lincoln soon disappeared."

"Rumour indicated she fled England with the Duke of Cumberland's money," said Nicholas.

"Regardless of how or why, her departure was a blessing for her sister." Gran shook her head. "I was thankful for Lady Ormonde's presence when Anthony was injured by that horse last Season. I will be forever grateful she helped Amelia return him to Audley Place. Isabella would be pleased Lady Ormonde has taken Amelia under her wing."

"She mentioned to me her friendship with my mother," said Nicholas. "She offered me some of Mama's drawings and paintings. I had been unaware they were such great friends. Lady Ormonde mentioned she and the marquess are my godparents."

His grandmother nodded. "That is true, though they were busy with their own children for a time, then distanced themselves after her sister's scandal. They had no wish for others to be affected by the rumours."

"Are they also Amelia's godparents?" asked Janey.

Grandpapa made a disdainful sort of grunt. "No, your father and mother were. Bennet seemed to forget as he did so many things after Sophie's death."

"Oh, Janey, before I forget, Lizzybeth wrote that the Hursts returned to town last week. I thought to call on them tomorrow. Would you care to join me? After what occurred with Mr. Bingley, I shall understand if you do not."

His cousin gave a slight flinch at the mention of Mr. Bingley, but as soon as she swallowed her bite, she nodded. "I do want to join you. No matter what occurred with Mr. Bingley, he caused me no harm, and I am acquainted with them from Netherfield, so I do feel I should. Besides, I would adore seeing the baby if Mrs. Hurst will allow it." Janey was too good. Only she would still associate with the family of the gentleman who attempted to court her for her fortune or would want to see that man's young daughter.

"Well, now that is settled, I require a brandy. Nicholas?" Grandpapa stood, his expression still rather dark. He had not said all he desired on the topic of Ireland. Nicholas was certain of it.

With a deep inhale, he rose and followed his grandfather towards the study. How long before he could reasonably excuse himself and retire for the evening? If he confessed to what had occurred in the past between him and Rebecca, his grandfather would be appalled. All Nicholas could do was continue arguing of the necessity of the journey and hope his grandfather relented. He had no other options. He rarely lied to his grandparents, and though he had not told them the whole truth, he had not told a falsehood about Moydrum requiring his attention. Yes, he was running away, but what other choice did he have?

Nicholas alighted from the carriage and entered the inn. The innkeeper and his wife greeted him with a gracious welcome as they always did and showed him to the room he usually occupied when he travelled to Mablethorpe. The establishment was clean and comfortable, and the food was excellent, which was why he always returned.

His gut gnawed at him for not stopping at Pemberley. He was so close, after all, but Lizzy and Darcy could not be a party to his scheme. Yes, he journeyed towards Mablethorpe, a Hatton property in northern Wales, yet he had no intention of actually arriving there. In fact, this inn was where he would inform his driver of his true destination and divert his course.

Once he had refreshed himself and removed some of the dust from the road, he made his way to the common rooms but came to a sudden halt at a familiar face. "Darcy? How did you know I would be here?"

His cousin's husband shook his hand. "Your grandfather sent me an express. He wanted me to ensure you had no intention of changing your course."

"Why am I not surprised?" He almost groaned the words while motioning for Darcy to follow him to the dining room. "Come, you must join me for dinner."

"My meal will be awaiting me when I return to Pemberley, but I will have an ale while we talk."

Nicholas nodded, then they both requested ales of the maid who attended them without delay. "Are you to lecture me as my grandfather did?"

"Lecture you? No, I had not thought to do so. May I ask why you are so intent on Ireland? You could escape anywhere in England without taking the additional risk."

"You are convinced I am going?"

Darcy directed a heavy stare at Nicholas. "If you were simply travelling to Mablethorpe, you would have broken your journey at Pemberley. I see no other reason you have tried to avoid Elizabeth and me."

"I did not want Grandpapa to blame you for any part in my scheme."

Before he could answer, Darcy's chin hitched up and he waved his hand, making Nicholas glance behind him and exhale. "Really? Pray, tell me Greene did not drag Amelia from Dereham for this. 'Tis truly not necessary. I know what I am about."

"Is he whining like a child already, Darcy?" asked Sir Anthony Greene, who was married to Nicholas's sister, Amelia.

"Of course, he is." Darcy gave a crooked grin and motioned to the serving maid. "One more ale, and no matter what he tells you, this lout does not want food. He has no money anyway."

Nicholas scoffed and batted away Darcy's finger pointing in his direction. "I have already paid for my rooms, and my driver is in need of rest. I shall not be going anywhere."

Greene leaned back in his chair and crossed his arms over his chest. "Amy saw through your ruse, you know. From the letters she has received from your grandmother, grandfather, and Janey, she insisted you yielded to Richmond's demands too easily. She knows your demeanour quite well."

"As much as we have teased each other over the years, we spoke of more than idle chatter after our parents died." He took a draw from the glass that was set in front of him.

"She expects us to bring you to Pemberley," said Greene. "Do not make me disappoint my wife. I am certain she shall mount the first available stallion she finds and ride here to make her displeasure known should you refuse."

Nicholas propped his elbows on the table and rested his head in his hands. "I am in no mood for her reprimand as well."

"I do not believe she intends to deliver a rebuke. She is more worried than anything else and seeks reassurance that you are thinking your options through."

He stared at his brother for a moment. "So, you expect me to travel a few hours back to Pemberley?"

"Yes," said Darcy while Greene nodded. "We have my carriage outside with a fresh team. Your carriage with my horses will be brought to Pemberley on the morrow. When you are ready to depart Pemberley, you may use my carriage team, which you may swap for yours here. I shall have my stable hands fetch mine the day after."

Greene held up a finger before Nicholas could so much as open his mouth. "If the prospect of visiting Mrs. Darcy and Amy is not enough to persuade you, what of your new niece? Isabella has yet to meet her uncle. You would not want to snub your only niece."

"That is low," he said, laughing. "Isabella will never remember meeting me at this time. She is too young."

"I am certain Alexander would appreciate a visit from his favourite cousin."

Nicholas let out a great bark of amusement. "That was laid on with a trowel—by both of you. Very well. I can see that I shall receive no quarter until I agree, so pay for the ales and let us be gone." He rose from his chair. "I shall notify my servants."

His brother laughed as he stood. "What do you think I was doing before I entered? Your valet has your trunk strapped to the back of the carriage and will ride with Darcy's driver. Your driver and tigers will accompany your carriage and Darcy's horses to Pemberley tomorrow."

"I see you have thought of everything," said Nicholas. "I have no choice but to accede to your wishes."

"We were certain you would bow to our persuasion." Darcy wore that ridiculous grin he never failed to sport when he was correct. That countenance was truly insufferable.

"Yes, well, let us be off. I have been travelling all day and was anticipating my dinner and a warm bed, not being harangued by my sister and cousin."

After throwing a few coins on the table, Darcy joined them. "Yes, but you will have an excellent meal surrounded by your family, a hot bath if you desire it, which I imagine you will appreciate after three days of travel, and a warm, and likely more comfortable, bed than you would have here."

"I am not certain of that, Darcy. The Bell may not look like much, but I have yet to find an inn I prefer."

His cousin's husband clapped him on the back. "If I should have need to travel this way, I shall make a note of that."

True to their word, Darcy's equipage stood outside the inn with fresh horses and Evans, his valet, atop with the driver. Nicholas would have a word with him later. Evans was his servant. Darcy and Greene did not pay his wages, Nicholas did. Apparently, his man required that reminder.

When he climbed inside, he sank into the plush squabs and sighed. He was in no rush to reach Ireland, yet this delayed him by at least a week. Amelia and Lizzy would never allow him to depart after just one day at Pemberley. Yet, the situation could be worse. He could still be in London and attending many of the same events with Rebecca—no, the Duchess of Clarence.

Regardless of what they once were, he should never think of her with such familiarity again. He had held his anger and indignation for long enough. Part of his escape from all that was familiar was to release her and what she once represented. If he was to do so, he needed to begin anew—and needed to begin now.

Chapter 3

"**N**icholas!"

He braced himself when Amelia lunged at him and embraced him with a huge smile. As much as he had not wanted to put her and Lizzy in an awkward position with his grandfather, now that he was here, he could not bemoan the situation. Richmond Castle and House had been quiet since their marriages. He had missed them—not that he would admit it to them!

"Greene has been raving about your daughter since we entered the carriage, so I suppose I must see this most impressive child for myself. Where is she?"

Amelia laughed and wrapped her arm through his, leading him to the drawing room. "She is asleep in the nursery with Alexander at the moment."

Nicholas gave a slight lean towards his sister. "So, when are the marriage contracts to be signed? I am certain Darcy is eager to follow the footsteps of Lady Catherine by engaging the cousins in their cradles."

With a chuckle, Darcy took his wife's hand as they walked beside the pair with Miss Georgiana Darcy following on Greene's arm. "Bite your tongue, Hatton. While I would be pleased if Alexander chose Isabella as a bride, I shall let *him* choose. I believe we are far happier than those who marry to align families and estates."

"Yes, well, some may consider that you married a lady with fortune, Darcy, as did Greene. By the view of the marriage mart, you both made excellent matches."

"Even though Fitzwilliam did not realize Lizzy was a lady of standing when they met?" When he glanced over his shoulder, Miss Darcy's lip curved upward.

Lizzy's merry laughter filled the drawing room. "No, he did not, yet I bewitched him all the same."

"Is that what you were about when you argued with me at every turn?"

"Could you not tell?" Lizzy pursed her lips, prompting her staid husband to chuckle.

Upon entering the drawing room, Amelia and Greene sat side by side as did Lizzy with her husband while Miss Darcy excused herself to attend her studies. As soon as she departed, Nicholas returned his attention to the couples in the room. They were such examples of marital felicity. He had never been able to open his heart with ease. Moreover, he had never been certain how the duchess had wriggled her way inside, but somehow, she had managed the feat. A part of him hoped for a marriage with such happiness and love, but how could he achieve what was before him? What if he lost himself once again? He had lost too many who had held significant pieces of his heart.

"Sir," said the butler from the door, "your steward is in your study and requires a word."

Darcy groaned and stood. "Forgive me. Two tenants are squabbling over a tiny piece of land along the joined border of their plots, and I have been at my wit's end dealing with their ridiculousness."

"Would you care for another opinion? I had a similar situation at Dereham, even though the tenant allotments are clearly marked so they had little argument."

"They are laid out on a map here as well, but one is insisting the division is impractical and he should have the portion to make their allotments even. Never mind that the family with the larger plot of land has been farming on Pemberley for three generations." Darcy waved his hand. "I would welcome any advice you have. Come, let us leave Hatton to the ladies. Perhaps they may talk some sense into him without our presence."

Nicholas flinched. "I may have a valuable opinion on your problem." The last thing he wanted was to be interrogated by his sister and cousin!

"No, I believe a conversation with Amy and Mrs. Darcy may do you a world of good," said Greene. His brother gave him a wide grin before departing behind Darcy.

Lizzy rose as soon as the men departed. "I shall check on the children. Alexander should be waking at any moment."

"Lizzy, wait—"

With an amused glance over her shoulder, his cousin left him alone with his sister. What an unfeeling thing for a cousin to do! She demonstrated absolutely no mercy for the torture he would endure. Until Janey had mentioned Amelia's knowledge of his feelings for the duchess, he had no inkling she was aware of even a tendre on his part. As his sister levelled a look he knew well in his direction, he braced himself.

"I had a letter from Janey just before Grandpapa's arrived."

"I think I should like to refresh myself." His ruse would not work, but he had to try.

"No, Anthony said you had the opportunity to do so at the inn. I know you travelled two hours here, but I should prefer to speak to you now. Otherwise, you may sneak out of Pemberley before first light to avoid me."

"You know me too well, Sister."

"What were you thinking, Nicholas? Rebecca is married, not to mention has a small child."

He stiffened and faced Amelia. "I am quite aware of that fact, and if Janey told you all, she also said that the duchess followed me. I sought out a quiet room to escape the crush, and she entered bold as brass no more than five minutes after I sat before the fire."

"You could have left her there."

Nicholas shoved himself from the sofa and began to pace. "I had no desire to attend the Ormonde's ball and attempted to cry off, but Gran would not hear of it. You know she wants me to marry and keeps insisting for me to select a lady to court."

"But you are too enamoured of Rebecca to do so, and she has been present at most events since last Season."

He came to a sudden stop and pivoted to face his sister. "No, I am no longer enamoured of her."

"Nicholas," said Amelia in a drawn-out manner. "I have seen how you stare at her."

"I shall admit to you and only to you that I once had tender feelings for her, but those have long since been replaced with resentment and anger."

Amelia rested an elbow along the back of the sofa and lifted her eyebrows. "Why have you never told me what happened between the two of you?"

"Because I would never speak so with my younger—maiden—sister."

She made an unladylike noise through her nose. "As if I had never heard the gossip in town of the scandals. You had no need to tell me particulars—if what I am assuming is what occurred."

"What are you assuming?" He should have never said "maiden."

"You and Rebecca were on more intimate terms than an infatuation. You bedded her." She spoke so matter-of-factly. Not one hint of trepidation or bashfulness accompanied her statement.

Nicholas raked a hand through his hair. "I wanted to marry her. Although I am uncertain when she first entered my heart, I suppose I saw the beauty she was becoming when I came home from Eton at thirteen. If you remember, our families spent the summer together, picnicking and such."

"As we did for the next five or six years," said Amelia. "That last year, when you came home from Oxford, I do recall that the two of you would disappear to collect strawberries during our picnics."

"I kissed her while picking strawberries that summer, confessed my feelings, and begged her to be mine." He could not look at Amelia while he made such confessions, so he stared into the fire.

"What did Rebecca say?"

"She was in love with me too and accepted my hand. I had intended to approach her father before they departed for their estate in Wiltshire, but a few days later, she found me while I was out on an early morning ride. We were along the north edge of the Richmond lands."

"Where the hunting lodge sits."

He nodded, picked up the poker, and jabbed it into the flames. "She was frantic and in tears. The Duke of Clarence had been visiting for the past week. He had formalised an agreement with the earl to wed her. Apparently, he and her father had been planning the union for some time. I begged her to elope with me. We hid the horses in the small enclosure behind the hunting lodge and went inside to talk. Every entreaty I made for her hand, she only sobbed harder and shook her head. The marriage contracts had been signed you see."

Amelia squeezed her eyes closed for but a moment. "So, the duke could take legal action against her parents and you if the two of you made for Gretna Green—not including the scandal that would occur."

After a sigh, he faced his sister. "Her father had invested a sum in a mine in Surrey. The man who approached him and several other gentlemen to back his venture was a fraudsman[1] who took the funds he was given and fled. The mistake forced the earl to retrench a year after his daughter's marriage."

"I remember."

"I suppose she told him of her feelings for me, so her father told her of his indebtedness. She felt she had no choice. The next thing I knew, her lips were on mine, and well..."

Amelia's eyes widened. "I hope the duke did not notice on his wedding night."

He shrugged with his hands and shoulders before dropping his hands back against his thighs. "I know not. She only mentioned her husband now has other diversions, and she wished   "

"To keep you as her lover?" Amelia blew out a heavy breath. "I would have never thought that of her, but I suppose if she is unhappy enough—"

"I refused her, of course. After she wed, it was a while before I stopped missing her, and when I heard of the birth of her son, I

---

[1] Fraudsman (1610) An earlier form of fraudster. From OED: https://www.etymonline.com/word/fraudster#etymonline_v_33374

somehow purged the last of those feelings. Now that she has returned, I do not know what has happened to me. I cannot cease staring at her, though I swear to you I am not in love with her."

"You keep saying that, but I believe your anger and resentment are what have become of your love for her. It simmers just below the surface, and I cannot blame you for attempting to distance yourself. I was in love with Anthony my first Season but learnt to bury my feelings when nothing came of the attachment. Once my heart accepted that I could trust him, my love was set free."

"I do not want her anymore, Amelia, but I cannot look at another while she is there."

His sister shook her head. "I can understand."

He studied her for a moment. "'Tis why you had those ridiculous excuses for never allowing another to court you, is it not?"

She laughed and crossed her arms over her chest. "I was a silly goose, was I not?"

With a huff, he dropped upon the sofa and leaned his head against the back. "Even if the duke somehow died and she was free, I still would not want to be with her. When I read the notice of her marriage, I was done with her.

"You retreated to Mablethorpe." She gasped, and he turned to look at her. "That is why you want to go to Ireland."

"Yes," he said. "I want to go where she does not haunt some corner or bring some unbidden memory to mind. Father wrote often of Moydrum and the Irish countryside in his journals, and I want to see it."

"We remember so little of him and Mama. I suppose I cannot blame you for that, but I do wish you had chosen a less dangerous time to travel. Anthony says the seas can have violent storms this time of year."

He rested his head on his hand. "You will not stand in my way?"

With a steady gaze, she held his eye. "No. While I understand Grandpapa's demands and concerns, your future is dependent upon your gaining your peace of mind. I think that takes precedence, regardless of the needs of the earldom. My grandparents are also terrified of losing us. When I was in my confinement with Isabella, Grandmamma was what I needed, but at times, she held me so tightly. They lost both of their children and our mother. I do not know how they would survive losing one of us—"

"This sounds remarkably like guilt, Amelia."

"No, I just believe I understand why Grandpapa is so adamant about you not going."

"I never misunderstood our grandfather's argument, but I cannot abide by it. While I have no want of accepting the Duchess of Clarence's charms, I cannot deny she still affects me, no matter how much I desire matters to be otherwise. I cannot risk being drawn into a situation with no happy resolution for either of us."

"Would you care for my opinion?"

He chuckled and dropped his head back to its previous position. "Do I have a choice?"

"Do not worry over our grandfather's reaction if you depart for Ireland from here. The Darcys and Anthony and I can manage Grandpapa. We shall also stand behind your decision. You need to find a lady worthy of your love, which you will not do while the duchess is always present."

"You are speaking for Darcy and Lizzy as well? Does your husband even know what you have just promised?"

"Without giving names or particulars, I told Fitzwilliam and Lizzy that you hold a tendre for a lady that cannot be reciprocated. Fitzwilliam knows enough of loving someone he thought he could not have, Anthony wished to court me for years before he finally made his intentions known, and Lizzy desires nothing more than for you to be happy, which you have not been in some time—not truly. You could not have a more sympathetic group supporting you."

His eyes burned as he blinked to keep the sting at bay. "I appreciate all of you."

"So, we make arrangements for your journey from here. My husband will be of aid to you as will Fitzwilliam, who made mention of travelling to Ireland when he was younger. When all is prepared, you will depart from here. Agreed?"

"Agreed." He had to admit remaining at Pemberley until he needed to board a ship was infinitely preferable to the alternative. He took his younger sister's hand and squeezed. "Now, can we speak of anything else? How about this astounding young lady you bore? I keep hearing such raptures of her, I am beginning to think she is a figment of our grandparents' and Janey's imagination."

They spoke of random matters for a short time before a knock came from the door and a maid peeked inside. "I beg your pardon, mistress, but the young miss has awakened and does not seem inclined to go back to sleep."

"Come in, Georgette," said Amelia as she sat up. "Is she hungry?" The girl Nicholas had believed to be the maid stepped inside, revealing herself to be the nurse.

"She has not fussed as yet, but I am certain she will make her demands known soon. At the moment, she is quite alert, though." Once the babe was in Amelia's arms, she gazed down upon the small child with an expression he had never before witnessed upon his sister's countenance—pure unadulterated love and happiness. A part of his heart settled at the sight. With the forced nature of her marriage, her contentment had been a great cause for concern. He could not have asked for a more perfect gentleman for her to wed. Greene was the best of men.

As soon as the nurse departed, Amelia turned with a beatific smile. "Since you returned to London before her birth, may I present Miss Isabella Greene."

He took in the two-month-old infant for a moment, her grey-blue eyes watching him with an expression that made him squirm. Could she see into his soul? "She is a beautiful child, but what does she know that makes her upbraid me so with her quiet stare?"

Amelia laughed. "Do not be ridiculous. She has started following people with her eyes, so I am certain she is fascinated by no more than a new face." Isabella's tiny fist pumped, and a crooked grin stole over her countenance.

"She is laughing at me already," he said. "She will certainly fit in with the Montfords."

"Here, you must hold her." His sister began to settle the babe in his arms.

"I know naught of babies, Amelia. What if I drop her?"

"You must learn, Uncle Nicholas. Now, support her head." She lifted his elbow a hair as Lizzy entered with her own bundle and began to chuckle.

"Well done, Amelia. He will make an excellent nurse. I am certain of it." Both of them began tittering away as he sighed. Perhaps Pemberley was not the perfect place for him to stay after all.

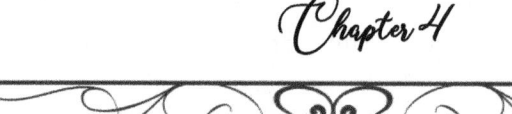

Chapter 4

<u>Early March 1813</u>

His mount's hooves pounded the earth as Nicholas galloped across the field and towards a sloping rise. Even with the cold weather and the thin layer of pristine snow across the ground, what little grass poked through appeared green—an oddity in March, to be sure.

The innkeeper at the last stop had given him the direction to Moydrum's lands, so this afternoon, as soon as the weather had warmed enough to tempt him to ride, he set out on horseback, eager to see for himself what his father had written of with such fondness. His father had been taken by Ireland and had always hoped to return with his wife and children, except he had never lived to carry out his plans. As Nicholas rode closer and closer to Moydrum, a restlessness inside him settled for the first time in years. He was finally here.

When he passed through the gates of the estate, Nicholas gave the horse his head to explore some of the countryside before he approached the house and introduced himself to the housekeeper. With ease, he jumped a dry fence at the base of the rise and began to draw back on his steed's reins at the sight of another horse and rider ahead of him. Whoever was on his lands wore a long cape, covering their head, and galloped as though they were being chased. No steward would be dressed so. No one who belonged on Moydrum would cover themselves as this person had, would they? Who the devil was trespassing on his property?

Without further consideration, he urged his horse to gallop, but as he did so, the rider disappeared around a bend of trees. Nicholas pressed the gelding forward, rounding the corner. After a moment or two, the rider glanced behind him, then urged their mount faster, making Nicholas hold his breath as the stranger took the next turn. He tugged the left side of his reins to follow, not slowing as he took the well-worn path. Before he could get the rider in his sights, a solid, sharp blow smarted across his chest and shoulders as his mount continued forward and he flew free of the saddle. At his contact with the unforgiving ground, the breath was forced from his body with a massive "whoosh."

Nicholas gasped and rolled to his side while he struggled to catch his breath. Blast that hurt! As he began to drag himself to a seated position, the cloaked figure stood before him, his hood pulled down— no, *her* hood pulled down and her long, vibrant red tresses escaping their pins and falling about her shoulders. In her hand, she held a small pistol pointed straight at his chest. The mysterious rider was a woman? Good God, a stunning woman at that. He clamped his jaw shut to keep from gawping.

"What do you mean to be doing, trespassing on Lord Hatton's land?" She held the gun steady without one sign of nerves or trepidation while her emerald eyes upbraided him. By her steady hand with her weapon, she had handled one before if he had to guess.

"*I* am Viscount Hatton. These are *my* lands," he finally managed. He could hardly speak as he was still struggling to catch his breath.

"I have met Lord Hatton, and you are not him."

He frowned and pressed a hand to the back of his neck before looking up to a tree limb still swaying above him. He choked out a chuckle. "You pulled back the limb and released it, did you not?"

Her chin hitched up a hair. "Seemed the best way to stop you from chasing me."

She had used her intelligence to great effect, delivering him a heavy blow and unseating him from his mount. He would be devilishly sore on the morrow. "While I appreciate your defence of my lands, I should like to know the identity of the dog who attacks wary travellers by day—or do you do so by night as well?"

She flicked the pistol at him. "It is no matter who I am. You have not answered my question."

"As I told you before, my name is Nicholas Montford, Viscount Hatton. These are my lands."

The young woman straightened and relaxed a mite. "Nicholas Montford? Viscount Hatton is James Montford."

He dragged himself up to his hands and knees and sat back on his boots. Lord, but he hurt! "James Montford was my father. He and my mother died in a carriage accident twenty years ago. I assumed the title with his death, though I had no understanding of what that meant at the time. I would give up the title happily for one more moment with him."

Her vivid green eyes narrowed. "No, I do not believe you. 'Tis a heartfelt story, but you are surely lying so I let down my guard. Tell me the truth, or I will..." As she said the last in her thick accent, the small pearl-handled pistol shifted to aim between his legs. "So, who are you?"

One hand covered the sensitive region while he held the other one up, palm towards her. "What do I have to gain from lying to you? I cannot be poaching as I have no gun or weapon with which to hunt.

If I had set traps previously, would I be able to collect any game alone and with only a single horse? If you look, I have naught to aid in that endeavour." His pitch had reached a level never heard before from him. He was in danger of squeaking it was so high. If only she would take her aim from his nether regions!

She glanced over her shoulder but back at him with haste. "What of your saddlebags?"

"I left ahead of the carriage carrying my valet and my trunk. Within those bags are nothing more than a change of clothing. If you wish to rifle through my small clothes, then do as you will." If she would aim at his manhood, then he would do his best to discomfit her too.

Her cheeks pinked, and she opened her mouth once or twice. "Quite impertinent for a stranger, are you not?"

He let out a bark and gave her a cursory glance from head to toe. Whomever this spitfire was, she came from means. Aside from the pearl-handled gun, she was well-dressed. Her cloak was of a heavy grey wool and a glistening yellow jewel peeked from the fastening. She was a gentleman's daughter. He was certain of it—though a hoyden if he ever saw one.

"Impertinent? Me? One could say the same of you—taking down the owner of the estate with a limb and questioning him at gunpoint. You must have a bevy of callers at your doorstep."

The woman gasped. "That is none of your affair."

Having recovered most of his breathing, Nicholas stood and brushed off his breeches, wobbling on his feet. If she had not removed his balls with a bullet by now, it was unlikely she would. She was amusing, to say the least, but he was already aching. He had no desire to remain on his knees arguing with this woman for the remainder of the day. A hot bath and a warm fire would at least do a little to put

35

him to rights. "Enough of this. How old are you? Twenty? One and twenty? You have never met my father. You are not old enough. Now, away with you, else I shall call on *your* father when I discover his identity and tell him of what you have done."

"Unlike you, I do have permission to ride here." Her voice had turned somewhat brittle. Was she doubting her earlier conviction?

He rested his hands on his hips. "I should like to know from whom."

Her eyes darted down to his greatcoat, which was open at the front to reveal his travelling clothes. She pressed her lips together and darted for her horse, mounting as deftly as any man in a great hurry and racing away. Was she riding astride?

When he looked about him, the horse he had been riding was gone. Blast! With uncertain steps, he turned in a circle until he saw a glimpse of stone between some trees and began walking...nay, hobbling. Without a mount, he could not give chase, so he may as well find the great house.

He had never been so relieved to see his destination as he was when after a half-hour of walking, the trees cleared and Moydrum sat proud and tall in a level valley surrounded by rolling hills and fields as well as a sizeable pond.

Lord but his chest and buttocks smarted. She was not a petite lady, by any means, and may have stood two or three inches shorter than his six feet, but he still would not have expected her to deliver such a decisive blow.

She was certainly a puzzle to be solved, however. Who was she? Who was her father and his estate? And, most importantly, why did she have such a protective attitude towards his lands?

Those questions ran over and over in his mind as he made his way to the great house. What he had thought was a chimney proved to be no more than part of the old house—or perhaps he should call it a castle, for that was what it was. His father had never mentioned that in his journals.

As he approached, no one was outside, so he rapped upon the door with the knocker. After two or three attempts, a slender, older lady opened the door. "I thought I heard somethin' when I was passing. Forgive me if you have been waiting." She poked her head outside. "Are you on foot, sir?"

He closed his eyes and prayed for patience before opening them once more. He seemed to do that often of late. "Yes, I am on foot. I am Viscount Hatton. I had chosen to come early and on horseback, but I seem to have met with an accident. May I come in?"

The lady flinched and opened the door. "Oh, how foolish of me, but if you will forgive me, we were not expecting you so soon after the snow. You must have journeyed through."

When he stepped into the hall, he had to pause. The stone walls and pillars were carved and arched over a wide staircase that led to the upper floors. He lifted his eyebrows. The lavish interior was not to be expected when one approached from the outside.

"I was rather eager to arrive. I must admit I have grown weary of inns and ships."

"Well, we will ensure you are made comfortable at Moydrum. May I say how sorry I was to hear of your father's passing? If we had known, we would have hung a hatchment over the door and laid out the house for mourning."

He shook his head. That explained a great deal about the events of today. "I was young, so I do not know what word was sent and when it was received. I apologise for any oversight. You were not meant to be excluded; I am sure of it."

The lady gave a wave of her hand. "Oh, I never meant to imply we were. I only wish to express my condolences now that I can. I was but a young maid here when he visited, but he was quite handsome and very kind. If I am not too bold, you resemble him a great deal."

Nicholas attempted a smile, though it surely came out rather tight. "Thank you. Speaking of his death, I assume no one in the neighbourhood would have been notified either, then?"

She shook her head. "No, I doubt they were." After almost startling, she pressed a hand to her chest. "Oh, where is my head? I am Mrs. Murphy, the housekeeper. Forgive me for not introducing myself properly."

"I am not offended, but my journey ended with a shock, to say the least, so if I could sit down, I would greatly appreciate it."

"Oh, of course, sir." Her gaze roamed over him. "I say, sir. Did you take a fall?"

He dropped into a chair in the hall, wincing at the frisson of pain that shot up his back. "Of sorts. A young woman removed me from my horse with the swing of a tree limb. Whomever the chit was, she informed me in no uncertain terms that I am not Lord Hatton, and that I was not welcome on my lands."

Mrs. Murphy gave a slight titter before covering her mouth. When she dropped her hand, she fought a smile from overtaking her expression. "Would the lass boast of red hair and be riding like a banshee leading the hounds of hell through the fields?"

"That is a fair description."

The housekeeper tsked with a sigh, though her amusement never left her countenance. "That would be Lady Fiona Fitzgerald, the only daughter and child of the Earl of Kildare. She is as headstrong and wild as a March hare, and her father indulges her."

"Lady Fiona?" The horse she had been riding was indeed a fine specimen, but he would not have thought her the daughter of an earl, even with the heavy, well-crafted wool of her cape. She deported herself like no lady of means he had ever met. Perhaps a lower gentleman or country squire, but not as the daughter of a peer.

"I wager, sir, you will meet the earl before long, particularly when word reaches him through his daughter. He and your father spent a great deal of time together when your father visited Moydrum all those years ago. Lookin' at you, you must have been quite young when he was here."

"I believe I was three. My sister was born in the year after he returned."

"I am sure you are correct, sir. I remember he arrived early summer but left before winter set in, eager to return to his wife and son."

"May I ask the age of Lady Fiona? She seems young to know what my father looked like, much less that I am not him."

Mrs. Murphy's eyebrows drew down a little. "She was too young to remember him, that is correct, but she and her father visit from time to time to ensure the steward is managing well enough. Your father has a portrait hanging in the gallery. Lady Fiona has walked past it on more than one occasion."

Nicholas glanced around as though he would see the image at any moment. "He does? How have I never heard of this Lord Kildare checking up on the estate?" Why would the steward not make mention of it?

"As I said, the earl and your father enjoyed each other's company a great deal and spent many evenings talking. I am not one to spread the business of others, but the earl's wife had run away not long after the birth of his daughter." Mrs. Murphy practically whispered the words in her thick brogue. "The earl was quite lonely, as was your father without you and your mother."

"His wife ran away?" Why did he sound more like a confused child rather than the grown man he was? Though at the moment, one could say he resembled more of the gossips of London.

"Yes, they said she was quite sad after the birth of little Fiona. Not even a half-year after the little lass was born, Lady Kildare disappeared—had run off with a young man from a nearby village. Broke the earl's heart, she did."

He made to stand with a groan. "If I could see my rooms and have that bath you offered, I would be most grateful."

As he began to shuffle towards the stairs, the housekeeper bustled after him. "Are you sure I should not send for the apothecary? We have no physician or surgeon close by, but Mr. Ryan the apothecary in Ballymena is as skilled as they come."

"No, I merely had the wind knocked out of me. I shall be well— probably bruised, but no more, I expect."

Mrs. Murphy chattered on as they made their way to the top of the stairs and a long corridor lined with windows came into view, several portraits visible on the far end. As he started in that direction, she stepped up beside him. "That be the gallery, sir. See, and your father is there, in pride of place. Perhaps we should have your portrait painted to hang alongside him."

His breath caught in his chest when he set eyes upon a countenance he knew better from portraits than from memory. He shared the same sandy brown hair and green eyes as his father while Amelia seemed to have their grandmother's hair colour and her mother's eyes. While not particularly sad, his father was rather straight-faced as he posed. "Was this painted while he was here?"

"Oh, yes, sir. Your grandfather, from what I am told, insisted a likeness of him belonged here. As you can see, your grandfather's portrait hangs on that wall and was also painted when he visited as a young lad."

The image of his grandfather was not difficult to find. While he had changed over the years, Nicholas had seen more than one of Grandpapa's younger portraits to know it was him—even without the similarities between the earl, his father, and himself. If Grandmamma was to be believed, their voices held a similar timbre as well.

"Come, sir," said Mrs. Murphy. "Let us get you cleaned up, and I'll have Cook make some willow bark tea for you. That will be of help for that stiffness."

"Thank you, but I shall require a sizeable amount of honey to get down the willow bark, especially if the cook here makes it as strong as Mrs. Brewer at Richmond Castle."

"If I had to guess by the bloody colour, I believe it likely she does."

He swallowed hard. A brew that shade would be bitter and stronger than Mrs. Brewer's. "Pray, bring the honey."

The housekeeper nudged him with her elbow. "Perhaps a bit of whiskey might help the tonic go down better than honey."

He could not help but let one corner of his lips curve upward. "I believe we shall get on well, Mrs. Murphy."

The housekeeper scoffed. "I do not know why you would doubt it in the first place."

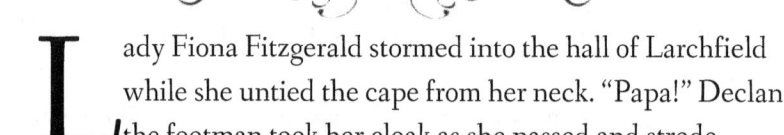

Chapter 5

Lady Fiona Fitzgerald stormed into the hall of Larchfield while she untied the cape from her neck. "Papa!" Declan the footman took her cloak as she passed and strode straight to her father's study. She entered without knocking.

Her father was grimacing when she came to a halt in front of his desk. "Good God, Fee. You would think I was deaf by that caterwauling. What is it that has you bellowing in the house? You know I would prefer you to bellow out of doors." He gave his usual crooked grin that always followed one of his pitiful attempts at humour. As if she would spend her time out of doors bellowing. She was not uncouth!

"Well, pardon me for believing you might want to know that I just met a man claiming to be Viscount Hatton on the Moydrum estate." She turned to depart, though he would not let her get far. She had not gone straight to him for no reason.

"What did you say?"

With a smile, she pivoted back around and crossed her arms over her chest. "Oh, so now you are interested?"

He exhaled and let his hands drop to his desk. "Of course, I am interested...when you speak like a lady, that is." He shook his head. "I should have listened to the nurses and governesses I hired. They all told me I indulged you, but I could not believe spending time with you as I did would lead to a daughter who would prefer to shoot with the men than have tea with the ladies in the drawing room. Heaven forbid someone ask you to do needlework. They may not survive the request."

"I am perfectly capable of serving tea and acting as hostess, Papa. Now, do you want to know of the man I encountered or not?"

"Fee," said her father with a downcast expression. "As much as Lord Hatton and I were friends when he was here, he did not maintain our correspondence. I ensure Moydrum prospers out of respect and courtesy because I promised and because I still consider him a dear friend. Regardless, I would never presume he would want to become reacquainted. He never sent word of his plans to travel, so I shall await an invitation."

Fiona pinched the bridge of her nose. Patience! "Papa, it is impossible for this man I saw to be Lord Hatton. He is far too young."

Her father's forehead furrowed. "Too young? How old would you believe him to be?"

She narrowed one eye a bit and bit her cheek. He was young but had surely finished university. "I did not ask, but perhaps between five and twenty and thirty."

Her father set his pen on its stand and began to tap his fingers on his desk. "Describe him."

She sort of flinched at the sharpness of his request. "Well dressed, sandy brown hair, green eyes."

"And he claimed himself to be Lord Hatton?" Her father dropped back into his chair. "What could have happened to Hatton and when?"

"What?" said Fiona in a higher tone. "You believe him to be the viscount? Your friend Lord Hatton would be closer in age to you, not the same age as this lout—whomever he is?"

"James Montford, Viscount Hatton when I knew him had a son who was two or three years old named Nicholas."

She scratched the side of her neck. "Nicholas?" Her voice was weak, but was not that the name of the man she knocked from his horse?

Her father turned his head slightly and regarded her with a wary eye she knew well. "Yes, Nicholas. Why?" He drawled out the words, making her stomach tighten.

"Well, um, the lout may have said his name was Nicholas Montford."

The earl scrubbed his face then let his hands slide down, pulling the skin some with the movement. "Dare I ask how you came to speak to him? You said he was riding on Moydrum lands."

Fiona turned her attention to the toe of her boot. "He was."

Her father cleared his throat. "Fee?" She detested when he said her name in that long, drawn-out way.

"I may have knocked him from his horse with the branch of a tree."

"Fiona Máiréad Eileen Fitzgerald, you knocked a man off his horse?"

"I turned into what you always told me was a fairy wood and grabbed the branch I usually duck under." Her father nodded and waved his hand for her to get on with it. "When I had pulled the limb as tight as I could, I released it, allowing it to swing back and hit him in the chest."

Her father shot to his feet. "You could have killed him!"

"I thought he might be poaching." The excuse sounded pathetic to her too at this moment, but she could not change what had passed.

With an odd inaudible noise, her father dropped back into his chair, and his forehead dropped upon his desk with a thud before he lifted it once more. "Tell me. Was he carrying a weapon?"

"Well, no." She stuck her thumbnail between her teeth and began to chew with vigour. Should she tell her father she was carrying her pistol, and that she had aimed it at the man?

"Fee, I love you with my every breath, but at times, I could..." He sighed. "You are too headstrong. Of all the stubborn and foolhardy things you have done, I believe this is the maddest. What if you had killed the poor man? What if he is grievously injured?"

"I do possess some intelligence, Papa. I knew it would not hit him in the head."

"Good Lord." He rose and began to pace back and forth behind his desk. After a glance at the clock, he stopped before the window where the sun was already beginning its descent. "'Tis too late to call on our neighbour, particularly under the circumstances, but we shall do so on the morrow. I shall discover what became of my friend, God rest his soul, and *you* will apologise."

She stiffened. "I was merely trying to help."

He faced her and pointed at her chest. "Be that as it may, you knocked the young viscount from his horse without learning his identity first."

"Would you prefer I introduced myself to a strange man on horseback and enquire of his identity when he is chasing me across the Moydrum lands?"

"No!" Her father slammed his fist on the desk. "I would prefer you ride with a groom as I have requested, nay ordered, repeatedly. I would prefer if you saw a strange man riding on Moydrum, you inform Mr. O'Shea or me and allow us to identify him. You are a lady, Fiona. You may be the heiress of Larchfield, but you behave as if you were born a son."

"I had no need for a groom as I had my pistol. And, no, I am not a son, but I must bear one for the sake of the earldom," she said in a bitter tone. "I must marry some poor sop and have his child and be under his control for the rest of my life. I have told you I shall not do it, and I mean what I say. I like my life as it is. I shall never marry and give away my independence. I should rather die."

A weary exhale left her father before he rubbed his eyes with his fingers. "Yes, so you have said over and over again. I can still hope some gentleman will appear who can manage your temper and maybe even soften it a little."

"Papa!"

"Pray, Fee, no more. I am now fairly certain my good friend died without my knowing, and I wish to have a drink in his honour. Would you join me? Perhaps I could fetch you some wine."

She stared at her father. How many times would he ask her the same question in the same hopeful tone? "Wine is to be drunk with dinner. I shall join you for the whiskey." He never drank wine other than with his meals. Why should she behave any differently?

He held out his arm. "One day—"

"You taught me to favour whiskey. 'Tis your own fault."

"Aye, but if only I could repair what I have wrought." Her father shook his head.

"I see nothing objectionable."

"Of course, you would not," he said dryly.

Nicholas stretched and groaned at the soreness of his chest and the stiffness in his back. Once upon a time, he could fall from his horse at breakneck speeds and not feel more than a sting upon impact or perhaps suffer from a slight bruise. It seemed being thrust from a horse by a swinging branch at six and twenty had an entirely different effect.

He shifted again. "Damn." He pressed his hand to his forehead while he contemplated the best way to rise.

"Good morning, sir," said the familiar voice of Evans, his valet. "Cook and Mrs. Murphy sent me up with some willow bark tea in case you required it, which by that moaning and groaning, I would say you are."

"A mad woman hit me with a swinging tree branch and knocked me from my horse. All I can say is I was not expecting such a blow when she rode around that bend—not that I could tell she was...well, a *she* at that moment." After a sizable and rather painful inhale, Nicholas sat up all at once, letting the sheet fall and cover him at his waist. Evans had not arrived by the time he had finished his bath, so the man who had assisted him the night before had found an old banyan in the dressing room that Nicholas wore until he went to bed. Regardless, he had never been fond of a nightgown while he slept. He was always too hot when he wore one and they wrapped around his legs, trapping him and making it impossible to sleep.

"Sir!"

When Nicholas looked at Evans, the man was staring at his chest with wide eyes. Following Evans's line of sight, he found a black and blue mark across his chest from the base of his ribs on his right to his armpit on his left. It was no wonder he had no desire to move.

"Did they send for a physician?" Had Mrs. Murphy not mentioned that to his valet? It seemed off for a woman who seemed to speak so freely the day before.

"An apothecary is the closest. Despite my claims that I had no need of the man, they sent for him. He said I may have a broken rib or three, but he thought they were more likely bruised, and to take care. I cannot ride for a few weeks, so I suppose I shall spend my days in the study with the steward, acquainting myself with the particulars of the estate."

Evans handed him a glass. "I was told this is willow bark tea, though it looks nothing like what the cook makes at Richmond Castle."

After two glasses the evening before, the ingredients were no mystery. "The housekeeper let it cool and added whiskey." He let the mixture slide down his throat, then handed the empty glass back to Evans, who stared at it as though it was poison. "The addition does make it more palatable."

"But will you be able to walk straight or conduct your business?"

"At this moment, I care not," said Nicholas with a grimace. He could not even laugh without pain.

Evans aided him in donning his breeches, boots, and a shirt, but when it came to the waistcoat, he grabbed his valet's wrists to stop him. "For the love of God, pray, no more. If I offend the sensibilities of the servants by walking around the house in my shirtsleeves, then so be it, but trussing me up in such tight-fitting clothing only causes me more pain."

"Perhaps you should rest for the day, sir."

"No, I did not come here to lay about." He closed his eyes and breathed. "Forgive me for my sharp tone."

The valet sighed and removed the waistcoat with care. "Perhaps if the waistcoat remains unbuttoned?"

"No, where is that banyan from yesterday? I shall wear that."

"Banyan?" Evans's voice was high. "You never wear banyans."

"Without other options, I gave in last night. Today, it seems the best course if I want to leave these rooms." In all fairness, they were not bad rooms, but Nicholas had never taken to being confined. Evans had been his valet since he first had need of one. His man should know his disposition well by now.

The willow bark seemed to have had some effect by the time Nicholas made his descent into the hall and glanced around. "Sir, if you are desiring the breakfast room, 'tis through there," said a footman who entered on some duty or another.

"Thank you."

Before he could depart, a loud rapping came from the door, and since the footman was presumably the closest, he opened the door. "Good morning, Lord Kildare. Are you in need of Mr. O'Shea? I can fetch him for you."

"No, I heard the most alarming news yesterday and hurried over to see if it was true."

Nicholas took a few steps back towards the centre of the room, allowing himself to be seen by the gentleman at the door.

"Good heavens," said the man with wide eyes. The footman moved to the side to allow the gentleman to enter and stand directly before Nicholas. "You are the very spit of your father." He shook himself and bowed, as though he suddenly realised his manners. "Pray, forgive me. I am Seamus Fitzgerald, the Earl of Kildare, and your closest neighbour. My estate Larchfield is but a few miles east of here. Your father and I were friends...for a time."

Nicholas began to lean forward a hair to return the bow, but the stiffness of his back somehow warned him to go no further. "I hope you will forgive me as well, my lord. Due to a fall from my horse yesterday, I fear bowing is beyond my capabilities this morning."

"Yes, my Fee told me of her actions."

"Fee?"

"Yes, my daughter Fiona. May I offer my most heartfelt apologies for her behaviour. I was appalled when she told me of what she did. Unfortunately, by the time I learnt of it, the sun was setting and with the new moon—"

Nicholas held up his hand. "Do not trouble yourself. I would not have set off either. The housekeeper sent for the closest apothecary, and I should be well. My grandfather was concerned about the crossing this time of year. If he had known of your daughter, I would have never been allowed to leave London." Nicholas chuckled, then winced.

"Your grandfather? So, by what Fee told me, I was correct when I assumed your father is no longer living."

Nicholas's eyes met those of the earl's that were open and seemed to be seeking information important to him rather than gossip. Mrs. Murphy had said his father had been friends with Lord Kildare during his time here. Had they not kept up a correspondence? It appeared the earl was not the only one with questions.

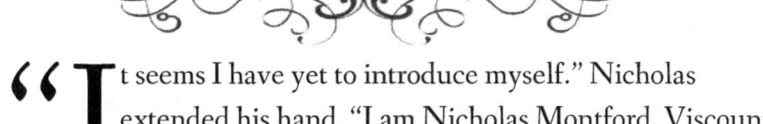

Chapter 6

"It seems I have yet to introduce myself." Nicholas extended his hand. "I am Nicholas Montford, Viscount Hatton. And, as much as I regret to inform you, yes, my father and mother died in a carriage accident when I was six."

Lord Kildare's eyebrows drew down some for a moment. "That was when his letters ceased. I wrote, but with the way the post travels between here and England, we sometimes had letters that were never received. I sent more than one. I suppose matters were rather hectic at that time."

"Yes, from what I remember of it, it was. I am sorry you never received word. Somehow, no one thought to inform the staff here either, it seems."

"No," said the earl. "I would have been notified had they done so. I am grieved. Grieved indeed. I am terribly sorry."

"Sir, your breakfast is ready." Nicholas turned at Mrs. Murphy's voice, allowing her to see the earl. "Lord Kildare, my but you are early this morning."

"Good morning, Mrs. Murphy. Yes, I came straightaway. I wanted to ensure the viscount was well."

"Lord Kildare, I thank you for your sincere condolences. If you should like, you may join me for breakfast, or if you have eaten, a cup of coffee or tea?" Nicholas held out his hand in the direction the footman had pointed earlier.

"Yes, I would be pleased to join you." As they passed Mrs. Murphy, the earl paused. "Fee is with Molly O'Shea. When she appears, if you could send her to me? She needs to apologise to Lord Hatton."

The housekeeper laughed through her nose. "You expect Lady Fiona to say she is sorry? Oh, now that is a sight I would pay to witness."

"Behave Mrs. Murphy," said the earl with a curve of his lips. Apparently, he did not mind people speaking so of his daughter.

When they were seated, Nicholas reached for the coffee pot but paused when it caused a burst of pain through his shoulder.

"Allow me, sir," said Mrs. Murphy. She poured them both coffee, and when the footman entered, she motioned for him to attend them.

"Tell me. Is there a butler here?" Nicholas had yet to meet or see one since his arrival.

"Our last butler left two years ago. I never found managing the few footmen we have to be a chore, so I never bothered. We have made do without since no family has been in residence in that time, but if you prefer, I can see about hiring one."

He shook his head. "No, do not bother for me alone. I was only curious."

As soon as the housekeeper departed, the footman picked up each of the offerings allowing him to take what he wished. "Thank you," said Nicholas. "If you need to attend to other duties, I can manage for now."

"Yes, sir."

As soon as the footman disappeared into the servants' passages, the earl sipped his coffee and regarded Nicholas for a moment. "I am almost afraid to ask how badly Fee injured you. You appear in more than a little pain."

"The willow bark eases the worst of it."

"Mixed with a healthy dose of whiskey which does not hurt," said the earl. At Nicholas's abrupt look, Lord Kildare chuckled. "I was here once and turned my ankle. Cook made me willow bark, and Mrs. Murphy served it in a large glass of whiskey. Thankfully, I was in my carriage and not on horseback. Otherwise, I might have fallen from my horse."

Nicholas could not help but let one side of his lips quirk upward, though he made great pains not to laugh. The ache in his ribs was too intense to do so. "I admit her tonic does render me a little light-headed, yet I cannot bemoan the effect. 'Tis preferable to laudanum."

After swallowing a sip of his coffee, Lord Kildare relaxed into his chair. "I must beg your forgiveness once again for my daughter. She has been without a mother since she was a babe, and I fear from a young age, I took delight in her ways. She was a precocious child, and when she became old enough, I taught her to ride and began taking her with me about the estate."

"She had no nursemaid or governess?"

"Oh, she had both as well as the masters I could arrange to come here, most of which would travel from Belfast. She speaks French, Italian, and Latin, she refuses to read gothic romances, preferring Shakespeare to Radcliffe, and excelled at mathematics. The masters bemoaned her a woman since she preferred those pursuits to needlework and tending a house."

Nicholas lifted his eyebrows. "Unusual accomplishments indeed."

"Yes, she is also a proficient rider and can handle a rifle as well as any man, and before you ask, yes, she fences. I had no part in teaching her to do so. We attended a house party in Scotland about seven years ago, and the young son, who was six years her junior, began teaching her. When his master arrived, the boy had enjoyed Fee's company so much, he insisted on her joining him. His father was appalled and begged my forgiveness, but I became resigned to Fee's unusual predilections long ago. She is the heiress of Larchfield, so I would prefer her to be prepared more so than most ladies who inherit. She will allow no man to cheat her. I pity the poor soul who makes the attempt."

As Lord Kildare spoke, Nicholas picked at his food. Would he condone such behaviour in a daughter of his own? In light of what Mrs. Murphy had said of Lady Fiona's mother, perchance in the earl's sorrow or grief of his wife's abandonment, he had created a sort of companion for himself. Granted, his daughter was not the usual companion of a man his age, but he could not criticise him for it.

"With that pistol she keeps tucked away, I doubt anyone would dare try to cheat her."

The earl squeezed his eyes closed. "She had not mentioned the pistol. She threatened you with it?"

Nicholas could not help but laugh, though he put a hand to his ribs with a grimace as he did so. "Stood over me with it. I must say she held it quite steady for a lady. Neither my sister nor my cousins would have been so bold." Well, Lizzy might have, more so now that she was with Darcy than before. She had gained confidence since her marriage.

"I believe I should hear the encounter from your perspective since I am certain my daughter did not tell me the whole of it."

The number of moans and groans from the earl were unable to be counted as Nicholas recited the tale from his first sighting until she fled the sight of her ambush. When he had completed the story, the earl shook his head and grabbed the footman who had just entered and passed behind him. "If you will forgive me, Lord Hatton, I believe I should prefer some whiskey if you will indulge me. A very large glass if you please."

Nicholas nodded at the footman, who with a crooked smile, hurried off. "While I would not wish to have been knocked from my mount, I am grateful for the defence of my lands. I had not expected it from such an unexpected quarter."

Lord Kildare laughed weakly. "I made a promise to your father before he departed to keep a watchful eye on Moydrum and any issues that arose. Mr. O'Shea is exceedingly competent, and I enjoy his company, so I never considered it a bother to converse with the man over a glass of whiskey every month or so. His daughter is a welcome friend to Fee, so my daughter would oft times accompany me and visit with Mrs. and Miss O'Shea. They have attempted to refine my daughter's temper where I failed. I must admit they have had more success than me. You should have witnessed her behaviour when she was ten. She was a wee lad in girl's skirts, I tell you."

"After dinner last night, I searched my father's journals from this time for mention of you. I had not read far into them as yet, but after discovering your identity, was curious. He thought highly of you. May I ask when your last letter from him arrived?"

The earl frowned and laced his fingers over his slight stomach. "I would have to look back through to be sure, but I think the last was in January 1793. He mentioned he and your mother would have their first Season in London since the birth of your sister...Forgive me, but I do not remember her name."

"Amelia."

"Yes, that is it," said the earl with a breath. "Your mother was loath to part with the two of you and wanted to bring you along when they departed Richmond, but your grandparents insisted the two of you remain and journey to London with them in a fortnight so your parents would have some time with each other without distractions."

"From what my grandparents have told me, my parents awoke for their second day of travel to snow. My father considered remaining at the inn, but my mother thought a carriage ride in the snow would be magical. My sister's lady's maid was once my mother's. Martin had been helping my mother to dress when they were discussing whether or not to depart."

"Your father could refuse your mother nothing, could he?"

"It seems he could not. We do not know much more. Martin and my father's valet proceeded in a separate carriage and reached the next inn, but my parents never did. Those who searched found the carriage north of Cambridge, turned over in a lode along the side of the road. The driver of Martin's carriage indicated that part of the roadway had been quite muddy. They believe the carriage overturned and slid. I know no more."

Lord Kildare let out a heavy exhale. "I attended Cambridge as a young man and on occasion journeyed up near Ely. I have seen the fens and the lodes. Those roads can be treacherous in good weather much less snow."

"My grandparents avoid travelling through them now."

At a light rap upon the doorframe, they both turned. Lady Fiona stood with her hands clasped before her, appearing much more the daughter of a peer than she had the day before. "Pray, forgive me for interrupting. Molly and Mrs. O'Shea needed to depart on a call to Father Ryan. Mrs. Murphy told me you were here."

"Come in," said Nicholas.

Though the lady was definitely the hoyden he met yesterday, her manner was markedly different, and she wore a silk gown more befitting of her status than the wool habit. The pale, fern green complemented her creamy skin, and her fiery locks were tamed and pinned atop her head. Curls framed her face as was the fashion, but they also escaped their pins at the base of her neck.

He pulled his eyes from her and cleared his throat. "You must forgive my attire. I fear I could not tolerate the confines of my waistcoat much less a topcoat this morning."

Lady Fiona pinked a bit after a glance at her father, who levelled her with an unforgiving glare. "Yes, about that, my lord. I am sorry for behaving as I did."

Lord Kildare gave a slight cough.

The lady's chin gave a hitch upward. "Yes, and it was impetuous of me to unseat a rider when I did not know their identity. I do hope your injuries are not too grievous. If I may do anything to be of aid…"

After raising his hand, Nicholas motioned to a chair. "Pray, no more. If you will sit, you may have tea while we visit."

"Thank you, sir." She sat beside her father, who poured her a cup of coffee.

"As I said, I taught Fee each and every one of my worst habits, though she does not abide smoking."

"Foul stench, that is." Lady Fiona crinkled her nose.

"When the footman returns, I shall request more coffee then, though I see nothing objectionable in a lady preferring coffee to tea. My sister has been known to prefer coffee some mornings."

"Your sister must be out by now," said Lord Kildare.

"She married Sir Anthony Greene of the Greene Baronetcy last Season. They recently had their first child, Isabella, and will remain at Dereham Hall for the Season."

The earl perked at the name. "The child is named for your mother."

"She is. I am very happy for my sister. Hers is a love match, even if she fought him every step of the way."

The man sighed. "I am pleased to hear her marriage is felicitous. We should all be so fortunate, should we not?"

Nicholas did not miss Lady Fiona's hand covering her father's and squeezing. "I agree. We were both raised with my grandparents to emulate."

"Your father mentioned his parents had a deep abiding love. I have never met your grandfather; although, my father did so when Lord Richmond visited. I was a mere boy at the time."

"Lord Kildare—"

"Oh, pray, Kildare is sufficient. I would not have you address me so formally."

With a nod, Nicholas set his cup back on his saucer. "Then you must call me Hatton."

"Hatton," said the earl in a murmur. "I shall try. While it is the custom, I only learnt of your father's death. It seems strange."

Nicholas stared at his plate for a moment. He had never had to accustom himself to being called Hatton as he had been referred to as such since he was a boy, except for by his family, of course. "I can understand your dilemma."

"I say, I have a fox hunt planned in a fortnight. I know it is late in the season for the diversion, but the pesky creatures have been finding their way into my henhouses of late, or so my gamemaster tells me. If you are feeling up to it, you should join us. You would be able to make the acquaintance of several of our neighbours. Fee will be riding with us."

His eyes darted to the striking redhead at her father's side, the lady's eyebrow arched in challenge. Why did that expression stir his insides so? "I do not doubt she would. From what I have seen, she could manage a fox hunt quite well."

"That I can, sir."

"Very well. 'Tis settled." Lord Kildare glanced between them. "Should you be able to ride by then. You will come." He settled one more glare on his daughter, who sighed.

Chapter 7

"You have failed to find a suitor here. Mayhap Lord Hatton could prove to be a match for you."

Fiona sighed at Molly's characteristic cheery view as they sorted through ribbons in a shop in Ballymena. Her friend was the same as most ladies, interested in fashion and finding an eligible gentleman to wed. Molly's latest suitor, a young barrister from Belfast, was promising, although, with his court schedule, he could only call on her when he visited his family nearby. He was in a better situation than most at his young age with a house left to him by a prosperous uncle who was a judge and a small fortune to accompany it.

With a hand propped on one hip, Molly frowned. "Do not sigh at me, Fiona Fitzgerald. What will you do if you do not marry?"

"I shall ride my horse and make Larchfield more prosperous than it has ever been. I shall be content. When I am an older spinster maiden, perhaps I shall take a lover and scandalise all and sundry with my wanton ways." She said the last in a low whisper near Molly's ear.

"You are wicked, Fee. If Father Ryan heard such mutterings, he would have you attend confession without delay."

"Except I am not Catholic if you recall. My grandfather came from England, fell in love with my grandmother, and remained for the rest of his life. My father never saw reason to leave as he loves Ireland, and I see no reason to ever leave myself, so I would never attach myself to a gentleman whose interests here were no more than a temporary diversion."

"I believe to see London would be grand," said Molly in a bit of a dreamy voice. "You could journey back and forth, spend your winters enjoying London and your summers in the peaceful green of Larchfield and Moydrum. Could you imagine attending Almack's?"

"No. I would prefer to be riding." She spoke in a firm tone, firmer than Molly should likely have received. "Forgive me. I just wish you would accept that I have no intention of ever marrying."

Molly turned an impudent grin to Fiona. "Yes, but I have seen Lord Hatton, and I must say he is a handsome man."

Handsome was an understatement. When she had knocked him from his horse, he had turned those glaring, green eyes on her, and her knees wobbled in a way she had never experienced. He was broad-shouldered, trim waisted, and his thighs spoke of his hours atop his mount. The dimple that had appeared in his amusement, which also happened when he spoke to her father, hinted at a mischievous character. The most disconcerting part was that she yearned to lick that dimple. A shocking thought indeed!

Who was Nicholas Montford, Viscount Hatton? Was he as worthy of her father's admiration and friendship as his father was before him? He had best be since her father spoke of him after their call as though he would become good friends with the young viscount. The proffered invitation to the fox hunt was proof enough of her father's unguarded nature when it came to friendship. She had to hope the viscount was an agreeable and upstanding man.

"Fee," said Molly with a giggle. "Where did you go?"

"I am sorry?"

"I was talking, and after you did not respond to my question, I turned to find you wool-gathering with the strangest expression upon your countenance."

Fiona held out the ribbons in her hands. "'Tis the choices you would have me make. You know I am hopeless. My maid helps me select my fabrics and patterns. If I could, I would send her to the dressmaker's without me, as you are well aware."

With a glint in her eye that told Fiona, in no uncertain terms, that Molly did not believe a word of it, she reached over and drew out a length of several ribbons. "The green would go well with your fern-coloured day gown, the blue embroidered would be beautiful with your white gown when you wear it to Lord Meath's ball, and the pink would complement the flowers in that sprigged muslin with the ivy embroidery come spring."

"Very well," said Fiona in a resigned tone. "I shall have a length of these." She handed the spools to the shopkeeper while Molly made her final selections, and soon, they returned to the Kildare carriage sitting along the kerb.

As soon as the equipage began its return to Moydrum to return Molly home, her friend bit her lip with a grin. "You could at least admit you find him handsome."

"Who?"

"Oh, do not be daft! Lord Hatton. He began wearing his waistcoat and topcoat again two days ago, appearing ever so well turned out. I still cannot believe you bruised him so badly, he could not wear them for seven days. A full week, Fee!"

"Yes, I know. My father has yet to cease reminding me." He was still cross with her, but what was she to do? She had been impulsive and headstrong for so long. She could not abandon her old ways in an instant, could she?

"I wish I could ride well enough to accompany you on the fox hunt."

Fiona frowned and faced Molly, who had never enjoyed riding. "Whyever would you want to do that?"

"Why, to see Lord Hatton ride, of course. I imagine he is even more appealing on horseback."

With an amused bark, Fiona shook her head. "Your father needs to find you a husband."

"Mr. Joy returns on the morrow. He has promised to call and has requested the first at Lord Meath's ball." Molly spoke so matter-of-factly. Had she any attraction or feeling for Mr. Joy?

"Do anything but wed without some depth of feeling, Molly."

"Mr. Joy is all a gentleman should be. I am not in love with him, but I also cannot avoid that when my father dies, my mother and I shall have little to live on and nowhere to go." Mr. O'Shea was not a young man but had fallen in love with a lady fifteen years his junior. As much as it pained them to consider it, the odds were his wife would survive him by at least a decade.

"You would have a place at Larchfield. You know that. And, if Lord Hatton is what he seems, I do not believe he would remove you from his lands. I am certain he would find you a small cottage to live out your days."

Molly shook her head. "Must we discuss this again? I do not want to rely on your charity, nor that of Lord Hatton's." Her friend threw up her hands. "Enough! Not one more word on the subject. Do I make myself clear?"

"Yes," said Fiona. She was familiar enough with Molly's demeanour. She had pushed too far. Her friend was never so defensive. That was a trait more suited to herself.

When Fiona entered the hall of Lord Meath's home, she shed her good cape and took her father's proffered arm. When they reached the end of the receiving line, the cheerful baron[2] gave his characteristic wide grin and bowed.

"Kildare! I am pleased you and your daughter could come."

"You know I would not miss one of your balls," said her father.

Fiona dropped a curtsey. "Lord Meath, 'tis a pleasure, sir." Despite what her father believed of her, she did try...most of the time.

After a few more genial words, her father steered her into the ballroom. "Do you think you will be asked to dance?"

"The gentlemen here will be the same as at every ball and event, and all dreadfully dull, so I doubt it."

"Fee, if you do not marry and have a child, the earldom will die with you."

She sighed. Must they discuss this yet again? "Yes, as you have told me time and time again. Must we?"

"Yes, we must, and I shall continue telling you until you understand the full implications of your decisions. Your plans have consequences."

---

[2] The title of baron in Ireland was once synonymous with earl, so barons are addressed as Lord. https://www.irishfamilyhistorycentre.com/article/peerage-of-ireland/

"Yes, as you have told me since I came out. You forget the gentlemen of the neighbourhood seem as inclined towards marrying me as I am towards them. Oh, look. Is that Lord Hatton?" She began walking towards the young viscount without relinquishing her father's arm. Perhaps his would help her father keep his opinions to himself. On this subject, she was fatigued of hearing them.

"Yes, I do believe it is." Her father perked up. "I had not known he was invited."

As they approached the gentleman, her father held up his hand. "Hatton, 'tis good to see you this evening. I was not aware you knew Lord Meath."

"Ah, he called a week ago to welcome me to the neighbourhood and invited me then. I must admit I am relieved to find you here. I have yet to meet many of the neighbourhood." He acknowledged Fiona with a slight bow. "Are you free for the first, Lady Fiona?"

She glanced at her father with a start. "I am. We arrived but a short time before you, sir."

"Then, would you do me the honour?" He held out his gloved hand.

"I—I...had not thought—"

Her father lifted his eyebrows. "She would be pleased to dance with you. Would you not, Fee?"

She pressed her lips together and tried to smile as she placed her hand in Lord Hatton's proffered one. Arguing served no purpose with her father standing so close. "Yes, of course, I would be *ecstatic*, my lord." Her father received the best glare as she could manage when they left him.

The music began just after they took their places, and Fiona made her way through the pattern while Lord Hatton seemed to watch her at every opportunity. Why? Was something amiss with her gown? Was her hair falling from the pins? What could possibly be so fascinating?

When her hands joined his for their turn, Lord Hatton's gaze caught hers. "Lady Fiona, I must say you look very well this evening."

"Thank you." Was that why he was staring at her? Because he found her attractive? Well, if so, she would need to put an end to those thoughts but quick!

He leaned a little closer. "If you will indulge me, can you tell me which lady is Lord Meath's daughter?"

Fiona's neck smarted with the force of her jolt to meet his gaze. He complimented her then asked her of another lady. How odd! Why would he ask her such a question and in such a manner? "Lord Meath's daughter?"

"Yes, the man spoke of her incessantly when he called as well as when he greeted me tonight. Forgive me for asking, but I hope to avoid her if possible. The way he spoke of her charms and accomplishments reminded me of a gentleman describing his best hunting dog, which is also a reason why I am not spending the Season in London. Who wants to hear a lady described in such a way?"

She covered her mouth and nose when the laugh she tried to withhold went terribly wrong. "Forgive me."

"Not at all."

"Miss Eithne Meath is the lady standing near the statue of Aphrodite by the terrace doors. She has the same eyes as her father."

Lord Hatton glanced during his next part of the pattern. When he re-joined her, he again leaned closer. "She does not appear wholly objectionable, though I would wager she has been out for some time. If I may be so bold to ask, why did she never marry?"

"She is one and thirty. When she was twenty, her betrothed died of grippe. It was tragic. The illness came on quick, and he perished from the fever. He had been the sole gentleman to call on her, and no other ever courted her. Her father invites any young man in the neighbourhood for dinner or a ball to introduce them to Eithne, but no one seems inclined as yet. And if you were wondering, I am not married because I am not so inclined." There! If he found her attractive, she had let her intentions, or lack thereof, be known in a manner that could not be misinterpreted.

He startled, and his eyebrows drew down. "You do not wish to marry?"

"No, I am content as I am. Does that shock you?" She tilted her head as she observed his response. Now, what would he say to that?

After a moment of quiet, Lord Hatton shrugged and grinned. "I suppose I should thank you for your forthright and frank confession. If I were considering you for courtship, I now know I should seek a wife elsewhere. I shall not waste my time with you."

When she took her turn with the person beside the viscount, something in her chest smarted. What? Waste his time? She drew her shoulders back when she rejoined Lord Hatton. "Yes, well, I am glad we have that sorted."

"Yes, of course," he said with a warm chuckle. Her breath caught in her throat. Why would that sound cause such a response in her?

Waste his time? Most gentlemen would laugh and ignore her. Was he believing her earnest confession without reserve? Only one thing could be said of Lord Hatton: the man puzzled her exceedingly.

Chapter 8

"Papa, tell me another story."

His father chuckled and tousled his hair.

"Another? Your Mama will scold me for keeping you up so late if I do. What do you want to hear that cannot wait for tomorrow?"

"I want you to tell me of Lady Fee and the leprechaun."

"Again?"

"Yes, again," said Nicholas bouncing in his bedclothes. "You tell the best Lady Fee stories."

"I am pleased you like them. I enjoy hearing of Lady Fee's exploits as well. She is a precocious wee thing."

"Preco...co..."

"Precocious?"

Nicholas nodded. "Indeed."

Nicholas shot up in bed, panting, a slight sheen of sweat covering him. "Lady Fee?"

He picked up the journal on the bed beside him where it must have dropped when he fell asleep.

I received a letter from Kildare, regaling me of stories
of his young daughter. He finds such joy in her antics,
not that I can blame him. Her battle against the duck
who wanted nothing more than her piece of bread was
amusing to say the least.

With a groan, he marked his page and swung his legs over the side. Lady Fee and the leprechaun? The name could not be a coincidence, could it?

"Good morning, sir," said Evans. His man strode in from the dressing room. "I have your riding clothes prepared and your boots polished. The stablemaster sent up word that he has several mounts for you to choose from and will have them saddled and awaiting your selection at the time you indicated. Mrs. Murphy said he expected you to try each of them before your departure. Would you care for a tray or to go to the breakfast room this morning?" Evans knew well Nicholas did not care for a large meal before a fox hunt.

"A tray would suffice, thank you. No more than some toast and jam."

"Of course, sir." The valet poured the warm water in the basin for Nicholas to wash and hastened back through the adjoining door.

As soon as he had refreshed himself from his sleep, Evans helped him dress, but when he held out his blue coat, Nicholas frowned. "I would prefer the green."

"The green?" He could not miss the hint of surprise in Evans' question. Nicholas was rarely particular about his dress.

"Yes, I believe I should like the green."

After a curt nod, Evans retrieved the requested coat and helped Nicholas button the front before brushing it down well. "Forgive me, sir. I would have had this prepared if I had known."

"I am not put out. I know I caught you unawares." His valet was so fastidious, but Nicholas's clothing was always impeccable as a result: no loose threads, no tears or frays, and always immaculately pressed.

Once he was dressed, he slipped out into the early morning chill and whipped his riding crop through the air. Lady Fee and the leprechaun? He shook himself. He could not let that keep running through his head all day or until he could ask Lord Kildare about the dream.

When he reached the stables, the stablemaster gave him a wide smile and a bow. "Good mornin', sir. I was unsure what sort of mount you preferred, so I ensured you would be prepared to depart on time no matter what horse you chose." The man took Nicholas through the four horses in front of him. Each of the four mounts had a superior conformation and an alert expression, a few pawing at the earth at the prospect of an early morning run.

In the end, Nicholas selected the last horse the stablemaster introduced, making the man grin widely. "Good, strong Irish Hunter that one is. He is who I would prefer if I were riding. Excellent choice, sir."

Nicholas mounted the sizeable stallion, slipped his boots into the irons, and situated the reins. "Does he have any foibles I should be aware of?"

"He is a bit ticklish in the sides, so a slight pressure is all you need for him to respond."

He nodded. His horse at Richmond was similar, so he should not have an issue. Within moments, he cantered along the paths he had learnt would take him to Lord Kildare's estate. The sleek, black stallion responded well to his cues and pulled against the bit in an effort to have his head.

"Calm yourself. You shall be allowed to run soon enough."

Upon his arrival, a group of men were gathered near the Larchfield stables with their mounts. Lord Kildare greeted him and introduced him to his guests for the hunt, many of whom he had met at Lord Meath's ball. Nicholas was speaking to the Earl of Kerry when a gasp came from behind him. "You rode Kelpie."

Before he could turn, Lady Fiona had approached his horse and was stroking the large white blaze down the stallion's nose while murmuring endearments. His mount clearly knew her as he leaned into her attentions before rubbing his head up and down her habit, making her laugh. Nicholas could only stare. For once, the headstrong miss he had become accustomed to seemed to disappear while she stroked his horse. Why had he the sudden urge for those same hands to touch his chest, his back, his...?

"Oh, miss!" A maid ran forward and began brushing Lady Fiona's coat, the girl's exclamation shook him from his reverie.

"Stop your fretting. I shall not be able to stay clean during the hunt. Why you insist I begin in such pristine condition..." She ceased her chastisement when her eyes met his. "Lord Hatton. I hope you are well."

"Yes, quite well, I thank you. You said his name is Kelpie?"

"Did the stablemaster not tell you?" She never relinquished the horse's head while he nibbled at her coat. He seemed to be comfortable with the lady, more so than most people were with her.

"The stablemaster described him, but he never gave a name. I fear I do not know what Kelpie means."

She laughed. "I suppose you would not have learnt many old Irish legends."

"No, I suppose I have not." Her laugh was so carefree at that moment.

"A kelpie is an evil water spirit who appears in the shape of a horse to lure people onto his back, allowing the creature to carry them into the depths."

Nicholas could not help but let his eyebrows shoot up. He and his grandfather had oft times named their horses for Greek and Roman tales or Shakespeare's characters, but an evil water spirit? "I have never heard of such before." The dark black of his coat leant well to the name. Nicholas liked it.

"He will be a superior mount for the hunt," she said in all seriousness. "Quick, agile, and eager to run. Your stablemaster made an excellent choice."

"He had four horses saddled and ready, then described them each to me. I chose this one."

One side of her lips quirked in an alluring fashion. "Then *I* am impressed with your discernment, sir."

He feigned a curtsey with one side of his lips struggling not to give away his amusement at the spitfire offering her opinion as freely as she had her intention not to wed. She could not have surprised him more when she had made the announcement while they danced at Lord Meath's ball. It had also not escaped his notice that he had been her sole dance partner for the evening. She had not seemed to mind and had passed the evening with a group of ladies that included Lord Meath's daughter, Lord Kildare, and on occasion with other members of the neighbourhood. Perhaps she had been so outspoken with the other gentlemen of the county as well.

"What of your horse?" He gestured to the white stallion being held by a groom. "Does he have an unusual name?"

Before she could respond, the hounds were brought out by the master of the hunt to the edge of the field where their party awaited them. They brayed and pulled at their leads, eager to set free.

"Shall we be off then?" shouted Lord Kildare to the group.

Nicholas would have offered his aid to Lady Fiona to mount, but somehow, he doubted she would accept or require the help. He was also proven correct on the latter since she climbed atop her horse with little effort and situated herself proud and tall. Once he was in the saddle, he turned his horse about and paused. He had suspected Lady Fiona was riding astride when she had knocked him from his horse, but now he had proof. As before, she was wearing a habit as any lady of means would, but a pair of high boots peeked out from beneath the fabric of the skirt she adjusted over them. Did she always ride astride?

She looked in his direction, but he schooled his features, so he did not give away his scrutiny of her attire. "My dressmaker is quite accommodating...so I do not shock anyone. She adds extra fabric, so my skirts cover my boots," she said. Blast! Apparently, he had not schooled his features well enough.

While the master of the hunt climbed atop his horse, a groom took the mass of dogs struggling against their leads, at which time the remainder of their hunting party mounted as well. The air around them thickened as every man sat poised to cue his horse forward until the hounds were released with a resonating blow of the master's horn. Just as always, Nicholas's insides jumped at the horn blast.

The dogs shot forward, running along and sniffing through the brush, while their tails wagged madly. The group followed for almost ten minutes and some of the gentlemen talked while they awaited some sign of their prey. With the earlier tension as they awaited the dogs' release, Nicholas could almost laugh at the sedate pace they had maintained thus far.

The largest of the hounds bounded into a wide ditch filled with tall grasses that would conceal any animal wishing for cover. Within moments, the dog brayed and chased a streak of reddish-tan from some undergrowth and across the field, the poor little beast moving as quickly as its legs could carry it away from the rabble of dogs who joined the lead in giving chase.

The group on horseback took off following the master of the hunt, who was clad in a red riding coat and carrying his horn before them, galloping east across the Kildare lands. Lady Fiona rode just ahead of Nicholas and to the right, and when the first fence approached, he gripped his reins as she prepared for the obstacle, clearing it with plenty of room and galloping ahead. After their first meeting, he should not doubt her abilities on a horse, but fox hunts were dangerous and even men had been grievously injured riding in them. Sitting astride was not enough to prevent injury to the horse or rider, one had to be skilled and thoughtful when controlling their mounts to do well with the pace of a fox hunt. Lord Kildare, however, did not appear concerned as he was near the front of the pack and galloping on without any hint of anxiety for his only child. The man was a peculiar one. Amelia was an accomplished rider, but his grandfather would have remained close to her in this situation, whether it was her first ride or her twentieth—not that Amelia rode astride.

At Richmond, fox hunts occurred when the need arose but were not one of Nicholas's favourite diversions. To tell the truth, though foxes were vermin and could kill a farmer's chickens and decimate an estate's game birds, he would have preferred to kill the poor beasts quickly rather than what happened at the end of the hunt. The tenants enjoyed a good fox hunt from time to time when the situation warranted, but his grandfather rarely held a hunt for his neighbours. Not many of the gentry did so. Nicholas, however, attended those offered for the challenge of the chase. The change of galloping across the countryside at breakneck speeds with a group proved to be a welcome diversion from the solitude of most rides.

The fox continued down through a valley and along the edge of the stream. Lady Fiona continued to ride with intelligence, taking no jumps unless necessary, unlike a baronet he made the acquaintance of earlier, who proved to be a larker, jumping any obstacle nearby and galloping recklessly. The man was a danger to those around him and a menace. Nicholas and Lady Fiona had not delayed in leaving him behind.

The hunt continued along the stream's edge until the hounds stopped and began furiously sniffing around a hole. "He went to ground!" yelled one of the men. As they slowed on their approach, the master of the hunt removed a terrier from a bag attached to his saddle and set the dog by the hole. Without pause, the dog darted in and continued the chase while those assembled waited and watched.

"Lady Fiona," called the larker. The baronet had sidled closer on his gelding—far closer than he should considering Lady Fiona's horse was tossing his head and snorting in objection to the approach. The man's mouth moved, though he did not speak loud enough for those around them to hear. Meanwhile, Lady Fiona reddened and raised her whip to the man's face, delivering a sharp slash along his cheekbone.

"You blackguard!" she said without care for who heard. Her horse lifted slightly to his back legs, and she skilfully shifted him away from the baronet. "Remove yourself from Kildare lands at once and do not return. My father shall hear of this. I promise you." She all but growled the last while those in the vicinity gasped and their mouths hung agape.

"You wench!" The man spat out the words with his hand covering his cheek. He still clutched the reins with one hand, manoeuvring his horse away from Lady Fiona.

Nicholas drew closer and ensured his expression was hard. "You heard the lady, sir. Remove yourself from Kildare lands." Where was

Lord Kildare? Nicholas kept his glare fixed on the baronet lest the man take advantage of his distraction. The man looked between them, his complexion almost crimson.

"What is the meaning of this?" Lord Kildare's low voice came from behind Nicholas, although he did not turn to look. Despite the crowd now gathering and her father's presence, Nicholas would not leave Lady Fiona unprotected.

The larker glanced at the earl, then at Lady Fiona, then at Nicholas before he gave an odd jerk of his head. "I believe the lady misinterpreted what I said. I apologise for any misunderstanding and will take my leave. Good day."

Lady Fiona held her head high as the man departed, the rest of the group watching with wide eyes. "That was no misunderstanding. I have always said he was a vile piece of baggage, Papa, and I maintain my opinion."

"What did he say?" The earl watched his daughter, who flushed as her eyes darted about them.

"I should prefer to tell you later and not in such mixed company."

The earl nodded before pivoting his horse to face Nicholas. "Thank you for your defence of my daughter, Lord Hatton." Kildare lifted his eyebrows at their group as he rode back to the master of the hunt. Most of the men followed and dismounted to continue the vigil over the hole in the ground while Lady Fiona exhaled. Her eyes lit as her gaze rested upon him and upbraided him.

"I am capable of defending myself, sir."

He stiffened. "I know well enough that you are, yet I would not have you confront him alone."

Her shoulders dropped and she squeezed her eyes closed for a moment before reopening them. "I do not relish being seen as the helpless lady. Sir Malcolm must have, or he would not have spoken in such a way. I know you could not have heard what he said to me, but I assure you, it was worthy of the utmost censure. I would not have struck him as I did if it were not."

"Which is why I stepped forward. What if he had forgotten himself and struck you with his own crop?"

"I admit to acting without considering that as a consequence. I suppose I should be thanking you." She glanced to where the men and the master of the hunt still waited for the terrier to emerge and steered her horse in the opposite direction.

"Where are you going?" Would she not wait to see if the dog flushed out the fox?

"To tell the truth, this is my least favourite part of the hunt. I enjoy the race and the thrill of galloping through the countryside in pursuit of the hounds, but I am not best pleased to watch the result. 'Tis not so different from the men who take pleasure in fighting dogs or cocks. They enjoy watching two animals kill one another for sport, which I cannot abide." Her gaze darted to him for a moment before she relaxed a mite.

He brought Kelpie beside her mount. "I agree with you."

Her head jerked to face him. "You do?"

"Yes, I enjoy the challenge of the ride, and I understand the necessity of controlling foxes on our lands, yet I wish they would do away with the animal quickly instead of allowing it to suffer." He had not realised he would share such an unusual opinion with Lady Fiona.

As they rode, they remained silent as they approached Larchfield. The quiet was not uncomfortable, but more that neither seemed to feel a need to fill it with idle chatter. He should not be following her, but once he saw her safely home, he would continue on to Moydrum. Upon their arrival, two grooms hurried out from the stables and took their horses.

Before she dismounted, she turned to him. "I should like to show you something."

"I should like to see it." The tilt of her head and the unusual glint in her eyes pulled at him. Why was he agreeing? He was supposed to be leaving for his estate not trailing after Lady Fiona like a puppy.

Chapter 9

With a lift of her eyebrow, Lady Fiona walked ahead as Nicholas took a few quick steps to reach her side. "You do not know what I intend to show you."

"I trust you." He gave a small startle. How odd! He did trust her. Regardless of the manner of their meeting and what had occurred since, she was not one of those ladies he was accustomed to in London. She bore no pretences—no artifice. She displayed her true self without reserve, though within the bounds of propriety—well, maybe some of the time. Her declaration during their dance a few nights ago was too forward, but he could not despise her for it. In fact, once they danced, she stood with her father or some of the older matrons for the rest of the evening. She did not hover at his shoulder as some unwed young ladies would. He had never made the acquaintance of a lady like her.

"You trust me? Do you not know it is dangerous to trust me? I may be a leprechaun or a banshee in disguise."

"I am unfamiliar with a banshee, though my father told me the story of Lady Fee and the leprechaun when I was a boy. I had not remembered it until recently. I happened upon a paragraph in his journal that said it was from a tale your father wrote of your adventures with a duck."

Her eyes widened. They really were the most vivid of greens. "Oh, no, what am I to do with Papa? He told someone of that?"

"Will you tell me of it?"

With a curve to her lips, she tilted her head at him. "You must understand, sir, that I was two. I remember naught of the adventures. You had best ask my father, though I daresay the tale may not live up to your expectations. Your father may have woven a much better story from my father's ramblings."

Before long, they approached an enclosure of sorts along the edge of a small wood and shaded by the limbs of a few large oaks along the forest's edge. Lady Fiona opened the door and stepped inside. "This was the orangery before my father built a new one closer to the house.

The air was moist yet cool; however, the plants housed within were curious. They were not exotic as most estate owners would keep in an orangery, but long containers of lavender and plants that grew in the fields were everywhere. A sharp, strong odour stung his nose, and he wiggled it.

"Pray, forgive the smell." Lady Fiona bent down and made a clucking noise with her tongue. Soon, a little long reddish-tan fox came bounding out of some plants, his tongue lolling a bit on the side and sporting an almost happy grin. He dropped in front of the lady and rolled to his back as one would expect a dog who wanted a belly rub. His gaze never wavered as Lady Fiona began to scratch the animal under his legs and on his chest. The fox gave a sort of "yip" before he bounced up and pushed at her hand, making her smile. Her earnest happiness at the animal's behaviour softened her—similar to when she interacted with Kelpie and he had caught a glimpse of true happiness upon her countenance.

"This is Robin. I found him injured when he was a mere kit and brought him home to Papa." She gave a delighted chuckle as the fox bounced around her and begged for more pets. "You should have seen my father's expression when I walked into the dining room bearing a bundle of a tiny fox. If I had not been so adamant about helping the poor mite, I am certain my father would not have gone to such pains for him, but I cajoled and cajoled until he relented."

"How old were you?"

"I was twelve, which makes Robin that age now. From what I can tell, he has gotten rather old-looking of late. I do not know if we shall have him for much longer, but I can say he can be as affectionate as a terrier pup and very playful. When I first found him, I had wanted to keep him inside the house with me as I would a small dog, but the master of the hunt could not train him to live inside as you would a dog. He will still mark what he believes is his, which is why it smells as it does in here. The grooms clean up, yet he does not understand that he must go out for that." She pointed to an open window on the side which led to a tall fenced garden of sorts. "He has room to play outside too."

"I am surprised your father did not insist you release him once he was well."

"My father remembered a tenant from his youth. The man had raised a hare after finding it alone and without its mother. The man released the animal, but it never strayed far from his cottage and had no fear of humans. It did find a mate and raise a family nearby. The young would not approach the man nor would the mate, but the hare he reared would always come to him. With that in mind, we feared releasing Robin when he became old enough. He has no trepidation around humans, and after living for a time in the stable, he does not fear horses either."

"He would make easy prey for a hunter."

"Precisely. I thought it cruel to release him. We did not know if he could even hunt, though, from his short time in the house, we do know he will ferret out mice and rats. Occasionally, a tenant will borrow him and let him live in their barns to rid them of vermin, so he is not always so confined in here. Grooms will take him out and walk him about the grounds in the evening as well. We have given him the best life we can."

Nicholas watched the animal who nudged Lady Fiona's hand, begging for more of her singular attention. "I believe you have done admirably given the situation."

After two or three more scratches behind the creature's ears, Lady Fiona led Nicholas back into the sunshine. She stopped and lifted her face into the sun's warmth for a moment, then looked off into the distance. "At the hunt, when Sir Malcolm drew his horse beside mine...he...he told me it would please him immensely if I would ride him astride." Once the words began to flow, they rolled out one after another while the lady's complexion deepened in colour and her eyes found a spot on the ground so interesting, they never returned to his.

"Good God." Nicholas ran a hand across his mouth for a moment. "I would never have forced you to tell me such a horrendous statement, but you do need to tell your father."

She pivoted around to face him. "I do not want Papa to call the man out, which is why I told you. Your aid may be required to keep my father from doing something foolish."

"If your father seems likely to challenge Sir Malcolm, send word to me, and I shall do my best to prevent it." His words were not obligatory or offered without the intention of following through. He could not explain it, but he meant every word. From his conversations with Lord Kildare, he liked the man. While Sir Malcolm's words deserved the severest reproof, he would not see Kildare injured or killed taking the man to task. However, what or how Nicholas could prevent it, he could not say.

Lady Fiona exhaled as she squeezed her eyes closed and reopened them. "I cannot express my appreciation enough for your willingness to be of aid. You must believe if I had anyone else to intervene, I would make the request of them. Mr. O'Shea would defer to Papa's rank and likely agree to be his second before making any effort to disabuse him of any notion of challenging Sir Malcolm."

He could not credit the lady's words. Since the baronet's insult, Lady Fiona had seemed more willing to consider him a friend. "If I may, your father would be within his rights to call out Sir Malcolm." She had to know.

"Yes, he would, but after the episode with his heart last year, I fear losing him. Besides, I already humiliated Sir Malcolm when I took my crop to his cheek."

Nicholas sucked air in through his teeth with a nod. "Yes, I am certain your rebuke will leave a mark, but the action may only serve to anger the man further. Is he one to create rumour and supposition? I cannot imagine him letting matters go." The man resembled most of the blustering peers in London who would not think twice about speaking against a lady in the basest of terms for revenge.

"He feels his importance keenly, so he may speak out against me, although I have no concern for what he says. As I told you at the ball, I have no intention of marrying any man, so other than concern for my father's honour, I have no reason to worry over lies damaging my reputation. The sole friend I would fret over losing would be Miss O'Shea, and she will surely be living in Belfast if she weds Mr. Joy, though he has not made her the offer of his hand as yet."

"What if you were shunned?"

She shook her head. "I require nothing more than Larchfield. I can be content living within its walls and riding the grounds for my lifetime. I need naught but my home."

His gaze lingered on her face for a bit before he sighed. "I have never known a lady such as you. Most fear for their future should they not marry." Of course, her attitude and habits, in all likelihood, ran off any suitors she may have attracted with her striking face and pleasing figure.

"Yes, well, I have no need to do so, and I should not enjoy a man courting me for my fortune. At least, this way, I know where I stand with those around me, whether they are friend, servant, tenant, or neighbour."

He startled and rubbed his forehead. "Forgive me. I should not pry. Your wishes and hopes are your business."

She shrugged. "You forget I am not most people. I was not offended. If Sir Malcolm spreads falsehoods against me. Naught will or can be done. I have no desire for anyone to be injured or killed defending my honour."

"I should go." He gestured in the direction of the stables.

"Yes, I should not keep you. Again, I thank you for the company back to the house, and your assurances of assistance should I require it."

After she walked him back and he departed on Kelpie, Nicholas stopped on the top of the rise and watched as Lady Fiona walked towards the house. She was handsome, yet so unusual when compared to most women who curried his favour and sought him out. For once, a lady wanted naught from him—well, naught but his aid should it be required.

What tore at his heart was her mention of Miss O'Shea as her sole friend. He had clenched his hands at his sides to keep from reaching for her. What impulse had inspired such a response from him? He had never been so tempted to comfort a lady before—other than family, that is.

Lady Fiona intrigued and confused him. She was not a classic beauty by London's standards, yet he had never cared what was popular when it came to a lady's appearance, and whether her hair or figure was fashionable made no difference in whether he was attracted to her, which he was. When he had followed her into the fox enclosure, his eyes had betrayed him and settled on the way her hips swayed under her skirt. Why could he not keep Lady Fiona from intruding upon his thoughts and his dreams, even if she was in a story told by his father?

As she disappeared through the door, he turned Kelpie back towards Moydrum and started for home.

Chapter 10

"Flee!"

Fiona winced at the volume and tone of her father's voice. As soon as she had struck Sir Malcolm across the cheek, a sharp pang had torn through her. Her impulsive act had been witnessed by their entire party and humiliated the baronet, who would not take kindly to being thus treated before their neighbours.

Fiona sighed. Her father would have been better off if she had never been born. If not for her, her mother would not have left as she had, and those of the neighbourhood would not joke of "Lord Kildare's banshee of a daughter," who ran wild through the fields and ate live fish from the streams—where the last bit had come from, she could not know. She could be an embarrassment, but by the time she was capable of understanding where she had failed as a lady, those habits had been too deeply ingrained. She could not help what she was, could she? Now she lived more to challenge those who appeared to question her nature. Her poor father deserved better. She sipped her tea and set the cup on the saucer as her father finally entered.

"Where is Lord Hatton? I saw the two of you ride away together."

"He accompanied me back to Larchfield, then took his leave. I have rarely been impressed by a gentleman, but his manner has been beyond reproach."

Her father closed the door to the drawing room and sat in the nearby chair, his filthy boots and breeches be damned. "I will know what Malcolm said to you. The entire hunting party could not stop speaking of what occurred. In order to defend you, I must know."

"You must make me a promise first," she said holding his gaze.

"I am *your* father, Fiona. Do not forget—"

"And if you want to know, you will make me your vow, sir."

He clenched his jaw then growled. "Very well. What did he say?"

Fiona closed her eyes tightly and repeated the words she had said to no one but Viscount Hatton. A part of her still could not believe she had been so open with him—that she had trusted him with the baronet's disgusting proposition. The silence that followed lingered until she finally opened her eyes to ensure her father was still present.

He was, but his cheeks and neck were turning a brilliant shade of puce. Oh God! Was he breathing? "Papa! Breathe!"

With a great inhale, he spluttered. "He said that to you? Why, the bloody revolting bastard! How dare he!" Her father stood and started for the door.

Before he could reach for the latch, she straightened in her chair. "Remember your promise."

Her father came to an abrupt stop, his shoulders dropped, and he sagged a mite. After a few seconds in that attitude, he stiffened. "Forgive me, Fee. I cannot keep my vow. Sir Malcolm's words are too scandalous."

Before she could rise from her chair, he had hastened through the door, and she hurried to the hall, grabbing Declan, the footman, as he entered. "Send to the stables for my horse and be quick about it."

Lord Hatton had said he would be of aid. What would she do if he refused now?

Nicholas snapped his book closed and exhaled. Why were the words of the baronet still causing him disquiet? He was not attached to Lady Fiona, by any means, but that a supposed gentleman should speak to her with so little respect rankled him.

With a huff, he stood and poured himself a glass of whiskey before returning to his comfortable chair by the fire. The library had proven itself to be decent and, in a manner similar to Richmond Castle and House, a sanctuary of sorts for him.

His first sip of the strong Irish whiskey slipped down with a slight burn. He had just resumed his place in the plush chair and re-opened his book when loud voices and commotion came from...He glanced around. Where was that sound coming from?

A door in the panelling opened and Lady Fiona rushed into the library. "Lord Hatton, you must help me. You promised."

He frowned and looked behind her. "How did you know of that entrance? I have not even seen the servants use it."

She glanced over her shoulder. "Molly and I found all the passages in this old castle years ago." After giving her head a shake, she grabbed the sleeve of his topcoat. "My father has gone after Sir Malcolm. Pray, you must talk some sense into him. I do not know of anyone else who can do so."

Nicholas looked down at his whiskey before setting it aside. A quiet afternoon after today's events was more than he could have hoped for it seemed. "I do not know the way to Sir Malcolm's estate."

"I can show you, sir," said Mr. O'Shea as he entered. "Lady Fiona, my Molly awaits you at the cottage. You can remain there until we return."

The lady stiffened, and her neck lengthened a little as she did so. "I beg your pardon, but I will be accompanying the two of you." She held out a pointing finger. "And do not try to guilt me with sad tales of your wife's worry or Molly's greatest friend coming to harm. It will not work."

The steward pressed his lips together for a moment while he stared at Lady Fiona, but she only returned his long look with her own, her eyebrows raised. Finally, the steward relented and turned his attention to Nicholas. "Our horses are being saddled as we speak."

A footman fetched his greatcoat, and without delay, they were atop their mounts and riding west. Lady Fiona did not slow their pace, riding astride at his side for the entirety of the journey. As they approached Sir Malcolm's home, the man himself was walking towards the house from the direction of the stables.

"Sir Malcolm!" Lady Fiona spurred her horse forward.

"Blast," said Nicholas in a mutter. Why could she not let the men approach the baronet? She would be the death of him.

The baronet came to a halt when he saw who was approaching and his hands clenched into fists at his side. "I do not know why you have come here, Lady Fiona, but you are not welcome on my lands. Remove yourself now."

"Where is my father?"

"How am I to know?"

As Nicholas drew closer, he winced at the bright red, angry slash that marred one side of the man's face. The baronet deserved what he received, but it still did not make the welt appear any less painful.

"Upon learning of what you said to his daughter, Lord Kildare left Larchfield to confront you," said Nicholas.

"Has he been here?" demanded Mr. O'Shea.

"If Kildare has called, he has not made himself known to me." A footman emerged from the house, and Sir Malcolm waved him over, said a few words, then nodded. "If he intended to come here, he never arrived. With a daughter such as his, he should not have been shocked at my comment. Why he should feel the need to defend her honour— why any man should—"

"How dare you, sir!" said Fiona. "I am a lady."

"You are a hoyden and a trollop." The baronet spit out the words with a great deal of venom. What had Lady Fiona ever done to earn his vehement displeasure? "No respectable gentleman should defend your honour."

Nicholas grabbed Lady Fiona's riding crop before she had a chance to raise it in the air. Thankfully, he had been close enough! "*I* would defend the lady's honour as would any true gentleman."

"Indeed," said Mr. O'Shea.

The baronet gave a derisive chuckle. "I saw the two of you riding off together after I departed the hunt. Are you hoping to be her next lover?" The words were sneered by the foul, little man before him. The rhythm of Nicholas's heart began to accelerate and pound through his veins. How dare he speak so before the earl's daughter!

"Why, I have never!" Lady Fiona urged her stallion closer. "Lord Hatton is a friend of my family as was his father before him. Why should he not behave with honour when one such as you will not?"

"Always so high and mighty, Lady Fiona. You are more of a man than your father, although, with a lady's intelligence, Larchfield will go to ruin under your care. I would bet my life on it."

Nicholas dismounted with haste and without heed, put himself nose to nose with the weasel of a man before him. His heart was hammering against his sternum, and he shook as he stared down at him. "She has more honour and intelligence than you, one who is a danger to himself and those around him on the hunt. Were you trying to impress her by playing the larker? You appeared more ridiculous than skilful." He had stepped even closer whispering the last in a low growl. He despised men of Malcolm's ilk. "You know you would never have any hope of Lady Fiona, so you belittled her then, and you continue to do so now, and if you do not desist, *I* shall call you out." His entire body continued to hum and vibrate as he towered over the man in front of him, the words flying from his lips with no thought or heed.

"You have no relation to the lady, sir. You would risk your life for a woman you have known for so little time? Perhaps you have already tupped her." Sir Malcolm gave a disgusting chuckle as Nicholas grabbed the grub worm by his lapels.

"I would for my betrothed," he said. "Which would you prefer, pistols or sabres? I assure you I am skilled at both and have no hesitation facing you with either weapon."

Lady Fiona gasped behind him and grabbed his arm. When had she dismounted? "What are you about?"

Sir Malcolm paled, making Nicholas give a strangled laugh that was odd to his own ears. Excellent! He had counted on the man being a coward. His grip on the man's coat tightened. "Now, you will apologise to the lady, and we shall take our leave—unless I require a second."

The man gave a twitchy shake of his head. At an odd odour, Nicholas glanced down. A dark brown stain was spreading over the front of Sir Malcolm's tan buckskin breeches. The man had pissed himself? Nicholas released the blackguard and shoved him back. He had no desire to be soiled by another man's fear. "You truly are a coward. If Lord Kildare arrives, send him to Moydrum. We take no leave of you. You have proven yourself no gentleman."

"I am not your servant."

Nicholas could have laughed at the larker's last effort to assert himself when he was obviously a braggadocio. Sir Malcolm had sputtered out the words, red-faced and with a dark patch so large upon his trousers, it formed paths down his legs to the tops of his boots. While Nicholas was not as knowledgeable on fabrics and tailoring as he could be, the boots Sir Malcolm wore to the hunt were more about fashion and less about practicality. Nicholas had only ever seen them in the most exclusive Bond Street shops, and at this moment, they contained the baronet's urine—a fitting revenge for a weasel.

"You may not be a servant, but you could show a modicum of sensibility should the earl appear."

Nicholas took step after step backwards so as not to remove his gaze from the baronet. He had angered the man, and angry people were not always wise. "Mount your horse." He spoke over his shoulder to Lady Fiona before climbing atop his own.

To her credit, Lady Fiona did not utter one more word until they were over the rise. She drew beside him. "What were you thinking?" she hissed. "Are you mad? We are not betrothed, and we shall never be so. As I have said, I have no intention of marrying you or anyone."

"Mr. O'Shea! We need to find Lord Kildare. Pray, ride ahead and assemble a party to search along the journey from Larchfield to Sir Malcolm's estate as well as someone to ensure he did not return home without confronting the baronet." His steward gave a curt nod and urged his horse forward into a gallop, leaving them behind.

"Lord Hatton, I shall not be ignored."

He stopped his horse and rounded upon her. His ire still simmered below the surface. "Do you wish to harangue me for challenging the man to prove him a coward, or would you prefer to search for your father? If considered in a reasonable manner, I believe the second should take precedence since he could be injured or ill. We can discuss the latter after he is found. Are we in agreement?"

Lady Fiona blanched a little at his curt tone and blunt words, then for once, mutely nodded. "If we are taking the paths between Larchfield and here, we need to return to the bridge and cross. My father would not be on this side of the river."

Her advice was practical and imminently sensible. "Of course, I shall follow your lead."

Chapter 11

They rode in silence for a long time, both taking in the fields and any obstacles along their paths that may have caused a hindrance for her father. He had to be here somewhere, did he not? But what would happen when they found him? Would the entire neighbourhood learn of Lord Hatton's heated claim that she was his betrothed? What would become of her if they did?

She squeezed her eyes closed for a moment before continuing her search along the edge of a dry fence. Her mind, however, despite her occupation, kept returning to the argument with Sir Malcolm.

What would she do if her father made her marry the viscount? He was handsome to be sure, but she had maintained since she was old enough to understand her mother's abandonment, that she would never wed, much less tie herself to a man of means who would take her from Ireland to London and thrust her into the middle of that nest of pit vipers. She would never be so dependent upon anyone.

Well, it was no matter what the neighbourhood thought! She would do as she wanted! As her gaze lit upon the viscount's broad shoulders, a frisson travelled through her stomach to the rest of her. She could not deny he was handsome. He would do for a lover, but if she were to be so bold she would never do so until she was older and her father was dead. Mrs. O'Shea once mentioned ladies eventually left their child-bearing years behind. She would not be too aged to take a lover by then, would she? However, if her father departed this mortal coil, she could hide away until any child was born and claim him or her as her ward. Put it about a tenant could not afford to keep the child and since she had never borne one of her own...She needed some happiness and companionship in her life. Did she not?

They passed into the next field where they would follow the hill down and return to the river's edge. She should not have told her father Sir Malcolm's offensive words. They spent little time in company with the baronet since her father did not care for him, and the coward was repugnant in the extreme, but since the rest of the neighbours had been invited to the foxhunt, how could they have excluded him? They were never so openly rude.

"Forgive me my earlier ire," said Lord Hatton. "I do not often lose my patience or forget myself, but I did with that man."

His gaze met hers for but a moment before she nodded and turned her attention back to their surroundings. As much as she could scold him, and desired to scold him, he had been right. They needed to find her father first.

"Sir Malcolm is not well liked in the neighbourhood. Few invite him to their balls or parties, and he spends part of the year in London where he claims to be welcomed by all of station and importance."

"I thought him a little man when he rode as he did during the hunt."

She could not fight the tug at the corner of her lips. "Yes, he has been so for a long time."

"Has he ever spoken to you in such a way before?"

"Sir Malcolm has made comments on my method of riding and deporting myself—mostly that I would not be accepted in London circles. Since I have never planned on being part of the Season, I never thought him worth rebuking. Besides, those sorts of barbs are easy to let go. They do not sting. At the last ball, he requested a dance and requested to call. I suppose he is becoming desperate to father an heir; I do not know. I refused him. He took the rejection with a bitter spirit, even though I did my best to be gracious. I could not imagine why he thought I would tolerate his revolting proposition."

"After your rejection and after the smaller insults he had delivered went without rebuke, he likely assumed a larger insult would go unchallenged."

She sighed. "My father was unwell in the autumn. He has rallied, although the physician from Belfast as well as Mr. Ryan the apothecary did say it was his heart. I inherit Larchfield as well as the title, so when word spread that Papa was ill, I began to receive the scrutiny of the eligible gentleman of the area once again. None would tolerate my riding astride or those diversions I enjoy, and I shall not be tied to a man who treats me as though I am feeble-minded."

"The Kildare title can pass through the female line? I was unaware. The current Countess of Orkney carries the title for her family. My grandfather has mentioned the scrutiny she received when she assumed the earldom. I am not old enough to remember."

"Yes, I do not know of another in Ireland, though that does not mean one does not exist. I have no intention of marrying much less giving control of my estate and myself to a man who values me more for my title and inheritance than my heart."

They rode in silence for at least five minutes, which caused Fiona no little consternation. Why was he so quiet? Was he put out that she had no intention of marrying when he had declared himself her betrothed only a short time ago? She had told him at Lord Meath's ball she had no intention of ever becoming any man's wife. Lord Hatton had no right to declare himself so attached, yet she was not one to criticise. How often had she let her ire get the best of her?

Her horse stopped without her cue, and his ears pricked forward.

"What is it, Diarmait?"

The stallion shook his head with a snort, then began pawing at the ground. She pressed her calf into him, but no matter what she did, he would not budge. "Something is amiss. He does not behave so without cause."

Lord Hatton pivoted around on his horse to face her. He opened his mouth to speak but an odd sound made both their heads turn to a tree at the river's edge. A large amount of brush and undergrowth concealed the rocky shoreline, so Fiona sidled her mount closer. Was that a boot?

She was out of the saddle and rushing into the reeds without heed. "Papa!"

He was on his stomach in the rocky shallow and wet through. When they turned him over, blood trickled down his temple, and his complexion was a pasty white.

"No, no, no, you will not leave me yet!"

She made to take him by his arm and pull him as best she could from the water, but Lord Hatton strode around and took her father's hand, hoisting him to his shoulder. "We need to get him to Moydrum."

"I can care for him at Larchfield!"

The viscount rounded on her and was close—too close, but she held fast. "Moydrum is closer, is it not? We could have him out of these wet clothes, warmed, and the apothecary called sooner than if we take him the further distance to Larchfield."

Standing her ground had been a challenge. When the viscount first turned, everything in her screamed to flinch back at his proximity, but she had managed to stand fast. "I suppose, when viewed in that light, what you say makes more sense."

"Well, I am glad you have deigned to agree with me, Lady Fiona." Her body gave a jolt, and she stiffened at his tone. Had it been necessary to be sarcastic about it?

Lord Hatton laid her father across his saddle, then mounted using a nearby boulder for a bit of aid. He shifted her father partly onto his legs and kept an arm across him while they began their ride to Moydrum at a fast walk.

She patted her stallion's withers. "Good boy, Diarmait," she said under her breath. "You always take care of me, do you not?"

"I daresay he has earned a treat when we reach the stables."

"May I ask why we are riding at such a slow pace?"

"Because I am not confident in my ability to hold your father atop Kelpie at a canter or a gallop. I would prefer he arrive without falling under my horse's hooves."

Fiona bit her lip. Maybe one day she would learn to trust and not question all. "Do you know if a tenant farm is nearby? I could ride ahead and see if they have a cart."

He shook his head. "I am not familiar with the location of every tenant farm yet. Mr. O'Shea and I visited the plots between my estate and your father's first. We are to visit these this week."

The pounding of hooves heralded the arrival of a group of men, who slowed as they approached. "Thank the Lord, you found him," said the man in the front, a groom from the Moydrum stable.

"Yes," said Lord Hatton. "Ride ahead of us. Send a cart back from the closest tenant farm in possession of one. Then send for Mr. Ryan. Lord Kildare will require care when we arrive at Moydrum." A chorus of "sir" came from the three men who galloped back in the direction from whence they came.

"We should be able to move him a little faster with a cart."

She glanced down at her father, so pale and hanging as though dead over the viscount's saddle. "His colour is not good."

"He is cold, but I can feel him breathing."

Her reins remained clenched in tight fists until the cart finally arrived, and they were able to pick up their pace. What would happen when they arrived at Lord Hatton's estate? Would she be allowed to remain with her father, or in light of what occurred today with Sir Malcolm, would the gentleman expect her to return home for the evening?

As soon as they approached the great house, servants flooded from the stables and the house. Their horses were whisked away to the stable with Lord Hatton telling the groom who took Diarmait that the horse was responsible for them finding her father. The groom had lifted his eyebrows and indicated he would see him given special treatment as soon as he was cooled.

Once inside the house, Fiona attempted to follow her father upstairs, but Mrs. O'Shea stopped her before her foot hit the first step. "Oh no, you don't, Fiona Fitzgerald. You let the men get him settled and Mrs. Murphy and Lord Hatton's valet prepare him for the apothecary. We sent to Larchfield for your maid and your trunk, and Mrs. Murphy has a bedchamber for you to refresh yourself. By the time you do so, I am certain your belongings will have arrived, and you can change."

Fiona looked down at her riding habit, the hems caked in at least six inches of wet mud. It should not be surprising after she hurried into the brush along the edge of the river. "Someone will tell me if Papa—"

"Yes, of course, we shall. We would never keep you in the dark."

Without further argument, she followed Mrs. O'Shea to a bedchamber she had always favoured, a large room with a delicate vine pattern wallcovering with the varied pink shades in the flowers that climbed the walls. She had never had reason to stay in the family or guests' rooms at Moydrum, and now that she was, all she wanted to do was go home.

This was her fault—just another thing to add to the ever-growing list of problems she had caused her father. She choked down a sob and ripped at the buttons of her coat, tossing it across a chair and unfastening the gown as best she could before shedding it from her body. The sound of a seam ripping accompanied her shoving it over her hips, but she cared not.

By the time she began trying to remove her boots, tears were pouring down her cheeks. She could have not stopped them if she had tried. She tore off her stockings and dropped onto the settee, collapsing to her side and giving in to her tears. What would she ever do if her father died? She was not ready to be alone in the world. Lord, what would Lord Hatton think if he saw her now? He would believe her an impostor, that is what he would think! A scared little girl. And how could she argue with him?

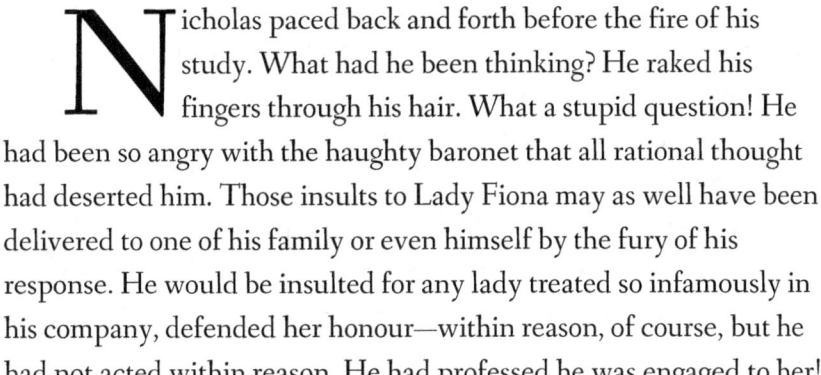

Chapter 12

Nicholas paced back and forth before the fire of his study. What had he been thinking? He raked his fingers through his hair. What a stupid question! He had been so angry with the haughty baronet that all rational thought had deserted him. Those insults to Lady Fiona may as well have been delivered to one of his family or even himself by the fury of his response. He would be insulted for any lady treated so infamously in his company, defended her honour—within reason, of course, but he had not acted within reason. He had professed he was engaged to her! Stupid, stupid man! What had possessed him to go that far?

Upon their arrival to Moydrum, he had seen to it Lord Kildare was placed in a suitable room before meeting Evans in his chambers to change. According to the reliable word of his valet, Lady Fiona was placed in the rooms next to her father's so she could help see to his care. Nicholas had not even considered providing her with a bedchamber or her remaining while her father convalesced, though he would have been rude indeed if he had neglected to do so. Thank heavens, Mrs. Murphy had made the arrangements for him.

At a light knock, he bid the person enter. When Mr. O'Shea closed the door behind him, Nicholas stopped to pour himself a whiskey. "Would you care to join me?"

"I'll not be turning down some of your fine whiskey if you are offering." As his steward took the first sip, the man watched Nicholas with a steady, penetrating gaze that made his insides squirm.

"Whatever you have to say, I beg you to say it." Yes, his tone was intemperate, but engaged to Lady Fiona? If he could, he would groan and bury his face in his hands. She had to wonder at his terse quiet while they had searched by the river, but as the initial ire had passed, the realisation of what he had done set in, making his heart race and his palms sweat. After years of avoiding the traps of eligible ladies, what a foolish and careless thing to do!

Mr. O'Shea merely lifted his eyebrows. "I think you know what I would say. After working for you this past fortnight, I know you typically consider every possibility before proposing a solution. You are quick with your wit, but that is a mark of your intelligence as you can best a man with your words rather than your fists. Your behaviour at Sir Malcolm's was...unexpected. I find that since Lord Kildare is abed, and we do not know if or when he will wake, I must act in his stead and enquire of your intentions towards his daughter."

For but a second, Nicholas's hackles prickled. Lord Kildare and Mr. O'Shea, despite the differences in their stations, were friends. O'Shea was doing no more than standing in for the earl while he was so ill. He needed to force that affront back where it came from. "I have no intentions towards Lady Fiona. As much as I respect her and Lord Kildare, we have no understanding."

Mr. O'Shea blinked, but his lip curved. "I see."

"You see? What do you see?" The words came out in a rush, but what could Mr. O'Shea believe that caused him...was that amusement writ upon his countenance?

The man chuckled and sat in a chair near the fire. "You surprised yourself when you claimed she was your intended, did you not? Have you ever been that angry before?"

"No," said Nicholas, pressing his palm to his forehead. "I...I do not know what happened. My first thought was to keep Lady Fiona from humiliating the man once again, but when Sir Malcolm began speaking of our departure from the hunt after the confrontation, I had no control over my words. They flew without thought or heed for what they meant. I shall admit that making Sir Malcolm cower was immensely satisfying. That worm does not deserve to be called man. He is a loathsome, foul creature and should be taken to task for his behaviour by someone. You know, I have heard of gentlemen in London who speak so and are called out, but the gossip does not always include what was said. I cannot credit the impudence of some men. My grandmother would leave a palmprint upon my cheek should I ever speak to a lady so.

"Lady Fiona mentioned Sir Malcolm once requested to call upon her." Why the man thought he could endeavour to deserve Lady Fiona was beyond him.

"Yes, a year ago. At the time, Lady Fiona told my wife, who fretted for weeks that Sir Malcolm might try to force the poor girl's hand." O'Shea sighed and stared into his drink for a moment before catching Nicholas's gaze. "Lady Fiona is...some might say she was indulged, which she was. I shall not tell you a falsehood. She seems a happy enough young lady, headstrong and impetuous, but usually wearing a smile. The Larchfield tenants love her since she spends a prodigious amount of time visiting them and ensuring they are well.

She will make an excellent Lady Kildare when the time comes. That said, I have overheard her speaking to Molly, and once to her horse, and I know she is adept at concealing her true feelings. Pray, I beg you to tread with care."

Nicholas waved his hands in front of him. "I had not planned on courting her. If I am honest, I travelled here to escape the presence of a lady I once held in some esteem. I am not searching for a wife."

O'Shea nodded while he glanced out of the window for a moment. "Still, I am requesting you to take care with Lady Fiona. Her reputation is based on her brash demeanour, but I have a suspicion that even Molly and my wife do not know all of Lady Fiona Fitzgerald's heart. My wife and I believe she is more sensitive than she seems."

Lady Fiona sensitive? He had never known so bold a lady. Could more lurk beneath the surface than what appeared to one and all?

After Mr. O'Shea finished his whiskey, he stood and placed his glass on the tray. "I was not searching for a wife when I met my Constance."

A strangled sound came from Nicholas before he could stop it. "Forgive me, but I do not believe Lady Fiona and I would suit. I do not plan on remaining in Ireland, and I am certain she would not wish to journey to England, so we would be at an impasse."

"I understand I have overstepped but do understand that neither her father nor I would want to see her hurt."

Hurt? Given the lady's first reaction to what he had said, she was as appalled and shocked by his impulsive declaration as he was. "You and Lord Kildare are friends. I am certain he would welcome your protection of his daughter given his situation."

"I thank you for your understanding, sir. Before I return to my duties, I thought you would want to know Lord Kildare's mount returned to Larchfield without him."

"That is good news. I thank you for informing me."

After the man excused himself to see to his work, Nicholas downed the last of his whiskey and poured another before resuming his previous occupation of pacing before the fire. How was he to manage this situation? He turned. Was there a situation? Would anyone other than Mr. O'Shea, Sir Malcolm, himself, and Lady Fiona hear of what he said? He turned again. What if he was forced to marry Lady Fiona? He halted and blinked. She was not wholly objectionable. She was not a simpering lady of the *ton*—that was a definite advantage. He could also not deny that she was beautiful; her dark red hair making a striking contrast with her pale complexion, and her green eyes blazing in his direction.

At a knock upon the door, he bid the person enter. Lo and behold, the lady herself stood upon the threshold with her hands clasped in front of her. "Forgive me, but Mr. Ryan is with my father, so Mrs. Murphy suggested I await word with you."

"Of course," he said, gesturing her inside. "Would you like some sherry?" Her eyes appeared a little pinker than usual. Had she been crying?

"No, but I should like a glass of whiskey if you would indulge me."

He poured her a small serving and handed her the glass when she passed on her way to the chair Mr. O'Shea recently vacated, leaving the door ajar. As she walked in front of the fire, the light behind her illuminated what was concealed by the layers of her gown. He swallowed hard. If they were forced to wed, her figure was not wholly objectionable either—what he could discern of it anyway. Shapely calves that led to a pair of thighs that were not sticks but were, no doubt, muscular and would wrap tight around his hips and...

He shook himself and cleared his throat. "I hope the rooms Mrs. Murphy provided are adequate." He conjured an image of Lady Catherine de Bourgh in his mind.

"Oh, yes, they are lovely. I must admit they have always been my favourite."

"I was not aware you were so familiar with Moydrum. First, you know the passages and now the guest rooms?"

She relaxed into the chair, her hand holding her whiskey on the arm. "I have been friends with Molly since we were wee things. We have played hide and go seek and other games in this house during the rain as well as explored the hidden passages."

At a knock upon the open door, Lady Fiona stood back up with a jolt. "Mr. Ryan, how does my father fare?"

"He has a good-sized lump on the side of his head, but I am more concerned with the time he spent in the water. Mrs. Murphy said he was chilled when he arrived. I also wonder if he breathed in any water since it was indicated you found him on his stomach."

"Where we found him was very shallow," said Nicholas. "The water was not covering his mouth or nose."

"Then we have some hope he will not develop pneumonia, but we cannot discount it completely. Mrs. Murphy and Mr. Evans have done an excellent job of warming the earl, so we can do no more than wait. No evidence exists of any broken bones, but we shall not know for sure until he awakens and can tell us what pains him. I have left laudanum and a tonic for cough and grippe that can be given if he needs either during the night. I told Mrs. Murphy to send for me should he take a turn for the worse, but I shall return on the morrow to ensure he is faring as expected."

"I thank you, Mr. Ryan," said Lady Fiona. "If you both will excuse me, I should like to see my father."

The moment she had departed, Mr. Ryan sighed. "I would have dissuaded her as he is asleep and little can be done at the moment, but I have learnt not to stand in the way of the lady. If you can remove her from her father's sick room—persuade her to eat and sleep—it would be beneficial. Otherwise, I fear she will remain at his bedside night and day until he returns."

"You expect him to wake soon, then?" That would be good, considering how they found the earl.

"The bump on his head is not too severe. He should not linger in his current state for too long. Do not tell Lady Fiona my expectations just in case her father does worsen. While he may be up and about by tomorrow, we do not know what occurred before he was found."

He did not want to raise the lady's hopes to have them crushed if the worst came to pass, which was likely wise. "I shall not alter what you have told her."

"Good," said Mr. Ryan nodding. "I shall return on the morrow. Good day, sir."

As soon as the apothecary departed, Nicholas dropped into the nearest chair and rested his head in his hands. Until Lord Kildare awakened, he would be in company with Lady Fiona. She had not mentioned Nicholas's challenge to Sir Malcolm since just after it occurred, but how long before she did? His presumption while angry affected more than just him. He was certain she wanted to marry him as much as he wanted to marry her. Yet, what if the earl attempted to force the matter? He cringed. What a happy couple they would make.

Chapter 13

Fiona straightened and propped her hands on her hips. "I beg your pardon?"

Mrs. Murphy did not flinch at Fiona's terse tone, but the Moydrum housekeeper had also known Fiona since she was a wee child. The woman had never been intimidated by Fiona's occasional ill temper. "I said you are expected in the dining room by Lord Hatton for dinner." The housekeeper held out her hand, palm out. "Before you raise your voice, know it will do no good. You cannot spend every waking hour at your father's bedside, nor would he ask it of you. Not to mention, arguing with me will get you nowhere, as you well know. I remember when you were a babe, so your ire does not frighten me as it does some. Besides, we both know your father will support me when he wakes. He always has."

As much as Fiona hated it, Mrs. Murphy was right. When she was little, how many times had Fiona's father punished her for speaking so to a respected servant? She was not at Larchfield, and Mrs. Murphy ruled the roost at Moydrum. Fiona had been reminded of that fact often enough. Of course, she had been an indulged child the last time she was punished by her father for her impertinence towards Mrs. Murphy.

She let her shoulders drop with her hands and huffed. Men! Without further argument, she marched past the housekeeper and stomped down the stairs, her insides shaking more and more as she drew closer and closer to the dining room. Officious, domineering, insufferable men! At the bottom of the stairs, she made a sharp pivot and strode into the dining room. She stopped just before she reached the table. "What do you mean by forcing me to come down for dinner? Courtesy would be to send me a tray so I may remain at my father's bedside."

"I would think it obvious," said Lord Hatton as he stood. The easy manner of his response merely served to raise her hackles further. "I am following Mr. Ryan's instructions. He feared you making yourself ill by tending to your father day and night, so Mrs. Murphy and I are ensuring you have a respite from time to time, meaning you will eat in the dining room with me for your meals."

She drew herself as tall as she could. "As a guest, I would assume I could eat where I please. You, after all, are not my father, nor are you my husband. You will also never be my husband, despite what you said to Sir Malcolm today." Her slipper-clad foot tapped in a furious rhythm under her skirts. Lord Hatton was too used to having his way. Goodness knows, he had gone too far when he had claimed her his betrothed—and he had still not apologised for doing so.

"*I* was defending *your* honour, my lady," said Lord Hatton in a slightly elevated voice. "You did hear the accusations and vile suppositions the man was making against you—against the two of us after the hunt?"

"I am accustomed to those who do not care for how I ride, that I do not prefer the pursuits or accomplishments of a lady, and that I am not soft-spoken. For the most part, Sir Malcolm and his vitriol are easily dismissed and carry no weight with me. So, you see, *I* do not need a man to save me. *I* can take care of myself."

The pinkie side of the viscount's closed fist rapped upon the back of a chair. "I never said you could not take care of yourself, but why should a gentleman not be of aid when he can? You could at least be a little appreciative!"

"Appreciative? Should word of what you said travel the county, my father could *make* us marry. You do know that, do you not? I have no intention of being tied to any man much less a stubborn, intolerable viscount who has no intention of remaining near Larchfield. I shall not become your brood mare!" As with the housekeeper, Fiona's hands went to her hips, and she lifted her chin. He *would* understand her opinion on the matter.

"That is well and good because I have no intention of being tied to you either. I am supposed to return to London next Season and find a suitable lady to wed. My grandmother will surely have a number of candidates for me to dance with and discover if they suit—"

"No doubt who has the best pedigree and the largest fortune." Fiona spat out the words. Lord, but she despised when her neighbours behaved so, but why did it stir her ire more that Lord Hatton would seek out a well-connected and well-dowered bride? She had no desire to be that lady. Why should she care if he married the daughter of a duke or the king himself?

"If I cared for naught but those considerations, I would have wed a lady before now."

"Perhaps what ladies sought your notice were not rich enough. You will likely do as most with means do, wed a lady you cannot abide to bear your heirs, then keep a mistress who is paid to be at your beck and call."

The viscount's chest swelled, and he spluttered. "I would not sully the Hatton viscountcy or the Richmond earldom, not to mention shame my family, in such a way!"

Fiona balked when he propelled forward while he spoke, stopping close, impossibly close, to her. What was that odd, fluttering sensation in her stomach?

"You know nothing of me or who I am, yet you assume I am the worst of libertines by how you speak of me. I shall have you know I would never behave so. Unlike some men, I do have some care for my reputation and what my family thinks of me! You, on the other hand, roam the countryside, drawing your pistol on unsuspecting gentlemen, accusing them of poaching on their own lands! Mayhap before you make further assumptions about me, you should look at your own hoydenish behaviour."

"Hoydenish? How dare you! I—"

Whatever she meant to say next died on her tongue when Lord Hatton yanked her into his arms and pressed his lips to hers. She held her arms out at her sides for but a moment, but his lips softened as he began to kiss her as though he were starved for her.

Her thighs clenched together, and her knees nearly gave way. A warm shiver travelled through her as her eyes fluttered closed, and she returned the pressure of his mouth with that of her own. That odd sensation in her stomach grew and travelled lower. Good Lord, kissing the viscount was like drowning in heat while her body burned from within.

His tongue darted between her lips with a groan while her hands moved to grip his lapels in an attempt to remain upright, which was impossible. This was a kiss? She had never expected a kiss to be so consuming. She could do no more than feel—her mind refused to work while his lips teased hers and his tongue stole all but sensation. Wait a moment! What was she doing? One minute, they had been arguing— had been yelling at each other, and now...This had to stop. But that fluttering low in her belly. What would happen if she gave it a moment more? No, she could not do that, no matter how much her body screamed to let him do what he would.

She shoved against Lord Hatton's chest until he released her, then let her hand swing, connecting with his cheek with a loud smack. After hastening two steps back, she shook her hand. Lord, that hurt! She heaved in breath after breath in a futile attempt to calm her body, which buzzed. Her breasts were heavy and every shift against her stays travelled straight to her lower belly.

The viscount's cheek bulged two or three times from clenching his jaw, then he turned on his heel and departed without a word.

Fiona squeezed her eyes closed. That could not happen again! No, never again. She would tend to her father, and Lord Hatton's demands could go to the devil. No matter what, she would not take any of her meals with him, she would stay as far away from him as possible, and with any luck, her father would wake soon, and they would return to Larchfield where she would no longer be in danger of happening upon the viscount.

As she made to return to her father's sickbed, she came upon Mrs. Murphy in the hall. "Lord Hatton requests a tray in the library." She was being presumptuous, but since the man left the dining room in such a hurry, he had to go somewhere, did he not? By his talk of books with her father, her best guess was that he would disappear into the library. "I would also appreciate a tray in my father's rooms."

Mrs. Murphy did no more than stare at her as though she had sprouted a horn in the middle of her forehead, the housekeeper's mouth agape, while Fiona continued as though naught was amiss and climbed the stairs to return to her father's bedside.

He sat before the fire in the library with his head in his hand. He, Nicholas Montford, was a horrible, hideous person. That was the only way to explain his recent actions. He was supposed to be a gentleman, so why was he having such difficulty controlling his responses to Lady Fiona?

First, he declared himself betrothed in some mad outburst meant to help the lady, then while her father convalesced upstairs in Nicholas's home, he kissed the man's daughter while arguing with her. Why? He had no interest in Lady Fiona other than his friendship with her father. What strange infirmity overtook him when in her presence? It must be an infirmity since he behaved so out of character. He had never, ever lacked restraint—until he met Lady Fiona Fitzgerald. Even with Lady Rebecca—nay, the duchess—he had never been so impulsive. They may have been on intimate terms the one time, but he had ensured more than once that the lady desired to continue. He had not lost himself to all rational thought as he seemed to do with Lord Kildare's daughter.

He closed his eyes and groaned when an image of Lady Fiona appeared in his mind instead of the darkness he craved. Her vivid red locks fell about her shoulders, and her green eyes upbraided him. When she was angry, they flashed dangerously, but in a way that stirred him like no other.

"Sir," said Mrs. Murphy. "I thought you should like to know that Lord Kildare woke for a few minutes. He recognised his daughter and took Mr. Ryan's tonic before falling back to sleep."

After kissing Lady Fiona so, he could not face the housekeeper lest he reveal his present state, although with her entrance, that predicament had faded some. "He seemed well?"

"He complained of a splitting headache and a chill. I brought him another coverlet and we built up the fire in the room. Thus far, he has no fever. I pray one will not come."

"At least he has awakened. Is Lady Fiona still sitting with him?" Why had he asked? What business was it of his whether she sat in his room all night or retired?

"Before he fell asleep, Lord Kildare ordered the dear girl to rest. I thought she would argue, but once she was assured he was comfortable for the night, she retired."

With a nod, he scrubbed his face with his hands. "Good. I thank you for seeing to the earl and preparing rooms for Lady Fiona. I had not considered her remaining until he could return home." Perhaps the earl would be well by the morrow, and they could depart. Nicholas would have done what he could for them, and he would not be tempted further by the lady under his roof.

"I would not have expected you to think of it, which is why I did so. 'Tis more a mistress's purview than a master's. Well, I shall leave you. Do you require anything before you retire?"

"No, I shall be going to my rooms before long."

After a quick curtsey, Mrs. Murphy departed, and he let his head fall against the back of the chair. He would pray Lord Kildare was well by the morning. To regain his peace of mind, he needed that man to take his daughter back to Larchfield!

Chapter 14

Fiona flinched when her father coughed. No fever had come, but the horrible, racking cough could have rattled Moydrum on its foundation. He had even been sick earlier after hacking and barking for a time so hard it caused him to gag and cast up his accounts. They needed to find some remedy. How was her father to sleep well or hold down food?

"Lady Fiona," said Mr. Ryan. "I should like to apply a poultice to your father's chest to see if we can calm his lungs, then I have a tisane and a tonic for him to take. It would be best if you departed while I tend to him."

She opened her mouth to protest. While they removed her father's nightgown from his chest, she could stand in the dressing room. Naught could be amiss about that. Her father squeezed her hand. "Go." The word was rasped out between coughs. With her lips pressed together to keep from letting an intemperate comment loose, she rose and left the room. Her father was so poorly that she would not argue with him. Once in the corridor, she paused and breathed for a moment. What was she to do? The weather was dreadful today, a heavy fog had covered the house and grounds, making those inside seem as though they were isolated from the rest of the world. Rain had begun falling near luncheon and had not stopped since.

Her feet began moving, carrying her down the stairs. She wandered through the drawing rooms and the ballroom before finding herself standing in the door of the dining room. A chair scraped the floor when Lord Hatton stood.

"Lady Fiona, how is your father this evening?"

"His cough is giving him a great deal of difficulty. Mr. Ryan is tending to him at the moment."

The viscount held out a hand to the opposite end of the table. "Would you care to join me for dinner?" He cleared his throat. "Unless you have been brought a tray already." He had not forced her to join him for a meal since his attempt three days ago, and Fiona had done her best to avoid the man.

"No, my maid has yet to bring me one. I would be pleased to join you." She would be as far from him as the table allowed. She should be safe. What occurred the last time she was in this room with him could not happen again! It would not happen again!

The footman pulled out the chair, a plate was set before her, and the man brought her the different dishes from the table so she could spoon some onto her plate. Then she chewed bite after bite, the sole sounds being the clinking of silver and when a glass was set upon the table.

They had not spoken since the confrontation three days ago—or should she say the kiss three days ago. The best of reasons existed for the separation: she could not take the chance Lord Hatton would kiss her again. Her toes still curled in her slippers at the remembrance of his lips moving confidently over hers, his tongue caressing and tasting, and his stuttered breathing coming in erratic puffs against her cheek. She shifted in her chair. Still, he was the most infuriating man! As much as they could not allow it, Lord but her body screamed to do that again and again. All the more reason to keep her distance!

As soon as she could be reasonably finished, she stood. "Forgive me, but I wish to look in on my father."

Lord Hatton stood and gave a slight dip of a bow. "Of course. I hope the meal was to your satisfaction."

She paused. "Yes, the food was excellent. My compliments to your cook."

A great exhale rushed from her when she reached the hall. What an awkward way to spend a meal! She and Lord Hatton seemed to be all that was polite and pleasant by appearances, but the tension made the air thick and heavy upon her shoulders.

When she knocked upon the door to her father's bedchamber, Mr. Ryan admitted her. "The earl is resting at the moment. The treatments brought him some relief from the cough. He insisted before he fell asleep, however, that you not remain tonight."

Her palm rested upon his forehead, careful to be gentle so she did not wake him. "It is no imposition since I prefer to know he is well with my own eyes." Papa's eyes moved under his eyelids and his breathing was somewhat laboured. What if he developed pneumonia?

"My lady, I shall stay for another hour or two to ensure the treatment's effects are lasting, then his valet will sit with him for the rest of the night. Your father was adamant you rest this evening."

Fiona pinched the bridge of her nose. "I insist on staying with him."

The apothecary sighed. "Your father ordered me to wake him should you defy his wishes. He is sleeping comfortably. Would you have me rouse him because you will not accept his request?"

Gah! Her father had instructed Mr. Ryan on how to manage her. She was certain of it! "Very well." As if she had any choice in the matter! She threw her hands up and let them drop back to her sides before departing the room. Insufferable men! How she despised the lot of them! They were full of their own self-importance, officious, and infuriating.

Once in her bedchamber, Walsh helped her to ready herself for the night, and as soon as the maid was excused, Fiona climbed into bed, sat against the headboard, and twirled her thumbs. She always read before bed and had no book to make her drowsy.

What time was it? When she consulted the clock, the hands told her it was but seven. If she crept downstairs to the library to find a book, would anyone be about to see her? Since she was avoiding Lord Hatton, she had no way of knowing when he retired. She bit her lip for a moment, then grabbed her dressing gown. As she shoved her arms into the sleeves, she toed on her slippers. This house had a myriad of passages. As long as she could make it to the old mistress's bedchamber, she could take the staircase behind the hidden door in the panelling to the library.

She peeked her head out of the door and smiled when no footman or maid was hovering nearby. With care, she ensured no sound was made as she closed her bedchamber door and tiptoed to the end of the guest wing. She could have shouted with glee when no one was about, and she could continue into the family wing. As she lifted the latch and slowly opened the door to the mistress's suite, she bit her cheek and winced awaiting an errant creak. She crinkled her nose at the decoration when she stepped inside. Her response to the outdated and worn rugs and wall fabrics was the same every time she entered this room. It was in sore need of redecorating. No mistress had lived here in generations, so likely no one thought to decorate a room for a lady who would never visit.

Her palms pressed against the panel, and she pushed, making the door open to reveal the staircase within. After she closed it behind her, she continued to creep along on her toes in case someone heard her moving within the walls. Mrs. Murphy knew of the passages, but how many had she revealed to the maids or the footmen?

The small space was dark, but she had been in these corridors how many times? She knew them so well; she had no need of a candle. Her fingers trailed along the wall, then the railing as she followed the stairs to the ground floor.

The entrance to the library was heavier than the panel upstairs, so she had to shove the door harder to fit her head through. A fire still burned in the grate, but the room appeared empty, so she stepped inside and began running a finger along the spines of the books. What did she want to read? She had not considered it since she was unsure if she would be able to reach the library in the first place.

Most of the tomes on farming methods on the shelf she was perusing were old and outdated, so she glanced down the stacks. The family visited so rarely, it was not worth purchasing the latest books for the library's collection. She glanced down the shelves. Perhaps some poetry would not go amiss, or Shakespeare? Surely one or the other was somewhere.

"What are you seeking?"

She whirled around and pressed herself back against the shelves, her palm to her chest. "When did you come in?"

Lord Hatton sat in the corner of the sofa near the window, tilting the glass in his hand to make the liquid swirl around the inside. He wore naught but his shirtsleeves, his topcoat, cravat, and waistcoat laying over the chair next to his. Was that a hint of chest hair peeking from the part in his shirt? She swallowed hard. Did he often wander his house in such dishabille? She glanced at the door. It was closed. Perhaps he did not.

"I have been here since you sneaked inside. You peered out at the chairs near the fire, but I sat here after dinner to watch the fog settle upon the grounds."

Fiona crossed her arms over her chest. "I see. I should go."

"You should. This is no place for a lady."

No place for a lady? "What is that supposed to mean?" She stepped forward to better see his expression in the low light from the fireplace.

"Only that I have had more than one glass of whiskey, and I believe we have already proven we should not be trusted alone with each other."

"Well, as long as you do not kiss me again, there is naught to worry over, now is there?"

She turned and continued to run her finger along the spines of the books until she found two, which she pulled from the shelves and set on the table.

"What did you select?"

"*Much Ado About Nothing* and *Twelfth Night*. I have read them before. They are both favourites of mine."

Lord Hatton lifted his brows. "You prefer Shakespeare's comedies to his tragedies?"

"Whether I read a tragedy or comedy depends upon my mood. When I am anxious or maudlin, I may prefer a comedy, while other moods may inspire me to read *Julius Cesar* or—"

"*Romeo and Juliet?*"

She balked. "Lord, no! I have never been fond of that particular tale of woe." She did not consider suicide romantic, even when done for love.

His low chuckle washed over her and made her warm. "I happen to agree with you."

"You do?" She stepped over to the decanter and poured herself a glass of whiskey before she sat on the opposite end of the sofa from Lord Hatton. He had surprised her. Most argued the merits of *Romeo and Juliet.*

One of his eyebrows hitched up as he took a sip of his drink and swallowed. "You are willing to be caught thus with me?"

"I am willing to wager you locked the door before you removed your coats."

"Are you?" One side of his lips curved in that insufferable manner he used when amused. What about her was humorous? "And you are willing to risk your reputation for an assumption?"

"My reputation is not perfect as you well know. My preferred diversions—"

"I would call them accomplishments." He tipped his glass in her direction when he spoke.

"To most, they are not."

"Most of the gentry are addle-pates. Would you not agree?"

She nearly choked on her whiskey before she could swallow. The liquid almost escaped when she struggled not to laugh. "Most emphatically."

The glass in Nicholas's hand sat empty while Lady Fiona extolled the ills of riding side saddle. She was amusing, to be sure. The lady who sat across from him was decided in her opinions and, unless the argument was reasonable and could be proven, she would not waver.

"What makes you smile so?" She gave him a side-long look.

"You."

"Me? What have I done to have diverted you?"

He rose to refill his glass. "I never disagreed with your observation about riding astride, but you have been defending your position for the past quarter hour."

"You did not? I thought you said..." She covered her mouth with her hand. "I suppose you did not." As soon as her mirth subsided, she threw back the remnants of her third glass of whiskey, then looked inside the glass before tipping it over with a pout.

"Would you like more?" He should not give her more, but since she seemed determined to remain with him, regardless of the possible damage to her reputation, he would not be rude.

"Oh!" She stood and took a crooked step towards him. When she set her glass on the tray, he poured a small amount, but she frowned. "You have more."

"I am not a lady." He needed to keep his wits about him.

"Neither am I," she said with a noise from her nose.

Her feelings were not surprising but made his heart squeeze. "I disagree. You may not enjoy the usual diversions of a lady, but..." He swallowed and kept his eyes from dropping to where the shoulder of her dressing gown had loosened. The shift she wore boasted of no sleeves, so the pale flesh of her upper arm was exposed. She had to have no idea the picture she painted in her state of dishabille. He gripped his glass to keep from reaching for her, from burying his fingers into her hair—from slipping his hand into the front of her shift and caressing—

"But?"

He shook himself and cleared his throat. "You are indeed a lady. Your comportment at Lord Meath's ball and in company warrants no censure. I believe you are too severe on yourself."

"I doubt it." Her fingers toyed with the folds of her dressing gown as she resumed her seat on the sofa, her feet tucked under her.

With his index finger, he nudged her chin up so her gaze would meet his. "I am in earnest." Her eyes flooded with an emotion he could not identify before she flinched back from his finger with a gasp.

She tilted her head. "Tell me of your family."

Nicholas gave a small start. "You want to know of my parents?"

"I would not object to hearing of them, but I am curious of who raised you. Who awaits you when you return to England?"

After a glance into his whiskey, he made his way back to the opposite end of the sofa where he spoke at length of his grandparents, his sister, and his beloved cousins. The subject was near to his heart which made the conversation quite easy.

Lady Fiona rested her arm against the back of the sofa and leaned her head upon it. He swallowed hard and trained his gaze upon her face so it would not wander to her exposed shoulder. Her company was not objectionable, but the restraint required to maintain any sort of decorum was a trial indeed!

Chapter 15

"**S**ir!"

Nicholas shifted and inhaled. His eyes fluttered open at the whispered exclamation to the ornate plaster ceiling of the library above him. His head was pounding, and his tongue was dry, as though he had been sucking on musty towelling. He swallowed. Ugh! He needed toothpowder as well. Maybe Cook had some peppermint leaves. He would even chew them dried and shrivelled if that was all she had.

"Sir?" His arm shook with the insistent voice, making him turn to Evans, who took a hasty step back. "Forgive me, sir, but you were not in your rooms. I just managed to divert the scullery maid to the breakfast room instead of the bedchambers, but the maids will be coming to clean soon. Lady Fiona must return to her rooms before her abigail discovers her gone and finds her thus."

"Lady Fiona?" He made to stretch, but a weight pressed upon his left side When he looked, Lady Fiona's head rested on his chest, just below that shoulder with his arm wrapped around her and the palm of his hand seemingly pressed against her lower back.

"How did you enter?" He kept his voice as low as Evans had. Lady Fiona would be mortified to be found in such a scandalous position.

"The doors were both locked, so I requested the key from Mrs. Murphy to the servants' entrance."

"Does Mrs. Murphy know of Lady Fiona's presence?"

"I do not believe so, sir."

He pinched the bridge of his nose while he attempted to think. How much whiskey had he drank? "We shall require time to return to our bedchambers. Lady Fiona knows of an unknown corridor in the panels on the far wall. Pray, do ensure no one enters the library for the next five minutes so I may have time to wake the lady and we may make our escape, then return to my dressing room."

"Of course, sir."

Evans hastened through the servants' doorway. Thankfully, the door to the gallery was locked as Lady Fiona had assumed the night prior. He had not wanted to be disturbed.

"Lady Fiona." Nicholas raised his voice a mite from the volume he had used with Evans. "Fiona," he said in a louder tone near her ear.

"Mmm..." She shifted and nuzzled her nose against his chest. He bit back a smile at the almost childlike response. That amusement died a swift death when her left leg lifted and brushed across his morning erection. He hissed and grabbed her thigh before she moved it again.

"Fiona!" She writhed and moaned, and he gritted his teeth. The softness of her breasts pressed against him, and the rub of her thigh did nothing to alleviate his current predicament. Was that a nipple pressed against his ribs? Likely his imagination, but his free hand grasped the fabric beneath him.

She lifted her head and blinked with her forehead furrowed. "When did I fall asleep?"

"The last I remember we were resting our heads upon the back of the sofa while we talked. I do not recall anything after."

"Oh!" She made great pains to place her hands upon the cushions to lift herself. "Forgive me. I did not realise I was on top of you." Her cheeks turned a colour that rivalled that of her hair. When she tried to move, she slid back over his erection, and he groaned as he grabbed her hips to still her, forcing her to shift her hands to his chest lest she fall. Was she attempting to torture him?

"Careful. I beg of you."

Wide-eyed, she glanced down at his hands upon her and frowned. "How am I supposed to remove myself when you are holding me in place?"

He squeezed his eyes closed. "Lady Catherine. Lady Catherine, Lady Catherine." Blast! The warmth of her core was pressed against that part begging to be freed.

"I beg your pardon?"

"Darcy's harridan of an aunt has proven helpful in alleviating trouble of a more delicate variety, but with you seated where you are, the remedy is not as effective as it would be otherwise."

"What would the lady think of your method?"

"She does enjoy being of use." He gave a tense bark of a chuckle as he glanced down at their current situation. How to remove Lady Fiona without further enticement or even her inadvertently hurting him? "Perhaps if I roll to the side, you may put your foot upon the floor and step away without making matters worse."

Her eyebrows lifted high upon her forehead. "I make matters worse?"

"Good God!" He covered his eyes with his hand. "Fiona, you are a lady and a handsome one at that. While this happens every morning, your presence combined with the feel of you against me...the movement...Well, all of that serves to make the matter more insistent."

"Insistent?" For an intelligent woman, she was being quite stupid at the moment.

"Yes, insistent. Now, I shall roll, and you will remove yourself." The longer she remained perched atop him thus, the more aroused he became. "Ready?"

As she nodded, he began to shift, and she stood in a similar motion to how she would dismount a horse. When he rose, Lady Fiona was not looking at his face but down to where his manhood was straining against the buckskin of his breeches. Her eyes widened, and she had just begun to bite her fingernail, a curve tugging at one side of her lips when he cleared his throat.

"Forgive me," she said. With a gasp, she put her shift and dressing gown to rights.

"We need to return to our chambers undetected. My valet is watching the servants' entrance to this room, so we are not found alone together and in such a state. How did you come down last night?"

"The passage starts behind that panel." She hurried over, shifted two books, and reached into the bookcase. "There is a latch here. Just pull the lever and the door unlocks." When she did as she said, the panel opened, and Nicholas followed as she entered and climbed the stairs. When she led him through another panel into a strange bedchamber, he could have groaned. This was the last place he should be with Lady Fiona!

She pointed to a door on the wall beside them. "That leads to your bedchamber, if you are in the old master's rooms."

"How will you return to yours?"

"I shall need to make my way to the guest wing through the main corridor. I can only hope, given the hour, that no maids are yet about." She had glanced at the clock on the mantel, which gave the correct time despite the outdated decoration in the room. Perhaps when it was cleaned, they maintained the clock. Who knew, but the time meant the servants had long been awake and would be beginning their duties around the house.

As she reached for the door, he held out his hand, palm forward. "Wait. Allow me to fetch Evans, my valet. He can go ahead of you and ensure you reach your room without incident."

"You said he was keeping watch outside the library. He found us, did he not?"

"Yes, but do not worry. He will not tell a soul."

"No, but his discretion does nothing to help my embarrassment."

Nicholas strode through his bedchamber and into his dressing room as Evans entered. "Lady Fiona is in the adjoining suite and needs your aid to return to her rooms undetected."

"Of course, sir."

Nicholas exhaled heavily once he was alone. Would his erection never subside? He unfastened his breeches and freed himself, breathing a little easier without the painful confinement.

Despite his hope for matters to abate, the image of Fiona straddling him would not leave his mind, thus keeping him in this state. With her astride him, he could imagine her curls falling free about her creamy shoulders and breasts while she rode him to completion. Lord, he would never be able to watch her ride a horse again!

He had to remember that his duty was to find a wife, to find a mistress for his homes, not one to warm his bed for an evening—not that Lady Fiona would be appropriate for an evening's pleasure. He was also not in the habit of seducing young ladies, despite what had occurred in his past. In terms of marriage, he and Lady Fiona would never suit. The two of them argued more than he would prefer for one he intended to wed, not that she would accept him if he asked.

With a groan, he grabbed a towel from near the basin and took himself in hand. This was what Lord Kildare's daughter had reduced him to. He fell to his knees at his peak, his legs unable to hold him. If a mere image of her in his mind could render him so weak, what would it be like to bed the lady herself?

Fiona thanked Evans, and closed the door behind her, dropping back against the panel and squeezing her eyes closed. She groaned and clenched her dressing gown in her fingers. The feel of him under her still made her knees buckle. When she had climbed over Lord Hatton, that hardness in his breeches had rubbed just so between her legs and had stirred something within her. The way he had grabbed her hips had served to increase the sensations. But why had she been tempted to rub herself against him? She squeezed her thighs together in an effort to cease that hollowness that remained.

The kiss during their argument a few days ago still made her breathing quicken. What was it about Lord Hatton that made her lose herself when his lips met hers? Would engaging another gentleman so create the same sensations—the same wanting ache within?

She conjured up an image of Mr. Joy and tried to imagine kissing him. No, not the same since just a dream of Lord Hatton made her body come alive.

No! It was no use. Even if she were inclined, she could not wed Lord Hatton. She would be forced to leave Ireland and her father for who knew how long, although perhaps the viscount could be persuaded to travel back and forth during the year. They could pass the summers here at Moydrum and the winters with his family.

The Season? How would she ever fit in at Almack's? Having tea with Lady Jersey and her ilk? Her father received a London broadsheet in the post, so she had read of the *bon ton*. They would never accept an Irish lass, even if she was the daughter of an earl and not Catholic.

Her eyes stung, and she pressed her lips together. Why would she even consider Lord Hatton? They would not suit and that was that. Such imaginings did her no good, so she needed to rid herself of them now.

Would that the ache would go away?

"Good morning, my lady. Your father will be pleased you had a good night's sleep. Would you like a tray before you dress?" Walsh glanced at the bed, which she had done no more than sit on. Could her maid tell it had not been slept in?

"How is my father?"

"He is still sleeping, but according to his valet, he passed the night without the cough waking him."

"I imagine he will sleep for some time then. He was exhausted yesterday."

"Yes, my lady."

"I require toothpowder and warm water. I believe I shall have breakfast downstairs this morning."

Her maid's eyebrows lifted. "Yes, my lady."

Fiona made quick work of her morning toilette, and when she entered the breakfast room, Lord Hatton was swift to rise to his feet. "Lady Fiona."

"Lord Hatton, I trust you slept well."

One corner of his lip twitched. "I initially had some difficulty falling asleep, but once I finally succumbed, I slept well." His eyes flitted to the footman against the wall. "I trust you had a peaceful night?"

"My night was very similar to yours actually." She selected what she wanted to eat from the sideboard before she joined Lord Hatton at the table.

"I understand your father rested well."

"I looked in on him on my way here, and he was still fast asleep. Mr. Ryan's remedies yesterday appear to have been of great aid."

"I am relieved to hear it."

After another glance at the footman, Lord Hatton turned his attention back to his food while Fiona watched the gentleman a moment longer. He had such lovely thick and wavy hair. Her gaze wandered down to his ears, then to his neck, now covered by a cravat. The cedar scent of him this morning had prompted the urge to bury her nose in his unclad neck until she awakened fully and realised the impropriety of her position. Still, his cologne and the outlines of his muscles discernible through the lawn of his shirt gave a more thorough glimpse of the handsome gentleman before her. She longed to run her fingers along the plane of his chest, and some odd notion of licking his Adam's apple had flitted through her mind.

Lord Hatton looked up, and she diverted her gaze. She needed to purge the viscount from her mind. Her first impulse had been to join him for breakfast. Her heart quickened at the prospect of seeing him again, but he was the forbidden fruit. She had no desire to wed anyone, much less Lord Hatton whose deep voice and penetrating stare made her body quiver. No! She had to cease this—whatever this was!

The footman departed, and Lord Hatton cleared his throat. "I must beg your forgiveness for last night. My behaviour was not that of a gentleman. I shall endeavour to do better."

"When examined, my behaviour was just as poor. I should not have challenged your request that I leave. I am uncertain what occurs when we are together, but we seem to find ourselves in the most improper predicaments."

He rested his fork and knife on his plate and curled his hands into fists. "I agree. I have never experienced the like, but you have said you do not want to marry or leave Ireland so we must ignore whatever this is and hope to one day become friends."

She gave a little jolt. "With our frequent confrontations, how would we be friends?

His eyebrows drew down. "I disagree. We did not argue when we danced at Lord Meath's ball, or when you introduced me to Robin after the fox hunt, or last night. I believe we got along admirably."

"I suppose we did, yet you were not ordering me about at the time."

"Ordering you about?" His voice had become a bit higher pitched.

"Yes, telling me what to do or making decisions for me. I can do so for myself, you know."

With a derisive chuckle, he pushed himself back from the table. "I believe the time has come for me to leave you."

What was that supposed to mean? She stood and followed him out into the gardens. "Why would you laugh as you did?"

"Go back inside, Lady Fiona."

"See. Why must you give me an order and expect me to obey? I do not need you to take care of me or stand in for my father while he is ill." He took the well-worn path towards the stables while she followed behind. "I shall one day be required to make all of the decisions for Larchfield, and I shall do so without you or any man telling me what to do."

I told you to return to the house for your protection—"

"Protection from what?" She lifted her chin. He would not intimidate her!

He whirled around and threw up his hands. "Why must you be so infuriating?"

She never had the opportunity to answer since Lord Hatton grasped her cheeks and covered her lips with his. His lips were hard for but a moment before he groaned and pulled her to him.

A throng of butterflies took flight in her stomach, and her knees knocked together. He teased her lips apart, and his tongue darted into her mouth to touch hers. That hardness she had accidentally rubbed in her attempt to remove herself from Lord Hatton pressed insistently into her hip, making the ache she had tried so hard to rid herself of return with a vengeance.

The gentleman turned away all of a sudden and covered his mouth. She gasped and sagged against the tree behind her.

Lord Hatton closed his eyes and inhaled. "Return to the breakfast room. If you must, consider it a request and not an order."

She put a hand on her hip and raised her eyebrow. "You did not say 'pray.'"

His jaw clenched and released before he growled and strode towards the stables. As soon as he rounded the bend, she peeled herself from the bark of the tree and returned to the house. *That* could not happen again!

Chapter 16

A week had passed since their return from Moydrum, and Fiona was restless in a way she had never experienced. Somehow, in the three days after the kiss on the path to the stables—their last encounter—she had managed to successfully avoid Lord Hatton. Her behaviour when in his presence was truly quite a mystery. She had never taken orders well, but when given by Lord Hatton, a prepossession to prove him wrong overtook her. Where had such an urge come from? She commonly challenged orders and what was expected of her as a lady, but not in the manner she did with him.

The morning of their departure, she had even taken an early morning ride which she ended at Larchfield. Her father arrived an hour after she had left Diarmait at the stable and had scolded her without mercy for being so rude to their host. She could not argue that they owed him dearly for not only defending her from Sir Malcolm but also for finding and having her father cared for until he could manage the carriage ride home, yet on two occasions, he had kissed her so that she had been tempted to abandon propriety.

By the time they left Moydrum, her father had improved but still had a racking cough, which thankfully, had tamed some since. Mr.

Ryan now called every two or three days to ensure her Papa was improving and to leave tonics to remedy what remained.

She whipped her crop through some tall grass on her walk back to the house from the stables. Today, she had ridden her stallion out to Lough Beg where she preferred to walk and think, the island in the centre with the old church steeped in history drawing her eye as it always did. When she entered the hall, she made her way to the staircase.

"Fee."

She paused with her foot on the first step. "Yes, Papa."

"I should like to speak with you. Now."

"I just returned from my ride and was going to refresh myself."

"'Tis just me. I shall not be offended by you smelling of horse." One corner of her father's lips curved, but it did not reach his eyes. Something was amiss.

As soon as they reached his study, he closed the door behind her. "After the events of the fox hunt and after..." He dropped his chin and gave her a look over his glasses. "I am of the opinion you should marry as soon as may be."

Her stomach leapt into her chest. "I beg your pardon. I am not marrying anyone."

After a weary exhale, Papa sat upon the edge of his desk. "I have penned a letter to a friend of mine. We attended university together. He is an earl whose estate is in County Clare to the south."

"I know where County Clare is, but I am aware of no such friend." Her tone was hard, but what was he about? She had never hidden her aim to become a spinster.

"We journeyed there once when you were six to visit, but he and I have kept up a correspondence over the years. His son is a year older than you and has finished university. He has just returned to Ireland after spending the year following in England. Before his son finished Cambridge, my friend suggested we arrange a marriage between the two of you, but I still hoped you would change your mind when a worthy gentleman came to call. Now, I am of the mind it is not such a horrible idea and have enquired if the union would still suit."

She searched her memories for any remembrance from when she was six before settling on one. "We went to the cliffs."

"Yes, and I told you the legend of the mermaid and the fisherman."

At such a young age, the cliffs had seemed almost other-worldly. How could something be so tall? And she had stood at the top. Perhaps that is why the recollection was so clear in comparison to most from when she was a little girl.

"I shall not wed a stranger, Papa. Why would you ask it of me?"

"Because I am not as young as I once was, because I could have died and left you without protection, and because part of your duty as my heir is to have an heir of your own, which you seem determined to defy."

"As I seem to tell everyone, I can protect myself, and I have an entire estate of servants to be of aid as well."

"They cannot protect you from unscrupulous gentlemen who are desperate for your fortune, Fiona! Without a male relation, you could be kidnapped and forced to elope. Any nature of ill could befall you— even widows are not always safe. They will also not bear an heir for this estate."

Tears prickled at her eyes. "I beg of you to reconsider. I shall behave. I promise." Damn that quivering of her voice!

"Fiona..."

She straightened and sniffed. Wait a moment! What if she could find herself a husband before any contract with this other man was signed? She had considered in the past week or two that she could tolerate Lord Hatton. She had no desire to ever leave Ireland, but despite dealing with the *ton*, would not a betrothed who was known to her be an improvement over one who was not? "Would you be amenable if I chose a gentleman to wed?"

Her father gave an incredulous bark. "You choose a husband? When have you ever thought a man worth your time?"

"Mayhap I know of a gentleman who may suit. If I am willing to approach him, would you give me a week or two to arrange matters for myself?"

Papa coughed a couple of times, not nearly as deep or consuming as they were, thank goodness, then walked around his desk to sit. He watched her until she could have squirmed under the scrutiny. During most conversations, he would enquire of the gentleman. Why was he not now? Did he have some idea of who she meant?

"Very well. You have a week."

"A fortnight. What if this gentleman requires convincing?" She did not doubt that Lord Hatton would require a great deal of persuasion, but she would never tell him a falsehood or endeavour to trap him. He would have to agree on his own terms.

"Are you certain you would want to spend your life with someone who requires convincing?"

Could she spend her lifetime with a man who curled her toes with his kiss? Yes! They shared an attraction, and her father desired an heir. Lord Hatton had never mentioned love when he spoke of finding a wife who would suit. An arrangement of this sort may not be objectionable in his eyes. Their inability to control themselves would be of great aid in begetting an heir, even if their arguments tended to be rather volatile. "I believe I could. Yes."

"Very well. I shall give you a fortnight, and no more."

Her shoulders and spine relaxed for the first time since her father mentioned the ultimatum. Now, all she had to do was convince Lord Hatton. He had said that maybe they could be friends, but would friends who were husband and wife do just as well? All she could do was ask.

Nicholas handed Kelpie's reins to the groom. "He will need a good walk so he is cool when you put him up."

"Yes, sir."

As his mount was being led away, hoofbeats from behind him made him turn as Lady Fiona atop her stallion approached and stopped a few feet away. She dismounted as another groom came running out of the stable.

She handed off her horse to the boy. "I do not expect to be here long."

Once the groom had led the horse inside, Nicholas took a step forward as she adjusted the skirt of her habit. "I had not expected you to seek me out. You avoided me for the last few days of your stay and departed Moydrum without taking your leave."

"I had not meant to offend. At the time, I thought steering clear would be in the best interest of us both."

"I took no offense, although I found it difficult to justify to your father why I did not find your actions objectionable." And he had. Lord Kildare had been exceedingly mortified, apologising for his daughter multiple times when he departed, but Nicholas could not very well explain that he had kissed the earl's daughter on more than one occasion, not to mention spent the night with the lady in the library. He would not have taken well to such a confession of his sister or his cousins much less a daughter.

"I understand," she said. "However, I should like to speak with you for a moment if you have the time."

"Do you think it a good idea?" He could not help but chuckle with the question.

"Whether it is or not, I need to talk to you if you on a matter of some import. Do you have somewhere we can speak without being overheard but where it is still proper?"

Her coming here was hardly proper, but to say so would likely raise her ire. As much as he enjoyed seeing her eyes flash and upbraid him, doing so now would only serve to bring about the situation they were attempting to avoid.

"Very well."

She followed when he took the path that led to the house. When they reached a small clearing near the pond, he paused and turned to face her, clasping his hands behind his back. If he kept them bound so, mayhap he would not touch her.

Her hands began to wring at each other, and her foot began tapping in a furious rhythm. "I must beg your forgiveness, but this morning, after I returned from my ride, my father requested my presence in his study. I suppose what occurred with Sir Malcolm as well as Papa's recent illness has made him needlessly worry for me. What will become of me, who will protect me from unscrupulous suitors, and the like? His intention is to betroth me to the son of a friend from County Clare."

"While I can understand why you would prefer to maintain your independence, I can sympathise with your father's concern." He would have felt the same were Amelia in Lady Fiona's position. An unprotected lady of means was a vulnerable one.

She pressed her lips together. "Yes, well, I have been allowed a fortnight to find an alternate option."

He started and clenched his hands tighter. "An alternate option?"

"Yes, I proposed to my father that I believe I know a gentleman who would suit—who is not unknown to me—and who I can tolerate."

His insides tightened and the wind was almost knocked out of him. She could not possibly mean him! "Are you asking me to marry you?"

Lady Fiona's arms crossed over her chest, and she could not look at him for a moment before she nodded. "Yes, but before you say no, pray, hear me out. You made mention that we could be friends, that we have spoken amiably on several occasions, which is true. We also seem to hold an attraction for each other that we find difficult to control—we would not need to keep our desires restrained should we wed. Lastly, you indicated you were to search for a wife who would suit next Season. While I may be Irish, I am Anglican, possess a fortune of thirty thousand pounds, and am the heir of an earldom as well as the properties that accompany the title."

"I thought you had no desire to leave Ireland." Was that not what she had said?

"I do not, yet I would be forced to leave Larchfield and live in County Clare should I marry this other gentleman. Not only would I prefer to know my groom before I am expected to marry him, but since you also have an estate that neighbours Larchfield, I hoped we could compromise and spend part of the year at Moydrum so I may see my father."

He could not argue with the reasonableness of her plan but to wed Lady Fiona Fitzgerald. Would he be satisfied—other than in his bedchamber, that is? Aside from her riding astride and her forthright manner, she was not wholly objectionable. In truth, he did not mind her education or manner of expression, but some in London would find her uncouth...but did he care?

Most of the ladies who sought him out in London desired his title, a connection to the Richmond earldom, or the ability to live in a means higher than that they were born into or one equal to it. Fiona was not seeking fortune or connections, but life to a gentleman she found agreeable to her temperament.

"I do not know. The decision is not one I would leap into without thought."

Her shoulders dropped a little. "I had expected as much which is why I bartered with Papa for an extra week. I am to give him word in a fortnight, so when you have made your decision, meet me at the southern tip of Lough Beg where it meets the River Bann. I will come every morning unless it rains."

He nodded. "Your father only presented his ultimatum this morning? You have had little time to consider your options. Are you certain of your request?"

"I am. However, if it will appease you, I shall find a way to send some correspondence should I change my mind."

Not one hint of trepidation was in her eyes nor in her expression. By the set of her shoulders and stiffness of her spine, she had been nervous to request this of him, yet given her situation, what she asked did make some sense.

The proposition was still somewhat odd. They had never courted. In truth, they knew little more than a night's conversation with each other. Was that what he truly wanted?

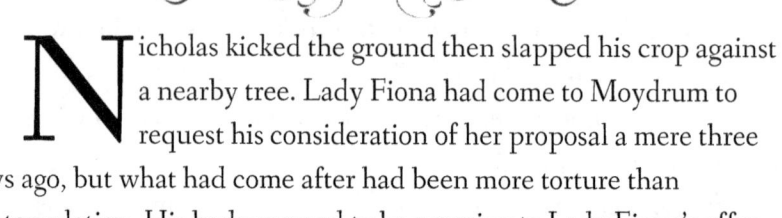

Chapter 17

Nicholas kicked the ground then slapped his crop against a nearby tree. Lady Fiona had come to Moydrum to request his consideration of her proposal a mere three days ago, but what had come after had been more torture than contemplation. His body seemed to be agreeing to Lady Fiona's offer since the dreams of her had intensified as had his physical responses to them.

He ran a hand through his hair and paced. Would she be willing to accept his request in return? He could do no more than ask. If it meant he was more amenable to her proposal, she would have to accept, would she not?

At the sound of hoofbeats approaching, he pivoted around as she came to a stop and dismounted. "I had not expected you so soon."

"Yet you came," he said.

"I said I would."

She inhaled and held her crop in both hands in front of her. "Have you come to a decision?"

"Not yet. I feel we should have some sort of courtship before I give you my answer."

"A courtship?" Her voice was higher pitched. He had surprised her.

"Yes." He stepped forward, but she did not move in response. "For what it is worth, I do not think you undesirable as a wife. We are obviously attracted to each other, so much so that we continue to break with propriety when we were not so much as courting." He glanced out at the large lake, then back at her. "Would you walk with me? We could talk."

"What do you want to speak of?" She fell alongside him as they began to stroll along the water's edge.

"I have told you of my family, though I do not believe I mentioned that my sister gave birth to a baby girl just after Christmastide."

"Then you have a new niece?"

"I do. Her name is Isabella, and her father will be insufferable when it comes time for a gentleman to court her."

She gave a light sort of laugh that made his breathing hitch. "By your manner when I was insulted, I would wager you would be insufferable as well if a daughter of yours came out."

"What made you ask me to marry you?" She had mentioned a few factors, but he had been obsessed with the definitive reason since she had made the request of him.

"I think you tolerable."

A bark of amusement burst from him. "Tolerable? My friend Darcy once called my cousin tolerable."

Fiona smiled. "High praise indeed. How did your cousin take his assessment?"

"She decided he was prideful and disliked him heartily. They are now married with a son."

She laughed again as her small hand found the crook of his elbow, and they continued walking. The birds chirped and sang their songs from the trees while the water lapped against the edge of the lake. This place was very peaceful.

"I am not familiar with Lough Beg. Will you tell me why it is so special to you? What is the island in the centre?"

"You want to know of Church Island?" Her tone was again higher than was its wont. He seemed to be surprising her a good bit this morning.

"The building is a church?"

"Yes, the church ruins are said to be from the time of St. Patrick, who used the River Bann to reach the island. There is a stone on the island with a hole. Supposedly St. Patrick once prayed at that spot. Should you like to see it, you can walk to the island on a land bridge near Bellaghy during the summer, though the path is through the mud and muck. Most take a horse rather than go on foot."

She pointed out over the water. "That spire there was built in the 1700s for Bishop Harvey. He wished to see the sight from his home in Bellaghy."

"He sounds like a man who thought a great deal of his own importance."

Fiona turned to him with an impish grin. "I would have to agree with you."

They walked in silence for a time before Lady Fiona stopped and faced him. "Do you believe this attempt at courtship will incline you to my suit?"

To keep from touching her, Nicholas again clasped his hands behind his back. "I am uncertain what this is. What I do know is that more often than not, you are in my thoughts. At times, I may wonder what you are doing. I received a letter from my sister a few days ago, and it occurred to me how much she would enjoy your company. At night, I dream of you—vividly. I have tried to think of the estate or a book I am reading, but the effort is wasted since the moment I close my eyes, you are there. The dreams have only become more detailed since you came to Moydrum to offer your proposal.

"Yet, before I give you a decision one way or the other, I must tell you why I came to Ireland."

Fiona frowned. "You did not come to see Moydrum and ensure the estate was being run to your satisfaction?"

He bobbed his head from side to side. "Yes, but I would not have made the crossing in the winter if that had been the sole reason. I came when I did to escape the presence of a lady I once thought I loved, but from almost the moment I arrived, I have thought of her less than I have in years."

"Why do you think that is?"

"I believe it is because I think of you instead. I cannot explain it. From the moment you pulled the hood of your cape from your head, thoughts of you intruded and consumed me."

"Tell me of her."

He startled. "You want me to tell you of another lady?" How many ladies wanted to hear of the one who came before them?

"Yes, why not? I am curious what sort of woman drives you to leave England and your family to journey here." Her head tilted a little while she regarded him with such an open expression, he told her the entire pathetic tale while she listened. They began to walk at some point, coming upon a grove of old beech trees where they stopped once again.

Fiona leaned against one of the trunks. "She never loved you."

"Why do you say that?"

"I do not mean to injure you, but if she had truly loved you, she would not have married the duke. She has been selfish if you ask me. By meeting you at the cottage and allowing you to take her maidenhood, she ensured you were tied to her for the rest of your life—she hoped you would carry a *tendre* for her even after she was bound to another. Now, she wants to have her cake and eat it too. She remains married to the duke, but she believes she can have you whenever she wants."

"Yet, Rebecca never tried to do so before."

Fiona lifted a shoulder. "When she first wed, she was in a precarious position. If her husband discovered he had been cuckolded, he could treat her in any manner he pleased. He could send the child away, he could see her locked up at their estate until she bore his heir, or he could call you out. Perhaps I have the wrong of her initial intentions, but I still maintain that if she loved you—*truly* loved you—she would have married you. She would also want to see you happy, even if that meant you found another."

Could Rebecca have desired that connection? Had she thought to keep him bound to her so they would be lovers once she bore her husband's heir? The thought of bedding another man's wife was simply not palatable to him. The nagging in his gut over taking Rebecca's maidenhead had plagued him for some time. As much as he had tried to deny the attraction between him and the lady before him, he needed to determine whether they could be more than friendly acquaintances. Her company *was* preferable to most ladies.

"Lord Hatton," she said.

He startled. "While we are alone as we are, why do you not call me Nicholas."

"Oh, I thought we were attempting proper discourse. As it is, you are the one who has your hands tightly bound behind your back so as not to touch me." One eyebrow arched in an alluring manner.

He shook his head and smiled. "How did you know?" She was too observant.

"You have never been so stiff in my presence, even when I threatened you with my pistol."

He glanced over to her horse. "You rode with no groom today. Do you have the pistol with you now?"

She laughed then scraped her teeth over her bottom lip. "Do not worry. I shall not shoot you...for the moment."

"Where do you carry it?" He stepped closer and examined her riding habit. Were there pockets? If she had the gun with her, he could not tell.

An affected gasp burst from her. "Sir, that question is hardly appropriate?"

His hands clenched and released. He did that a great deal when in her company, but he could not very well grab the lady and have his way with her.

"And a lady carrying a pistol is proper?"

"You know I have no care for what is proper," she said. Her voice was low and made his hands itch to touch her. Would he never have a reprieve from wanting her?

She walked up to him and traced a gloved finger down his cravat. Did she know how tempting she was? How he was holding on by a thin and rapidly fraying thread?

"Fiona, you know we should not." He grasped her hand, removed her glove, and kissed her palm. Her eyes widened a hair, and her breathing quickened. At least she was just as affected by him as he was by her. "You should go before we abandon propriety once again." She had to have no idea how much of a temptation she presented.

His lips pressed against her wrist, but before he could back away, her free hand wrapped around the back of his head and drew it down to touch her lips to his. The kiss was soft for but a moment before they allowed their passions to overrule their sense. He drew her into his arms, savouring the taste of her until he broke away. "Fiona, you need to go. Now."

When her tongue peeked out and licked her bottom lip, he closed his eyes to blind himself to the sight. "Someone could happen upon us at any time. We cannot behave so here."

She shrugged. "The worst that could happen is we are made to marry. Of late, I have come to believe our chances of happiness are better if we are together than if we are apart or wed to another. I would not have made the request of you if I thought otherwise."

His lips forged a path down her neck, and his trembling fingers unbuttoned the top of her riding coat so he could kiss the swell of her breasts. With a whimper, she clutched his head in her hands.

He lifted her against the tree and held her fast as his hips ground into the softness between her legs. At her gasp, the fog in his brain cleared, making him set her back upon the ground and put a few feet between them.

"Forgive me."

Before she could respond, he climbed atop his horse and cued him to a gallop. He required a good run across the countryside to clear his mind and to think. This courtship had seemed an ideal solution, yet he would need to keep his hands to himself!

Chapter 18

Fiona urged her horse forward and over the dry fence as she rode towards Moydrum. For the past week, she and Nicholas had been meeting every morning the weather was fair. They had happened upon each other once more at Lough Beg before she suggested another location would be prudent, so they were not always meeting at the same place. For today's assignation, she had proposed a small ruin on his lands that he would have been unlikely to have found. The remains were surrounded by trees and well hidden from passers-by. An ideal place for them to meet.

When she arrived, Nicholas stood at the edge of the wood.

"How long have you been here?" He was always early.

"I arrived but five minutes ago. I do not like the idea of you waiting for me alone, despite that pistol you carry." His grin was crooked, giving away his tease.

She scoffed and dismounted before leading her horse through the trees to where his grazed on a small patch of grass. "Mr. O'Shea claims this was an old friary, but only the one section of wall is all that remains. From the peak of the hill, you can make out the top if you know where to look."

His gaze travelled up what was left of the structure. "I believe you know my land better than I do. No one has mentioned this is here."

"Likely because not much is here to see." She trailed her gloved fingers along the stone as she had done when she was younger.

"*You* thought it worth the ride."

"You and I both know I am not like most people." She should not need to tell him that by now. He stared at her for a moment, then touched her pinkie with his. "Why are you watching me so?"

"I like looking at you." He entwined his fingers with hers and raised her hand to his lips as he had begun to do often when they saw each other. Her insides turned and flipped at the warmth of his kiss. Her response to him was bewildering. How could she be affected by so little? She still could not credit they were conducting this odd sort of courtship. Would he truly agree to her scheme in the next few days? Not much time was left for her to persuade him.

Today, however, Nicholas's countenance was too serious, so she pivoted to walk backwards. With the motion, he was forced to release her hand, which gave her a much-needed respite from that current coursing through her body. She smiled, then laughed before taking off in a light run around the end of the wall. After a moment or two, she slowed and glanced behind her. Why had he not followed?

She walked back to the edge, but when she made to peer around, strong arms lifted her into the air as he appeared before her. "Nicholas! Put me down."

He chuckled. "You were the one who began such a merry chase. Why should I release what I have so easily captured?"

"I am not your prey, sir."

His grip relaxed, and she slid down his body until her feet were once again upon the ground. She reached up and touched his cheek.

For the first time since she found him at the edge of the glade, he appeared relaxed. His hands were not clenched or clasped behind his back, his shoulders were not stiff, and the ends of his mouth turned up as if he was content.

He leaned forward, his palm cupping her cheek, and allowed his lips to meet hers. Since their kiss at Lough Beg at that first meeting, he had not kissed her again. He was trying too hard to be a perfect gentleman, though that pull between them, more often than not, made the endeavour trying.

Her eyes fluttered closed, and she murmured his name as he turned his attention to her neck, making her knees weak. How was she to stand while he wreaked havoc with her equanimity?

"God, I want to touch you. I think of it every moment of every day—how your lips feel against mine. How your body presses so perfectly against me. You must stop me, Fiona. I had little restraint before, but the more we meet, the more we have these glancing touches, the more difficult it is to regain my regulation." Every word was said between kisses to her neck, while his hands grazed along her arms, her shoulders, and along the edge of her bodice."

"What if I do not want you to stop?" Her breathing was coming in pants and made her words disjointed and breathy.

Nicholas groaned as he claimed her lips and pressed her against the wall of the ruins while she let him lead her as he would. His kiss seemed to claim so much more than when they were at Moydrum, but she could not consider why. She could do no more than let the sensation of his kiss as well as his hands moving confidently over her body consume her. Why could she not think when he kissed her, when he touched her as he was?

He made to press a lingering kiss in the cleft between her breasts, and her toes curled in her boots. "Nicholas." She had managed to say his name on a whimper.

His eyes were serious when he straightened. "You will marry me? You will not change your mind?"

"If you agree to my scheme, then no, I shall not change my mind."

His lips claimed hers once again with a groan and wandered across every inch of exposed flesh. He dropped to his knees, and when the coolness of the air met her calves, she gasped. Her fingers entwined in his hair as his hands caressed up her legs, taking her skirt with them. After a devastating quirk of his lips, his head disappeared under her skirts.

At this first touch of his lips to the seam of her thigh, her knees about collapsed allowing him to situate her legs further apart. He then separated her folds, and before she could enquire what he was about, his tongue grazed what was between before he latched on to some point that made her head drop back against the tree while she gave a keening gasp.

Oh, good Lord! Nothing could have prepared her for this. He continued to drive her mad with his lips and his tongue while she struggled to keep from falling. One hand grasped the wall over her head to help support her while her other, desperate to touch him, lifted the fabric of her skirt until her fingers once again threaded through his hair. The higher his lips and tongue drove her, the tighter she clenched his sandy brown locks as the pleasure became too much to bear. Her eyes rolled back in her head, and she panted aloud. This could not go on for much longer, could it? She would surely expire if it did. One last graze of his teeth, and her eyes squeezed closed as she saw stars, her cries echoing through the trees.

When the peak subsided and she could breathe again, she glanced down to where Nicholas rested his head against her thigh while he watched her. "I had planned to refrain from touching you today. It seems I failed."

She could not help the breathless laugh that escaped. "I cannot say I have any complaints." She sagged against the wall behind her. Her legs refused to support her.

His eyes lit, and one side of his lips curved. "I am pleased to hear it." He stood and ensured her skirts dropped down to cover her legs, then took off his greatcoat and lay it out upon the soft grass of the wood. "Come."

He drew her down to curl against his side. They said not a word until she propped her chin on her hand. "Am I to understand that was your acceptance of my proposal?"

After staring at her for a moment, he shook his head. "You deserve better."

"Better than that?" If marital relations were anything similar to what she just experienced, she would never lament being made to marry by her father. She might even thank him!

Nicholas rolled on his side and let his fingers trail down her cheek. "Lady Fiona Fitzgerald, will you do me the honour of being my wife?"

"You need not propose, you know. I rather enjoyed that I asked you first."

He sighed and let his head rest upon his arm which was stretched out upon the ground. "You always hope to be different than what is expected."

"I see nothing amiss in that." She lowered her head into a similar position to his, so they were eye to eye. "Yes, Nicholas Montford, Viscount Hatton, I shall marry you."

After he drew her back against his side, he sighed. "When shall we wed? I would prefer to know the particulars before I go to your father. I had thought to return to England by early autumn for the harvest ball at Richmond. My sister and my cousins will come, so you can meet them and my grandparents before we journey to London for the Season."

She lifted and propped herself on his chest. "We shall return to Ireland after the Season, shall we not?"

"As long as nothing of importance keeps us in England, yes. Should you fall with child, I would hesitate to embark upon such an arduous trip if you were nearing your confinement."

With a slight nod, she rested back upon his chest, his steady heartbeat soothing any disquiet at leaving her beloved home. "I suppose that is understandable."

"But will you be so compliant in the moment?"

"Probably not." They may not love each other, but at least he knew her well enough.

A groom took Kelpie when Nicholas stopped his horse in front of Larchfield. He swallowed hard in an attempt to quell the stirring of his stomach. Lord Kildare was a reasonable sort and not prone to dramatics. Since the earl and Fiona had made such a bargain, the earl should be expecting a gentleman's call for this very purpose; however, would Lord Kildare object to Nicholas since he would be taking Fiona from Ireland?

The butler admitted him without delay and showed Nicholas to the study where he was announced. As soon as he stood before Lord Kildare's desk, the earl clasped his hands with a huge grin.

"Hatton! I had not expected your call today. I hope naught is amiss?"

"No, all is well at Moydrum. I called to..." He tried to breathe. "I called to request your permission and blessing to marry your daughter. We hope to be wed in three weeks—as soon as the calling of the banns is completed."

Lord Kildare dissolved into a fit of coughing. He lowered himself into his seat and motioned to the decanters on the side of the room. Nicholas hastened to pour a small measure of whiskey which he gave to the earl.

"Forgive me for startling you. I thought the best way to ask was to get it out."

After taking two sips, Lord Kildare winced. "I recall what it is like being in your place. I believe I did much the same." He took another sip and cleared his throat. "You want to marry Fee? Forgive me, but I would never have expected such a request from you. To my knowledge, the two of you have not even courted. Has Fiona persuaded you to partake in some scheme to escape an arranged marriage?"

"She mentioned the bargain she made with you—that she had a fortnight to find an alternate betrothed before you made the arrangements with your candidate. Will you not keep your word?"

The earl blanched. "I never said I would not. I simply wanted to determine if you truly asked for her hand or whether this was a ruse."

"'Tis no ruse, sir. I asked, and she accepted."

He blinked and gulped down the last of the whiskey before rising to pour a second serving. "I should like another. You will join me."

The earl handed him a glass which Nicholas accepted in an awkward manner. While he did not object to whiskey, had he the option to refuse? He had never been told he would drink before.

Lord Kildare shook his head. "O'Shea told me of when you claimed her to be your betrothed to Sir Malcolm. I thought the idea amusing. I never considered—"

Nicholas's gaze lifted from his glass to meet that of the earl's. "I was unaware you knew of what occurred that day."

Lord Kildare shrugged and sat in the chair across from him. "O'Shea told me after I returned to Larchfield. Since at the time Mr. Ryan had not declared me fit to ride, I could not call on you, and I felt a letter to be imprudent. In the end, Sir Malcolm did not spread the tale, so I did not feel you were beholden to my daughter."

"Sir, you are well aware I have the means to support your daughter. I doubt I am wanting in connections, so may I ask why you have yet to give me a response?"

"You have not mentioned that you love my daughter." The earl's gaze was direct as he held his glass before him.

"Since you were willing to give your daughter away to a man you do not know, I had not thought love to be a consideration."

The earl flinched. "That is unfair."

"Is it, sir? While I do not find it surprising the gentlemen of the neighbourhood would ridicule your daughter, I have found her to be intelligent, honest to a fault, and capable. She told me of her intention never to marry, and though it is odd for a lady of her age, upon reflection, I could understand her reasoning. Most men would not accept her as she is. Why would she take such a risk as to wed a man who is unknown to her—who may not accept her—and allow him to remove her from all she knows and loves? I had not thought on her dilemma for more than an hour when that occurred to me. We have spoken on more than one occasion and have become friends. Lady Fiona knows and trusts me. We have taken morning walks every day this past week and spoken of our families, of our pasts, and of what we want from a future together, so for us, this is not so odd as you may think."

Lord Kildare appeared as though he was shrinking in his seat while Nicholas spoke. The earl then exhaled. "Very well, you have my permission. I would ask that you return to Ireland as often as you can. I should like to see my daughter from time to time and know my grandchildren if possible."

"Your daughter and I have already spoken of it. As long as nothing demands my attention in England and Lady Fiona is able to travel, we shall do so."

The earl nodded, though it appeared to give him no joy to do so. "You must remain and dine with us. I am sure my daughter would be pleased if you stayed."

Dinner had been an unusually quiet affair. Lord Kildare ate what was put before him while he watched Nicholas and Fiona while he chewed, making any attempts at conversation between them awkward. Upon his return to Moydrum, Nicholas had trudged to the study with weary legs. The thickness of the air at dinner had been exhausting! As soon as he entered, he pulled the bell and sat behind the desk.

"Sir," said Mrs. Murphy as she entered.

"In three weeks, I am to marry Lady Fiona Fitzgerald in a small ceremony at the Larchfield chapel. The breakfast will be held at Larchfield as well. While we shall be journeying to England in early September, the mistress's suite will need to be cleaned and aired as well as decorated. If you know of any other detail I am missing, pray, do not hesitate to speak."

"You are to wed Lady Fiona?" The woman's chin had tucked down a little, and her tone was flat.

"You heard me correctly."

The woman shook her head as if clearing it. "Forgive me. I am certain you will be very happy together." She did not sound the slightest bit convincing. "I must admit to some confusion over the mistress's chambers. I do agree they need redecorating, but 'tis a little more than two months until you depart. Lady Fiona will live in those rooms for so little time before you leave."

"Yes, I am aware of that fact."

"Perhaps she would prefer to do the decoration herself if you return."

He leaned his forearms upon the desk. "I appreciate your economy, yet I do believe we shall return. My wife will want to visit her father. If you believe Lady Fiona would prefer to decorate her own chambers, I can send a note for her to come view them and speak with you."

"That would suit. I should be more comfortable with her selecting the fabrics and patterns." Mrs. Murphy opened her mouth as if to speak, then closed it.

"If I need to know something, pray do not hold back."

"It is Walsh, sir: her maid. She was Lady Fiona's nursemaid, but when the time came, Walsh had no desire to find another family expecting a babe, so Lord Kildare invited her to become his daughter's lady's maid. I am uncertain if she will want to travel to England much less journey to London and possibly back to Ireland. Walsh may also not be prepared for what those of London would consider fashionable."

"This is precisely why I requested you mention what you believe me to be missing. I would never have considered her maid. I shall enquire of Lady Fiona and what she wishes. If this Walsh is willing to continue until we depart, then we can hire a new maid for her in England who is willing to follow us when we travel."

Mrs. Murphy nodded. "I agree."

"Very well. I must pen a letter to my family. If you think of anything else, pray, seek me out."

"Yes, sir."

The housekeeper closed the door behind her, and Nicholas pulled a piece of paper from the drawer and dipped his pen into the ink. What was he supposed to write? No matter how he delivered the news, it would come as a shock.

> *14th of June 1813*
> *Moydrum, County Antrim, Ireland*
>
> *Dearest Grandmamma and Grandpapa,*
>
> *I am well and enjoying my time here immensely. This evening, I am writing with the most exciting of news, I am to be married.*

Nicholas stared at the page for what seemed an eternity before he set his pen in the stand, crumpled the paper before him, and threw it into the fire.

Chapter 19

7th of July 1813

As soon as Fiona entered Moydrum, Mrs. Murphy curtseyed. "I wish you joy, Lord and Lady Hatton."

"I thank you," said Nicholas. Today's smile from the housekeeper was a far cry from her reserved reaction when he had informed her of his upcoming nuptials, but he would not complain.

In the almost four weeks leading up to the wedding, he had attempted to be an attentive suitor. He called at Larchfield daily with a nosegay of roses or other seasonal flowers he pilfered from the Moydrum gardens or conservatory, and he enquired as to his intended's likes and dislikes. Her father, however, never ceased watching them in a strange manner, as if Nicholas would jilt her at any moment. Until today, Lord Kildare behaved as if Nicholas and Fiona were conspiring on some elaborate prank.

The voice of Mrs. Murphy broke into his thoughts. "The work on your rooms was completed a few days ago, my lady. The choices you made proved to be lovely. If you require any further changes, do not hesitate to ask." They had undertaken the task with so little time until the wedding, he had not relaxed until the work was completed, even sending a man to Belfast to acquire the supplies. The state of the room before their betrothal left much to be desired. He could not ask her to live in rooms so badly outdated and worn.

With a nod, Fiona handed her spencer and gloves to a maid, who promptly excused herself, the housekeeper departed after her. "What are we to do?" Since departing Larchfield, a certain awkwardness had descended over them. Was she thinking of what was to come? He had spent the carriage ride keeping his hands at his sides lest he surrender to his baser thoughts and muss her gown. He would not embarrass her upon their arrival to Moydrum by having her hair and gown askew.

"Nicholas? What do you want to do?"

He started at the question. "Whatever you prefer. If you should like to rest, I can show you to your rooms, if you should care to walk, I would be pleased to accompany you for a turn of the gardens, or if you should like to read, we can spend the rest of the afternoon in the library."

"I should like to rest," she said with no hesitation.

He offered her his arm, and she allowed him to lead her up the stairs and to the outer doors to the mistress's suite. His entire body was tight. What he wanted more than anything was to accompany her inside, strip her of those layers of silk and muslin and touch every part of her, bury himself so deeply within her one could not tell where one ended and the other began. Lord, when had he ever been so desperate?

When she entered her bedchamber, she paused in the doorway to take in the changes since she had last stood in this room. New fabrics of pale pink with cherry blossoms adorned the walls, the pale green of the pattern now covered the chair and sofa by the fireplace, the canopy was in the same green, the coverlet was the same pink as the walls with the rest matching the darker pink in the pattern. Despite her penchant for a gentleman's diversions, she appeared to enjoy pretty, feminine patterns and gowns. She was always well-dressed but the revelation that she enjoyed such feminine decoration still made him lift his eyebrows.

"Mrs. Murphy is correct. This did turn out well." He closed the door and wandered around, touching this or that. After a moment, he straightened. She was surely desiring his absence. He should respect her and not intrude upon the solitude she required. "I shall leave you then."

Fiona stepped towards him. "I would rather you stayed."

"Fiona..."

The words died on his tongue when she drew closer and slipped her arms around his neck. "If I had wanted to rest, I would not have required you to accompany me as I know the way." After a quirk of her lips, she kissed him while she pressed every inch of her body against his. He remained stock-still for a second or two before a tremendous groan erupted from his chest, and he pulled her as tightly to him as possible. The kiss deepened, and she began fumbling in an attempt to untie his cravat, which eventually gave way and allowed her to graze her fingers down his neck. She struggled a little to unbutton his tightly fitted topcoat and waistcoat while he kissed along her jaw to just under her ear where he suckled, his trousers tightening at her quick intake of breath. She smelled of lilacs, delicate and feminine, and her skin was soft against his lips. He had never wanted a woman as much as he wanted Fiona.

The lady did not back away or push from him but clutched his hair in her fist and kissed him back without reserve. His mind was a muddle. He could not think of anything beyond Fiona's curves moulded to him from his chest to their hips. As soon as he had fumbled with the buttons of her gown, he drew the silk from her shoulders. How he wished to press her nude form against his—to have her velvet flesh pressed against him.

Once her gown fell to her feet, his fingers would not work as he dealt with the laces of her stays before finally ridding her of the blasted thing. Without looking, his hand found its way to her breast to knead through her thin muslin chemise while he nipped at her shoulder, drawing a moan from her chest. More. He wanted more, and by the noise she had made, she felt the same. Would the never ending layers between them never end?

The dainty ribbons of her chemise gave with ease, allowing him to push it from her shoulder. He groaned at the silky softness of her skin when his hand returned to finally touch her with no barriers. Her nipple hardened against his palm, and he rolled it gently between his fingers earning a gasp and a whimper.

He drew her hips flush to his and ground into her heat, but it was not close enough, so he ran his hands down her rear, lifted her, and set her upon the edge of the bed. His heart beat so hard in his chest that it echoed in his ears as he pushed her hips against his, allowing him to situate himself into the cradle of her thighs. He latched onto her nipple and suckled as her fingers wound into his hair and clenched, creating a sting he relished.

He drew back, and their gazes held, wide eyed, while they panted. "Are you sure?" he said between heavy breaths.

"If I was not sure, you would not be here." She pushed his topcoat and waistcoat off, then worked at the fastenings to Nicholas's breeches. Once the bottom of his shirt was free, her fingers slipped under the hem and hauled it upward until he drew it over his head for her.

He closed his eyes and groaned when she touched him over his heart branding his flesh with her palm. Her fingers grazed over his chest and stomach. Determined he would allow her this, allow her to become familiar with his body, he gripped the bedclothes with white knuckles and attempted to rein in his ardour.

She paused in her ministrations to remove her chemise before she slid her slippers from her feet, then slid to the centre of the mattress. With a crook of her finger, she beckoned him to follow.

He could no more refuse her invitation than sever a part of his own body! He impatiently removed his trousers and shoes before scrambling up to join her. She took his hand and pressed it against her breast. "I want you to touch me." Her countenance while he obeyed her earnest request was a thing to behold. Her lips parted and her head had fallen ever-so-slightly back while his fingers drew lazy circles upon the silky flesh. The response she had to him prompted him to let his hand drop to the inside of her thigh. He grazed over the seam between her legs several times, and she shifted her hips forward while holding him by his shoulders. Meanwhile, she watched him through heavy-lidded eyes and bit her lip.

As soon as his fingers touched her centre. A throaty whimper tore from her throat, and she pulled him closer, anchoring herself to him with an arm around his neck while he teased and sought the rhythm that would have her shatter. When they had been at the ruins, the warmth of her core had eliminated his reason and drawn him to pleasure her the way he did. Today was no different. Her breathing hitched then quickened, and she buried her face into his neck while he continued to touch her, letting her faint gasps and whimpers guide him. The scent of her perfume flooded his senses, and he caressed his nose against her shoulder and her neck, peppering kisses in its wake, seeking to drown himself in her.

He slipped a finger inside to join his efforts, making her cry out a strangled sound into his neck before she bit his shoulder. Her hips writhed against his hand while he gritted his teeth to withstand the temptation of her. How he yearned to bury himself in her warmth—to watch her passion peak while he loved her—but that would likely not happen tonight, so he wanted her to feel pleasure first. The least he could do was ensure her wedding night was as perfect as possible.

Those noises she had made began to increase in volume when he concentrated his efforts on those places which seemed to bring her the most pleasure while he drew her head back to claim her lips. She ground against his hand as he continued to torture himself with the sensation of her warmth around his fingers. He could not last like this much longer. She drew back, her eyes meeting his, which made him pause.

"Are you well?" His voice came out in the oddest of ways, as if he had been running.

Fiona frowned. "Why did you stop?" She grasped the arm between her legs that had begun its retreat and guided it back. "Do not dare do so again, or I will shoot you myself."

A strangled chuckle fell from his lips. Meanwhile, their gazes held without wavering while he continued what he had started. Her breathing quickened once again, and she watched him, her eyes struggling to remain open. Her back arched against his hand, and her hips shifted forward as she drew closer and closer to that precarious edge.

Her boldness was the most seductive thing he had ever seen. Her curls had loosened and had fallen around her head in a sort of halo, her lips were red from their kisses as were some patches of skin on her neck and chest, and her exquisite, uncovered breasts heaved with each panting breath. The lust writ upon her countenance was unmistakable. How was he to survive this?

Her eyes closed for but a second, but she reopened them a moment later, their gazes holding until her head fell back with a strangled cry.

He eased his ministrations but sustained her pleasure until she finally grabbed his arm. "Pray, 'tis too much."

He pulled the pins from her hair and released what remained bound. He had conceded before that she was a striking lady, but as she was, mussed from their activities, she was spectacular. Even in his dreams, he had never imagined her so.

While his fingers loosened her tresses, her eyes no longer held his but had wandered down to his arousal. Her hand reached for him, but he made haste to grab it and pressed her palm to his chest. "Not yet. I am too far gone for you to do that." To his shock, she did not argue as he shifted forward and guided himself to paradise. She angled her hips to receive him, a quick inhale accompanying his intrusion. Was she well?

"Fiona?"

Her hands grasped him by the buttocks and pulled him the rest of the way.

He nearly fell atop of her the pleasure was so great. "Wrap your legs around me."

He rolled them both over, so he lay on his back with her astride him. She lifted a little from him, then sat up as his gaze wandered over every inch of her, his fingers toyed with a curl that fell over her breast. "You are so beautiful."

For a moment, her eyes appeared glassy, but after a blink or two, one side of her lip quirked. "Are we to remain thus all night?"

"Are you always impertinent?" He grasped her hips and lifted her before guiding her back down his length. "Fiona—" he groaned out. Dreams of Fiona naked and riding him to his release, her supple thighs under his palm, and the feel of her centre under his fingers all flooded his mind and kept any rational thought from intruding. It was almost too much to bear. The living embodiment of his dreams since he had first set eyes upon her, the pistol in her hand and her gaze upbraiding him.

"You are tight as a glove."

"Is that a good thing?"

He gave a panting chuckle. "'Tis an exceptional thing. You feel so good, I fear I may spend myself too soon."

"Then we would do it again, so I am not cheated of the experience."

Again? He had no idea how he would survive this encounter much less partake of a second. "I may have married the perfect woman."

After several thrusts, she set her palms upon his chest and bit her lip while he tested the depth and angle until she squeezed her eyes closed. "There. Oh, yes, right there."

Without warning, she took command and began to ride him as she had in his imaginings, her hair cascading around her shoulders, her green eyes aflame, and her lips agape in her passion. She was the most magnificent creature he had ever beheld, and the freedom she embraced during their intimacy only made her more enticing. He had never experienced anything so exquisite. When he had first met Fiona, he never would have dreamt they would have such a strong passion between them. At his club, men spoke of relations such as this with their mistresses but never their wives.

Before long, he resorted to concentrating on the harvest, then remembering words in Latin to hold off his peak: pectus, papilla, stricta. This was just too much—she was too much. He reached to where they were joined and brushed a finger over her centre until her movements became erratic, and she bent over to kiss him until she cried out and could not seem to move. He attempted to draw out her pleasure, but her peak milked his from him, making him arch his back.

"Good God, Fee!" She was too perfect—the way she held nothing back despite her inexperience served to fuel his ardour until he broke.

When he became aware of his surroundings once more, Fiona had collapsed on top of him, her deep red curls covering his face and his chest. Not that he cared. She had been all he could have hoped for and more, and she was his wife. How had he been so fortunate? He considered himself fortunate anyway. Those he loved tended to die or leave—even if it was no more than to marry. He and Fiona were friends. They did not love each other, so they were both protected from that sort of heartache.

While they recovered, he held her in his arms and kissed her temple and her crown. His fingers grazed up and down her back, her shoulders, her sides. She had done him in.

Chapter 20

He had called her Fee. No one had ever called her by that name but her father. At that moment, she had been too wrapped up in him and the overwhelming sensations coursing through her, but now that she could form a thought within her head, his cry had shifted to the fore. Did she care that he used that name? Had he even known he was using it?

She lifted from his chest and propped her head on her hand, her elbow resting upon the mattress. He appeared so relaxed.

"You are staring." How could he tell with his eyes closed?

"I was thinking."

When his eyes opened, his fingers moved her fringe from her face. She must look affright!

He took her hand and held it when she attempted to repair the damage. "I have begun to believe both of us think too much." A tinge of humour laced his voice.

She looked at their joined hands. "Tell me something of yourself no one else knows."

His eyebrows drew down a bit. "I believe you already know my biggest secret, though I suppose others know some."

He must have meant the duchess. "Was she the only lady you...?"

"Yes. When I was at university, a man I was acquainted with through another became diseased from visiting certain establishments. The knowledge was enough to keep me from partaking without some feeling. A great number of gentlemen ridiculed me, but those I considered friends did not—or they were rather fastidious about those matters themselves."

She searched his eyes as the fingers on his chest toyed with the fine bit of hair under her hand. "Have you ever wanted to be someone other than who you are?"

The fingers of his free hand grazed between her breasts, then back up and down the slope. "I have no desire to ever be earl." His voice had gone softer with the admission. He also could not look her in the eye and watched his fingers as they bestowed those distracting caresses.

After a hard swallow, she closed and reopened her eyes as she attempted to concentrate. How could he eliminate her ability to think with such a simple touch? "I am not surprised you would prefer to remain as you are. You speak of your grandfather with great fondness. You likely want to assume your earldom as much as I want to assume mine. Neither of us desires to experience more loss than we have already."

"How is it that we understand each other so well?"

She let a light laugh escape. "I do not believe it to be so well, but we have enough similarities in our lives that we can sympathise."

"What of you?"

"I beg your pardon?" What did he mean?

"Well, what have you never told another soul?"

"You make it sound quite dramatic. I also have a difficult time considering the question when you do that." She glanced down to where he still played, but without warning, he set upon her, tickling her ribs. "No, stop." The great heaves of laughter continued as he dug his fingers into her side while he grasped her hands with one of his. No more than a moment later, she was pinned beneath him, one of his hands pressing both of hers over her head. His strong chest was before her, the muscles standing out with the exertion of holding her the way he was.

"Do not evade the question. I answered you." The boyish grin he wore made her smile.

Fiona stared at his chest. Other than a book or two she had found in her father's library, she had never seen a naked man before today, and if she compared Nicholas to the specimen in the drawing, he was much more tempting. She squeezed her eyes closed. He asked her a question, but how to answer. "I may seem bold, but I am not certain about meeting your family. I fear they will not like me, particularly if they know of why we wed." She opened her eyes. How would he respond to her revelation? Her stomach had tightened when she told him as she was rarely so open with another, but she told the truth.

He frowned. "I never had the impression you cared so for the opinions of others."

"I have no care for most people's opinions, but my father's is important—even if I do not always heed his words—but your family is now my family, and I am not a lady they would have chosen."

"My grandparents will never know that you approached me to escape a threatened arranged marriage. You must know that if you do not tell them, and I do not tell them, they will never learn. Besides, they are not ones to judge such things lest they cut most of the *ton*."

"I am Irish."

"My grandparents will not have a care for that. They accepted Mr. Bennet as their daughter's husband, and he was no more than a country gentleman."

"Mr. Bennet is your cousins' father?"

"Yes, my grandparents may speak of your father's English roots during calls and to those who can be of aid with your acceptance at events, but they will embrace you into the family. I am sure of it. I have never known them to slight someone without good reason.

"In the meantime, this is not how or when I should care to speak of my family." He reached down and tugged at the ribbon holding one of her stockings followed by the one on the other. He grazed down the side of each leg as he removed them both causing her supple skin to pebble under his fingers. All the while, he kept her hands pinned as they were, swapping hands to accomplish his task.

"What should you like to discuss then?" His touch had made her voice weak.

His teeth nipped under her ear while his fingers again found their way to her core. "I should like to spend the remainder of our time in Ireland in this room, to hear you whimper and moan, perhaps make you cry my name over and over again." Her breathing hitched. How could he reduce her to a puddle with no more than his words?

He moved within her with ease but kept his movements slow and deliberate while that one hand still held hers captive. His eyes roved down her body underneath him to where they were joined. "This is so perfect. I want to savour it."

She wrapped her legs around his hips once again, letting him lead her where he would.

Nicholas's eyes fluttered open, and he blinked for a moment. The presence first thing in the morning of an unclothed lady in his bed was a novel one. Fiona had been clothed when they had fallen asleep in the library, and his first thought upon waking and finding Fiona sleeping upon his side had been to hasten her return to her rooms before they were discovered. Yet, with her tucked against him, her back to his chest, naught was amiss in her presence this morning. She could remain as she was, and he had no need to rush her away.

He buried his nose into the space between her shoulder and her chin and inhaled the remnants of her perfume. They had spent the remainder of their wedding day in her bed until he rang the bell and had dinner brought to their sitting room. After, he had thrown her over his shoulder and brought her to his rooms. He had imagined her so many times in that bed that he had loved her before they gave in and succumbed to sleep. When he had awoken in the middle of the night, he could no more deny himself a hazy and sleepy interlude before drifting back to sleep. He could not bemoan having a wife!

He ground his hips into her firm buttocks while a lazy hand trailed over the flesh of her thigh then up and across her stomach. Yes, marriage had certain advantages. Thankfully, he found his wife attractive, and he enjoyed her company. How many men wed for mere fortune or connexions? He had not even been wed a full day, and he was of the opinion that those who wed for fortune and connexions were addle-pates indeed. They may not have married for love, but friendship was infinitely better than no feeling whatsoever The attraction they held for each other would also not be taken into account in a marriage of true convenience.

His fingers found her nipple, and he teased it to a hard peak. He could never get enough of her body—of her heat engulfing him, bringing him to a shattering peak. A low, breathy moan broke the quiet within the bed curtains. That noise was the most incredible sound—other than her crying his name, that is. His heartbeat quickened at those whimpers and moans, and his ardour increased at those tell-tale signs of her pleasure. Her eyes when she found her release flashed in a way that only rendered her more beautiful. He was addicted to Fiona. Thankfully, she was his wife because he was ruined for any other woman. They could not compare.

"Nicholas," she gasped.

"Good morning." He would ensure this was the best morning in her memory too.

"Enough!" Fiona pushed Nicholas towards the foot of the bed and covered herself with the sheet while she sat back against the headboard. "Firstly, I demand breakfast, then I want to do something besides..." She waved her hand around between them.

At his sad eyes and forlorn expression, she chuckled. "Oh, do not behave as though I have taken away your favourite toy. While I have enjoyed all we have done since we arrived home yesterday, if we continue, I shall not be able to walk. I am not so certain I can do so without a waddle as it is."

He picked up her foot that was sitting just outside the coverlet and began rubbing his thumb up the instep, making her eyes almost roll back in her head. Where had he learnt so many ways of seducing her?

"I have enjoyed you as well," he said in a low voice. Their gazes held until she shook herself.

"What if we have your valet or my maid lock the doors to the library? We could put on our dressing gowns and sneak down the passages with no one knowing we did not dress." She did not want to put on stays or take the time for a full toilette, but the library would at least give a new prospect.

While Nicholas made the arrangements, she visited her dressing room and put herself as much to rights as she could. Soon after she returned to her bedchamber, Nicholas joined her so they could sneak down the passage.

She closed the door when they entered the library, but when she turned with her back to the shelves, Nicholas's hungry gaze roved down her clothing.

"Nicholas," she said a little drawn out.

He swooped forward and kissed her, lifting her to a small ledge between the bottom shelves and the top. "This was a horrible idea if you wished to distract me." He pulled the shoulder of her dressing gown and shift from her shoulder and bit the slope. "You do not know how you tortured me that night we fell asleep in here." His hand slid up the back of her thigh. "You cannot know how much I wanted to rip the dressing gown down your arm where it had fallen and take you as you are or press you down into the sofa."

"Nicholas." His name came out as a feeble whimper. This was ridiculous! Would she ever be able to refuse him?

When he slid home, she sighed and welcomed him into her. One day, they would need to learn some restraint, but today would not be the day.

Chapter 21

10th of September 1813

Nicholas brushed the hair away from Fiona's sleeping face and sighed. She was still a little pale. Leaving Ireland, not to mention the crossing, had been difficult for her.

As soon as the carriage had journeyed far enough from Moydrum that her father could not see, Fiona had cried at leaving him but not long after, had straightened and declared herself well, determined to bear the separation with aplomb.

The journey to Belfast and boarding the ship had been easy; however, the crossing to England had been miserable with the storm they had happened upon. Nicholas had fared better than Fiona, who never ceased retching and retching until they had arrived and settled for a day in an inn near the port. He could not bear dragging her further in her pathetic state. He had been worried for her during the crossing, but by the time they docked, he had questioned the wisdom of leaving Ireland and putting her through such misery.

Due to her pallor and extreme discomfort, he had intended to remain in Liverpool to allow her to rest and recuperate some before they embarked on their remaining travel, but the inn was noisy, particularly at night, so at his insistence, they hired a carriage and drove two hours to a quaint inn in a small market town where they stayed for the next three days.

Fiona bristled at being confined, so they took walks in the small town and in the countryside. The food had been excellent, and his wife had regained some of her appetite—a welcome relief!

When her courses came the day before they had planned to depart, he had attempted to wait another few days, but his wife would hear none of it, insisting she would prefer a moving carriage to remaining shuttered in for another week. He was weary of travel and strange beds as well, so they continued; however, despite Fiona's insistence that they not prolong their journey, they never spent an entire day in the carriage, instead breaking the trip more often than Nicholas would have if he had travelled on his own.

The corners of her lips curved. "You are staring. Do not fret. I am well. My appetite has almost returned, the aching of my courses has subsided, and now, I only need to wait for the rest to end."

"You are still a bit pale."

"Such a charmer, my lord. A lady does enjoy being told she is pale, but 'tis sometimes a consequence of a lady's courses. Since I was so ill on the ship, I am not surprised my colour would be a little off." She opened those vivid green eyes, and he required a deep inhale Why did her gaze affect him so?

"Forgive me."

She sighed and sat up from where she had leaned against his side. "One would believe you have no sister at all with how panicked you became when my courses began."

He had found the evidence on the bedsheet and had sought her out to ensure she was not injured. How was he to know ladies had courses? No one had ever mentioned it to him. "Why would I know such an intimate detail about my sister? I would not want to know anyhow."

"I suppose that makes sense." She glanced out of the window. "Where are we?"

He lifted his arm to point at the gates of Richmond Castle. "We are crossing onto Richmond lands."

She gave a jolt. "Oh!" With shaky hands, she retrieved her bonnet from the seat across from them and proceeded to put it on. He had never seen her wearing the article considering she was either on horseback with her riding hat or inside when they had happened upon each other. For all he had known, she did not own one.

"Do not worry. 'Tis just my grandparents. No one is to arrive for the shooting party for another fortnight. I thought this a good time for you to become acquainted with them without other people vying for their attention." What he said was true, yet his insides were in turmoil. He drew in a sizeable inhale. His stomach was clenched in the most unforgiving manner, and he swallowed hard. Until now, he had been able to avoid thinking of what was to come by concentrating on his new wife and her health, but that ability was diminishing by the second.

Her gaze left the view out the window and settled on him. "I think I would have preferred the latter. Your sister and guests would have given me some freedom from the scrutiny of your grandparents."

He grinned and wrapped an arm around her shoulders. "Grandmamma and Grandpapa will not bite." He doubted they would her anyway.

"*You* are not meeting them for the first time."

"Very true, but I promise they are not hateful." He brushed his lips against her temple as they descended the hill, and the castle came into view. The statement was the truth. They would never treat Fiona with disdain, though their treatment of him in the next few days was in question.

Fiona gasped when they topped the crest and Richmond came into view in the valley. "I thought Moydrum large, but this is a grand castle indeed."

"It is only a building. While the castle appears large, those who came before us kept a portion for the house and have let parts they could not save fall into disrepair. That one low wall there," he pointed towards the remains of a wing that had been in ruins for at least two centuries, "is not whole. My great great grandfather took down a portion so they would not be a danger to anyone walking in them, and since, they have been used for kitchen gardens."

"I would imagine maintaining such an old and extensive house is quite expensive."

He took his wife's hand, and she squeezed it with a shaky breath. "They will love you."

A brittle laugh accompanied her shaking her head. "Do not make promises you cannot keep. I am well aware what most say about me in my own neighbourhood, and many of them have known me since I was a wee lass. Your grandparents have no such history with me."

The equipage drew in front of the keep, and he alighted and held out his hand to help Fiona. She looked up at the old stone edifice before them. Had she blanched?

Before he could settle her once more, the door opened, and his grandparents hastened outside. "Nicholas? We had not expected you for another week!" said his grandmother.

He kissed Gran's cheek, and his grandfather hugged him. When he drew back from his grandfather's embrace, his grandmother was looking at Fiona.

"Nicholas, will you not introduce us?" Her eyes darted back and forth between him and his wife. She was surely curious why he was travelling unchaperoned with a lady unknown to them.

He extended his arm to Fiona, who put her trembling hand near his elbow. "Grandmamma, Grandpapa, may I present Lady Fiona Montford, Viscountess Hatton."

His grandfather burst into a fit of coughing while Gran's eyes narrowed on him. "Perhaps we should go inside."

Damn! He had avoided writing them of the news since he could not find a way to tell them in a letter. How was he to inform them he was to wed—had wed—without them in attendance? He had not witnessed a countenance as severe as his grandmother wore today since he was fourteen and she had caught him daring Amelia to climb the giant oak in the gardens.

"Where is Janey?" Perhaps his cousin could diffuse the tension a bit.

"She was invited to stay at Pemberley for a month with Lizzybeth," said his grandmother in a terse tone.

Fiona's grip on his arm was unforgiving as they entered, although it loosened somewhat when they entered the hall, and she took in her surroundings. The castle was built in the 12th century, but the hall, while old, had been decorated with statuary, rugs, and plush settees along the wall, making it seem less like an old fortress of sorts and more the house befitting his father's status.

His grandparents led them into the closest drawing room and closed the door behind Nicholas and Fiona once they had entered. "Nicholas, what is the meaning of this?" asked his grandfather as soon as they were guaranteed their privacy.

He glanced at Fiona, who lifted her eyebrows. "You failed to tell them we are married." Her tone was not hard, but by the hint of ire in her eyes, she was not best pleased with him at the moment.

"No, he did not," said Gran. "Forgive us, but I plead shock at the news." She held out both hands to his wife, who took them, accepting the offered olive branch with a tense smile. "You are Lady Hatton? Would you tell us a little about yourself since my grandson seems inclined to remain silent?"

Fiona glanced at him then pressed her lips together for a second. "I am the only daughter of Lord Seamus Fitzgerald, the Earl of Kildare. My father's estate Larchfield neighbours Moydrum to the east, and I am the heir to the estate and the earldom—"

"Your father's title can be passed through the female line?" Grandfather's shock was evident in his voice.

"Yes," said Fiona. "Larchfield's lands are almost as extensive as Moydrum's, though the house is not as grand. My father once thought to add to it, but when he had no further children, he decided spending the funds to do so was unnecessary. My grandfather was English, but my grandmother and mother were Irish. I am unaware of any connections through—"

His grandmother held up her hand. "My dear, while we would enjoy hearing of your father's estate and your family, I want to know about *you*."

"Me?" Fiona glanced at Nicholas once again. She opened her mouth once or twice. It was unlike her to be speechless. He needed to help.

"She is an excellent horsewoman." He clasped his hands behind his back as his grandparents and wife looked at him.

"You enjoy riding?" His grandmother dipped her chin a little. He had seen that expression before. She was hoping to put Fiona at ease.

"I do. Very much so." Fiona swallowed again. "I fear I am not much of a lady." She glanced between them. How he wanted to alleviate her nerves! "Since my father never had a son, he taught me to hunt and shoot. I enjoy reading, though I detest novels and prefer histories and plays. I never took to needlework or other ladies' pursuits."

His grandmother patted her hand. "You must have been at sixes and sevens in the carriage before coming here, then to find out Nicholas told us naught of you—I am certain your nerves must be bothersome. That said, pray do not fret another moment. If Nicholas thought to make you his wife, I am certain we shall get along well, and I look forward to getting to know you better."

"I thank you, Lady Richmond."

Grandmamma waved dismissively. "When you feel comfortable enough with me, you may call me Grandmamma or Gran as my own grandchildren do. You are part of the family."

Fiona attempted a weak smile. "I shall do my best."

"Now, when shall we expect Evans and your lady's maid? I shall need to inform the housekeeper." She hastened to pull the bell. "I shall also need to have rooms prepared for the two of you. Nicholas's current rooms will not be appropriate."

"Evans and our trunks should be not far behind us," said Nicholas. "Fiona's maid wished to remain in Ireland, so my wife has been without since we departed. I had hoped you would be able to suggest a replacement."

He shrank back at Gran's withering glare. "This would have been wonderful information to be included in a letter announcing your intention of marrying—or even that you had married, do you not think, Lady Hatton?"

"Pray, I would be pleased if you called me Fiona. And yes, I do believe that would have been excellent information to include in a letter." Her gaze met his, and her lips curved on one side. Oh, no. His wife had aligned herself with his grandmother. He would likely receive no quarter for some time.

"I am glad we agree. Hugh, do cease standing there so quietly. You are never without something to say, and it is vexing me that you are silent."

His grandfather gave a start then a short bow. "Lady Hatton...Fiona, welcome to Richmond Castle." I do hope you will forgive our manner. We do not usually greet guests—or in this case, new family—in this way. I hope you will look past our boorish manners."

"Nicholas, do go to your grandfather's study. I am certain he should care to speak to you while I become acquainted with your wife."

His grandfather gave him a wave to follow, making his stomach flip. Whenever his grandmother sent him to his grandfather's study, nothing good came of it. Why did he feel as though he was eight and about to be punished for some grievous misdeed?

Nicholas was going to leave her with his grandmother? He would not even argue to remain to be of aid to her? She clenched her reticule in her hands. Despite the temptation to knock him in the head, Fiona longed to grab his sleeve and pull him back, but she clasped her hands together instead.

A woman she could only assume was the housekeeper entered as her husband departed with one last look and a tight smile. Well, that was hardly reassuring!

"You rang, my lady," said the housekeeper.

"Yes, it seems Lord Hatton married while in Ireland, so he will require more appropriate rooms as will his wife. Lady Hatton, may I introduce you to Mrs. Cox, the Richmond housekeeper."

The housekeeper straightened and glanced at her when Lady Richmond had announced her marriage thus, but gave a curtsey when introduced.

"It also seems Lady Hatton's maid was unable to accompany her to England, so we will require a suitable girl to help her until we can hire a lady's maid for her."

"May I suggest my niece, my lady? She is in Catterick visiting my sister after leaving a position with the house of Sir James Manning in Norfolk. If I send for her, she could fill the position on trial, and if she does not suit Lady Hatton, we can seek another maid, although I am certain my niece would perform admirably."

Lady Richmond looked to Fiona and raised her eyebrows. "What do you think?"

Fiona looked between the two watching her. She would not be intimidated! "May I ask why she left the service of this Sir James Manning?"

"The wife is known to have difficulty keeping servants in her household," said Lady Richmond.

"Indeed, my niece left the house after her employer slapped her for failing to respond quickly enough to her summons. In Hattie's defense, she was in the kitchen when the bell rang and hurried as quickly as she could through the house. The lady still found it not swift enough for her standards."

"She slapped her?" Fiona pressed her hand to her chest. "How old is your niece?"

"She is five and twenty but has served as a lady's maid for six years and learnt under Lady Richmond's maid."

Lady Richmond nodded with a fond expression. "She kept my gowns pressed, and the maids often had lovely and fashionable hair while she was here. I remember being impressed with her eagerness to learn."

"Then I am willing to hire her on trial if that suits her. My strictest requirement is that what is said between us or in front of her is in confidence. I would have her know that." She had trusted Walsh without question. If this girl could be circumspect, they would likely get along.

"Of course," said the housekeeper as though it went without question. "Hattie knows to keep her mouth shut, my lady."

"Then we shall suit admirably."

The countess grinned. "Wonderful. Pray, send for her. If she can, we should like her to begin this evening. Lady Hatton will have the final say on whether she is hired."

"Of course, Lady Richmond. Shall I see to the new chambers for Lord and Lady Hatton?"

"Yes, at once so they may refresh themselves. We should care for some tea while we await your word their rooms are ready."

"Yes, my lady." With a quick curtsey, the housekeeper departed.

Chapter 22

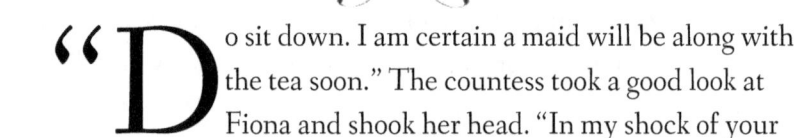

"**D**o sit down. I am certain a maid will be along with the tea soon." The countess took a good look at Fiona and shook her head. "In my shock of your arrival, the butler never took your coat or hat. One moment."

The lady departed and returned without delay, a maid trailing behind her. "This is Grace. She will take your belongings and put them in your chambers once Mrs. Cox sorts that out."

As soon as Fiona had rid herself of her bonnet, gloves, and travelling coat, she sat on the sofa with a relieved exhale. "I had not expected the day to be as warm as it is in September."

"I agree. 'Tis as though summer wanted one more warm day to say goodbye." A maid entered with the tea service and set it before the countess. "Now, tell me. How did you meet my grandson?"

A pang travelled up Fiona's chest and into her throat. "We happened upon each other riding on the day he arrived at Moydrum."

Lady Richmond paused and furrowed her brow. "That is a rather general statement. Where were you that you happened upon him?"

She bit her cheek. How was she to avoid the truth of the matter? "I have grown up riding on Moydrum's lands as well as Larchfield's. My father made a promise to Nicholas's that he would keep a watchful eye on the estate, so I was of aid to him in honouring his vow."

"How lovely of you both," said the countess.

"The day we met; I had been riding—galloping really—along the edge of a field. The hill was a favourite place to test my horse, and I had started up the incline when I heard hoofbeats behind me. I did not recognise the man, so when I reached the top, I grabbed the branch of a tree I would duck under most days and pulled it back tight. When the rider came around the path, I let the limb loose and hit the man in the chest—hit Lord Hatton in the chest."

Lady Richmond blinked and made to open her mouth while Fiona began to tap her foot. "I dismounted and confronted him for being on Moydrum's lands, only for him to inform me he is the current Lord Hatton."

"You were bold as brass to approach an unknown man such as you did."

Fiona cleared her throat and stared at her hands. Why? They held no secret to make this easier. "My father gave me a small pistol to carry since I prefer not to be followed by a groom. One would often ride out with me, but most of our grooms had difficulty maintaining my pace."

"You held a pistol on my grandson." The countess's tone was a little low. Perhaps Fiona should have made it romantic, woven a tale worthy of a poem, but what did she know about that? She had never read Radcliffe or that "lady" who everyone raved over.

"I was not certain why he was following me, so yes, I did."

After a moment, a strange sound made Fiona lift her head. The countess had covered her mouth with her hand, and her shoulders were shaking. "I must say that is a most unusual tale for how a husband and wife met. I have thought for years that Nicholas would require a strong lady as a wife. When I first saw you, you appeared a little pale and wide-eyed. I thought perhaps he had wed someone without the mettle to stand up to him."

"The crossing was...difficult. The sea was rough, and I spent the entire time sick. My husband put us in an inn in Liverpool and had planned to remain, but the tavern was boisterous in the evenings and uncomfortable, so we moved to another inn until I could regain some of my appetite. Nicholas still says my colour has not completely returned as yet."

"I am certain that is part of it. Meeting his relations with your marriage a fait accompli cannot be an easy affair either."

"No, my lady, it is not."

The lady's eyes flashed for a moment. "May I ask if my grandson was injured in your attempt to protect yourself?"

"He suffered from some bruised ribs and was sore for a week or so, but suffered no lasting effects."

"Well, after the many times Amelia had some bruise or bump from one of Nicholas's horrid jokes, I cannot be upset since he had no permanent injury."

"Jokes?" She had never seen him behave in such a way.

"That boy is as mischievous as they come. Have you never seen this in him?"

"I suppose a little. After our initial meeting, he teased me here and there, but for the most part, he has never been mischievous with me." Other than since their marriage he had taken to tickling her when he exercised his wit upon her.

Lady Richmond handed Fiona her cup of tea and sat back with her own. "How curious, but perhaps his feelings for you are why he is so different with you than his sister or cousins."

Feelings? Nicholas had spoken of his attraction to her. By his manner in her presence, he cared for her and was affectionate, but he had never claimed to love her. Did he now consider her more than an intimate friend?

"Well, now that we have your lady's maid in hand and I know how you and my grandson met, I should like to know how you were married. Are you Catholic?"

"No, since my father's family was from the Church of England, we continue to be Anglican. We were wed in the chapel at Larchfield. The Church of England united with that of Ireland in 1800, so I would assume our marriage should be recognised here."

Lady Richmond wrapped her hand around Fiona's forearm. "I was not questioning the validity of your marriage in our eyes, but if you had been wed in a Catholic ceremony, we may have had you marry in the chapel here at Richmond, to be certain your marriage is valid in England. If you were wed in the manner you mentioned, I am certain all is well."

Fiona's shoulders relaxed as she took a sip of her tea. "That is a relief."

"Have you thought to inform *anyone* of your marriage?" Grandpapa looked at him over the top of his glasses, finally breaking the silence that had prevailed since they entered his study.

"No, I could never think of a way to pen it in a letter. The words escaped me."

"So you practically give your grandmother an apoplexy arriving here with your wife—no notice and no warning that we are about to have the shock of our lifetimes. You know your grandmother will be sore for some time at missing your nuptials. I know I did not miss that grind of her teeth when you introduced the poor girl, who must have been nervous to meet us as it is. Then to discover we never knew of her in the first place..."

He could not help but let one side of his lips quirk. "Yes, I shall be put in my place. I have no doubt of it."

"Will she? She appeared pale and very quiet upon a first impression."

Nicholas laughed. "Then you are in for another shock. She is forthright in her opinions and can ride a horse as well as any man. Her pallor was due to the toll of the crossing from Ireland. She never ceased being ill while aboard the ship. She has recovered some, but I think her colour has not entirely returned as yet."

"I remember when I journeyed to Ireland, a storm came upon us during the crossing," said his Grandpapa." I had never been sicker. The ship rocked and swayed for a day and a half."

"Fiona will require a mount. As much as she would wish to have her stallion here, we thought to leave him in Ireland so he will be there when we return for the summer."

"You intend to return?" His grandfather straightened, his voice a little higher.

"We thought to go after the Season. We shall spend the summer at Moydrum and return in October or so for the shooting parties and Christmastide. I would not deprive Lord Kildare the pleasure of seeing his daughter, nor my wife of visiting her father."

Grandpapa frowned. "Yes, of course. I suppose I had not considered. We can always invite the earl to Richmond as well."

"I took the liberty of inviting him whenever he should like. He thanked me for the offer, though I did not get the impression he would come. He has had several trials with his health in the past couple of years."

After nodding, his grandfather rested his forearms upon his desk. "Do you have a mount in mind for your wife? You know better her skill as a rider."

"What of that young colt out of Hades? He is spirited and needs a firm hand. I believe Fiona could manage him well."

"Adesius? I would not put the most skilled of riders atop that horse side saddle."

Nicholas shifted in his chair and cleared his throat. "Fiona does not ride side saddle."

His grandfather lifted his eyebrows. "She rides astride? In a gown?"

"Her gowns are altered with extra fabric. She can fasten the excess, so it does not drag the ground when she walks but covers her legs when she is riding. For the foxhunt at Larchfield, she also wore tall boots. I have never seen her ride side saddle, though I am certain she could if required."

The door to the study opened, and Gran entered and sat upon the edge of the desk. "Mrs. Cox has your rooms prepared and is showing your wife to them. You should refresh yourself as well. Dinner is at the usual time. I mentioned purchasing your wife some new gowns. Hers are of expensive fabrics, and I am certain the latest fashion in Ireland, but she will require some more suited to what is popular in London at the moment. I purchased some fabric before we departed town that I packed in a trunk. I believe several colours will suit Fiona's complexion. I also know of a dressmaker in Leeds who is exceptional. She will come here to fit your wife if requested. I intend to pen a note to her today."

"Fiona agreed to this?"

His grandmother chuckled. "I do not believe she was pleased, but I do not think she will argue."

Was his grandmother speaking of Fiona? The one whose temper matched the vivid red of her hair? "If I were you, I would be prepared to argue." He stood and hugged his grandmother. "I thank you for being of aid to her. Fiona's hands were shaking before we stepped down from the carriage. I know you did what you could to put her at ease."

"I did. I look forward to getting to know her better."

He kissed Grandmamma on the cheek and quit the room. Tiptoeing as quietly as possible, he rounded the corner and entered the library. He approached the adjoining study door with careful steps.

"I cannot credit that he wed without us. What could have occurred in Ireland?" said his grandmother. "As much as I am loath to admit it, we shall need to do all we can to ensure she is accepted by the *ton*. Thankfully, she is Anglican. As you know, I have no quarrel with the Catholics, but being Irish will be difficult enough." Nicholas bit his lip. As much as he despised it, his grandmother was right.

"Nicholas wants to give her Adesius," said Grandpapa.

"That is a spirited mount indeed for a lady. Amelia is an accomplished rider, and I would not be comfortable with her riding that horse."

"He said she rides astride."

"She what?"

Nicholas cringed at his grandmother's tone. Her dismay was not a surprise.

"I enquired of how they met," said Grandmamma. "Do you know she knocked him from his horse, then drew a pistol on him?" Oh, blast! He should have known Fiona would not beat around the bush.

His grandfather spluttered and coughed. "Do you know how she unseated him?"

"She said she pulled the branch of a tree back as far as it would go and released it." Nicholas rubbed his chest. The mention of it still smarted!

"She is fortunate he was not gravely injured."

"Hugh, I believe more exists to their wedding than they will tell us."

Grandpapa sighed. "We cannot force it from him. As much as we would wish to, he is of age. If he wed this girl, we must accept it—unless she proves to be of poor character."

"She would not be so full of anxiety over meeting us if she did not care," said his grandmother. "I just want to know how this all came about."

"We may need to resign ourselves to the fact that they may never tell us."

His grandmother huffed. "You are asking me to do the impossible."

"I know." His grandfather chuckled.

Chapter 23

Fiona buried her face into the pillow while huddling back further into her husband's embrace. A fortnight had passed since their arrival at Richmond Castle and since she made the acquaintance of Nicholas's grandparents, and she longed to feel at home. She could not complain, however, of Nicholas's grandparents. Lord and Lady Richmond were adamant she was part of the family and did what they could to ensure she felt welcome, which helped immensely. So much had changed in so little time. Settling would take even more time it seemed.

The past two weeks had been spent ensuring she was ready for the guests who would arrive beginning today. A dressmaker had come from Leeds and created some lovely gowns, riding habits, and other *accoutrements* for her to wear. The woman had taken her foot measurements and new boots and slippers had arrived the day before to match the dressmaker's work. Fiona had not needed them, but Lady Richmond had insisted.

The most pleasing part of their time at Richmond had been when Nicholas took her to the stables to meet Adesius, her new mount. A beautiful grey stallion with white markings who required a firm hand she was more than capable of providing. He was heaven to ride! He sailed over the countryside and jumped the dry fences with at least a foot to spare. They had taken a long ride this morning before returning for luncheon. After, Nicholas had brought her up to their rooms. She had barely closed the door before he had pressed her against it. She bit her lip and blushed. If a servant had passed outside, they were sure to have heard her cries as well as the door rattling while her husband took her without regard for who might hear.

A lazy hand glided over her stomach to cup her breast. "Mmm, I do not want to get up."

"We cannot remain thus. Your sister and her husband are supposed to arrive at any moment."

"If this house fills with people, I shall never have you alone again." She had never considered whether she would enjoy an affectionate lover, but she could not complain of the way Nicholas laced their fingers when he held her hand, the gentle kisses he bestowed to her forehead and hair when he held her, as well as the small gestures he could manage when they were in company with his grandparents. Before that day at the ruins when he spread his greatcoat on the ground and held her, she would have never considered him to be so doting, particularly since they were no more than friends. The more she came to know him, the more she came to know his generous heart.

She rolled in his arms to face him. "How will we never be alone? Will someone be joining us in our bed each evening? Just so you are aware, I would not be amenable to such a thing."

His fingers attacked her ribs making her shriek as he tickled her. "You and your cheeky responses. My grandparents believe you to be shy, did you know?"

"I am not comfortable around them yet." She gasped in a breath as she attempted to cease his torment, her hand scrambling to grasp his.

"Yet you told them of aiming your pistol at me."

Somehow, she managed to press her foot to his hipbone and push. Ha! As soon as he rolled off, she straddled him and pinned down his hands. He could remove her with little effort if he tried, but he indulged her. "I am not proficient at lying. Your grandmother seemed to find the tale humorous. I believe she referred to you as mischievous, yet, other than tickling and teasing, you have never behaved so with me."

"Would you like me to put alum in your toothpowder or a snake in your dressing table?" He wore a boyish grin that made something within her long to kiss him.

"You did those things to your sister?"

"My cousin. Do not feel pity for Lizzy. She is capable of defending herself and did so after each of my pranks. My sister and Janey may not be as quick with their retribution, but they can manage."

"I anticipate meeting this Lizzy if she bested you."

"My sister once put sand in my sheets. Her husband aided her in the endeavour as well."

Fiona gave him a side-long look. "And what did you do to her?"

He chuckled. "I put vinegar in her rosewater the morning of her wedding."

Without warning, his hands freed themselves and resumed their onslaught of her ribs as she laughed uncontrollably. She dove to the mattress and attempted to cover herself before he stopped and pulled her flush to his body.

"If I had the choice, I would remain thus with you forever."

She blinked madly and swallowed that lump in her throat. When he said such heartfelt things to her, she could almost imagine he loved her as much as she loved him. She bit her lip and hid her face in the crook of his neck. Wait! As much as she loved him! Her eyes burnt, and her insides were a twisting, fluttering mess. She loved him? When had that happened? It seemed the feeling had not come upon her all of a sudden but had crept upon her. She could have wept. How was she to survive, especially if he never felt the same?

Her lips claimed his, and Nicholas showed no hesitation in accepting her kiss. Hands wandered and their tongues duelled until he rolled her on top of him. He ground up against her core, making her groan. "I can think of nothing but you, like this, all day long."

It seemed they would not be dressing as soon as they had planned.

Nicholas attempted to school his features as he descended the stairs with Fiona's hand resting upon his arm. As much as he wanted to see his sister, he had groaned at the necessity to leave their bed and have Fiona cover herself. While she was handsome in her new gowns, she was never more lovely than when she was unclothed, her creamy flesh his to enjoy. He had been insatiable since they married. Some might consider his appetite for his wife unseemly, but why should he care? He was content, and he ensured Fiona was satisfied. Nothing more mattered.

Grandmamma and Grandpapa came into the hall as they approached the bottom. His grandmother looked at them and lifted her eyebrows. "Refreshing yourself after your ride took a great deal of time. I am pleased you condescended to join us for Amelia and Anthony's arrival."

"We rested for an hour or so," said Nicholas. Fiona, meanwhile, bit her cheek as her complexion was overtaken with a delicate pink. So much for his excuse! His grandmother would, no doubt, notice that subtle change in his wife's complexion.

He opened his mouth to speak, but a baby's wailing stopped any sound from emerging or being heard for that matter. When Amelia and Anthony entered, Amelia appeared harried while Greene's jaw pulsed as he clenched and released it.

"My dear, did Isabella not take well to the carriage ride?" Gran held out her hands to the red-faced and squalling child in Amelia's arms. Isabella shook her head, screaming louder, then leaned with arms outstretched to Fiona as they approached. His wife, without hesitation, took the child and cuddled her to her shoulder.

His sister glanced between them. "Who is this?"

Nicholas straightened and placed his hand between Fiona's shoulder blades. "Lady Fiona Montford, Viscountess Hatton, may I present my sister, Lady Amelia Greene, and her husband, Sir Anthony. Amelia, this lady is my wife."

Sir Anthony began coughing and spluttering while Amelia's eyes bulged. She glanced between his grandparents and him as she removed her bonnet. "This is one of your awful pranks, is it not?"

He gasped, and his chin hitched back. "I would never tease you so. Were you not persuading me to take a wife before I departed for Ireland? Mayhap I simply took your advice."

His sister gave him a penetrating stare. "You have never taken my advice."

"I have seen the marriage contracts and papers, Amelia," said Grandpapa. "I assure you he is in earnest.

After another moment, his sister shook herself and curtseyed. "Forgive me, Lady Hatton, I seem to have forgotten my manners. I am pleased to make your acquaintance, and I thank you for indulging my daughter." Greene followed his wife's lead and bowed while he welcomed Fiona to the family.

Grandmamma clasped her hands. "I put you in your usual rooms, so if you refresh yourself and come out to the gardens, I thought we would take tea outside. The day is lovely and not too cool. We should take advantage of the pleasant weather while we have it."

Amelia faced Fiona who was whispering to Isabella. His niece had quieted in his wife's arms, though she was still snuffling and whimpering. Lord Kildare had mentioned Fiona was good with children. This was the first time he had witnessed her manner with them. She appeared comfortable and not at all apprehensive.

"I should take Isabella to her nursemaid." When Amelia made to take the babe from Fiona, Isabella buried herself into Fiona's arms with another loud wail.

"I do not mind, Lady Greene," said Fiona. "If she needs a bit longer, I am happy to provide you with some respite. Refresh yourself and my niece and I shall walk around the gardens and look at the flowers, shall we not, wee one?"

Amelia glanced at him. "If you are certain and do call me Amelia. We are sisters now after all."

"Then you must call me Fiona."

His sister seemed to have a difficult time leaving, continually glancing behind her at Isabella in Fiona's embrace until she rounded the corner at the top of the stairs. He could not blame her. Her daughter's insistence to a stranger had to be disconcerting.

Gran rubbed Isabella's back. "The poor dear must have been overwrought and needed someone new to listen to her woes."

His wife brushed a tear from the child's cheek. "She is likely overtired as well."

When they entered the gardens in what was once the ward of the castle, Fiona stepped over to a bed of roses and pointed at the flowers while Isabella watched with her head still pressed against his wife's chest. She still sniffled and hiccoughed but had calmed in a considerable fashion since her arrival. While Fiona settled the child, he sat at the table with his grandparents.

"She has experience with children," said his grandmother.

"Her father mentioned she helped their tenants, even holding new babies so the mother could rest from time to time."

"A thoughtful gesture; I am certain the mothers were appreciative indeed. A new mother is always in need of rest."

He could not resist the draw of his wife and stood, making his way closer. When he stepped behind her, her quiet singing could be discerned over the birds chirping and the other sounds of nature around them. He had never heard her voice before. Her lilting soprano was beautiful, even if he had no idea what she was saying.

"What language is that?" He asked in soft tones, so he did not disturb the babe.

"I learned that song when I was young from my governess. It is in Gaelic."

"You speak Gaelic?"

"I know bits and pieces—enough to understand the meaning of the words." She rubbed Isabella's back and walked in a slow, swaying gate through the flowers. After a few minutes, his niece turned her head upon Fiona's shoulder while he walked alongside them. When they turned back towards the group, the baby's eyes had drifted closed with a shuddering breath, Fiona's voice still lulling the child to sleep.

As soon as his sister returned, she hurried over, and her eyebrows rose. "She is sleeping." Her tone was a little high. Why was she so surprised?

Fiona continued to rub Isabella's back. "She must have closed her eyes but a minute or two ago. I would not move her yet. If she wakes again, it may be more difficult to put her to sleep a second time."

"We shall await your ability to sit down and join us for tea," said Gran.

"I am sure Sir Anthony and Amelia are hungry after their travels. Pray, do not delay for me. I am certain I shall be able to hand this little one over to her nursemaid soon. She is lovely, Amelia."

"I thank you. Forgive me, but I must admit that her preference for you shocked me. She tends to be timid of those she has never met."

"She surely recognised her aunt without being introduced." Nicholas pulled out a chair for Fiona. "Do you think she will let you sit?"

"I can only try." With slow movements, she sat, then paused and glanced up at him. "Has she opened her eyes?"

"No, I believe you are safe."

"Well, you can, at least, have a cup of tea if you are sitting," said Gran. When his grandmother set a cup before Fiona, he shifted it where she could reach better. When he sat back, his gaze met Amelia's as she glanced between him and his wife with a curve pulling at one side of her lips.

"What is it?"

"Why did you not write to say you are married? Or at least pen a note inviting us to the wedding?"

"Would you have boarded a ship to come to Ireland? After the journey you had with Isabella today, I wager you would not have made it to Liverpool, much less Belfast because you would never leave her behind. Fiona and I were happy to have a small ceremony in the chapel at Larchfield. Her father, her friend Miss O'Shea, and Mr. and Mrs. O'Shea were in attendance. I did miss you and my grandparents, but I would not have insisted you make that journey."

At his wife's wave, the nursemaid bustled over and took the baby with as much care as possible. They all paused and held their breath as Isabella was transferred, and once the nursemaid had departed with the babe for the nursery, they let out a collective exhale.

"You cannot know how much I appreciate your help with her today," said Amelia.

Fiona gave a one-shouldered shrug. "Oh, I was happy to be of aid. I have enjoyed caring for babies for as long as I can remember, so walking with her was no imposition."

"Gran!" They all pivoted about at Lizzybeth and Janey waving from the doors to the house.

His grandparents gasped and stood to greet his cousins and Fitzwilliam Darcy who now walked towards their merry little party.

As he stood, he held out his hand to Fiona. "You said you hoped to meet Lizzy. Well, it seems you will make her acquaintance a day earlier than planned. You will also meet her sister, Janey."

His wife gave a tight smile as she allowed him to help her stand. When they approached, Amelia's hands were gesturing in large motions.

"You have yet to meet Nicholas's wife!"

He and Fiona stopped when the Darcys came to a sudden halt and their wide gazes jolted to them. Lizzy's jaw was agape for a few seconds before she finally stepped closer. "You are married?"

"Lady Fiona Montford, Viscountess Hatton, may I present my cousins Mrs. Elizabeth Darcy and Miss Jane Montford, and Lizzy's husband Mr. Fitzwilliam Darcy. I hope you will forgive me for not introducing you first—"

Darcy held up his hand and shook his head. "No need to explain. I understood why you introduced us so."

After they bowed and curtseyed, Fiona squeezed his arm. "I am excited to finally meet the famous 'Lizzy.' My husband has told me of some of your pranks. I was curious to meet the lady who could best him."

"Best me!" Nicholas gave a bark. When had Lizzy ever bested him?

Lizzy watched him out of the corner of her eye. "Well, I am unsure if there was ever a clear victor, but I tried, as did Amelia and Jane to seek our revenge; however, Nicholas has always been a bit wicked. Since the two of you are wed, you should know of his teasing nature."

He held his breath while Fiona bit her lip. "I have actually never been subject to one of his pranks. Nicholas has always been a gentleman."

He was not *always*, but his chest puffed that his wife would say so.

His cousins and sister glanced at each other before bursting into laughter. "I suppose it is a relief that he would not behave so with you," said Amelia.

"Since our bedchambers connect, I would be an imbecile indeed to put a snake in her bed or tamper with her toothpowder. Her gaining access to my rooms would be far simpler than what we often went through to get the best of each other." To tell the truth, he had never considered treating Fiona as he would Lizzy or Amelia. He wanted to sleep in her bed or have her sleep in his. They had been married but a couple of months, and he had yet to be without her during the night.

Even during her courses, she allowed him to hold her while she slumbered.

"Come, children. Let us sit and enjoy this beautiful weather. Before long, the days will become cold and the sun will set early in the evening and rise late each morning, and we will long for days such as this."

Amelia, Lizzy, and Janey linked arms as they walked towards the tables while Fiona remained with him. He took her hand in his, entwining their fingers. After seeing her care for his young niece in such a way, he could not help but imagine her large with their child, holding and soothing her as she had Isabella. He had never given much thought to children before. Why was that? An expected outcome of their marriage would be children. He had always assumed he would have a child one day. It was expected of him, but why did a little, red-haired girl with a fiery glare suddenly sound so appealing?

Chapter 24

As soon as Fiona's new maid, Hattie Taylor, had placed the last pin, she stepped back. "How is that, my lady?"

"It will suit very well for an afternoon of shooting."

The young woman nodded, picked up Fiona's morning gown, and draped it over her arm. "Would you be needing anything further?"

"No, I believe you have everything well in hand." Mrs. Cox had not been exaggerating her niece's abilities. As a result, Fiona's new lady's maid proved to be polite, efficient, and capable of the latest fashions for hair. She could tame Fiona's unruly locks with what seemed like little effort. Walsh had never complained, yet she required more time when one considered she had been with Fiona since she was a babe.

As soon as Taylor curtseyed and departed, Fiona knocked on the door to her husband's bedchamber, but after no response, she made her way to the hall. Ladies' voices came from the drawing room, so she peeked inside.

Lady Richmond looked up and down Fiona's riding habit, which was what she usually wore when she accompanied her father at

Larchfield. "Are you not joining us for tea? We are expecting several more ladies whose husbands are shooting this afternoon."

"I am searching for Nicholas. He invited me to shoot with the gentleman."

"You shoot?" said Amelia. Her eyebrows lifted.

Lizzy, as she had requested to be called, laughed. "My father would have died of an apoplexy if I had so much as expressed an interest in the diversion."

"Today is a smaller party, so perhaps that is why he invited you." Lady Richmond pointed to the door to the courtyard. "I believe they are outside awaiting the hounds.

She nodded and followed the countess's direction. When she exited the house, she walked towards the stables where the gentleman awaited the gamemaster near the entrance.

Nicholas grinned when she approached. "There you are. I thought I would need to send a maid to ensure you joined us."

"Forgive me. I had not realised I was late."

"You are not. My grandfather enjoys shooting immensely and has been impatient. The dogs are by the river's edge. We are to walk along the water. Pheasants prefer to be near marshy areas."

The plan was sensible and not at all a surprise.

He stepped over to where two fowling pieces leaned against a tree. "This is a gun my grandfather gave me. I use my father's so I thought you could use this one. The servants have a second gun for each of us while they reload."

When he handed the piece to her, she inspected the scattergun from top to bottom, then held it to her shoulder and aimed at a tree limb. "'Tis an excellent gun. The fit to my shoulder is better than the one I used in Ireland."

They walked until they met the rest of their party and the dogs. Fiona was introduced to two neighbours who raised their eyebrows and chuckled in a condescending manner at the mention of her joining their shooting party. Their response was not unusual, so she paid them no mind and kept her head high. She had encountered similar before, but their neighbours at Larchfield had become accustomed to her presence.

As they made their way down the bank of the river, servants beat at the bushes to frighten out the pheasants who were resting before emerging to feed near sunset. After a good half-hour of being unsuccessful, birds finally bolted from the brush to escape the intrusion, and Fiona, without thought, put her gun to her shoulder and took aim. She followed the bird in her sight and shifted to account for his movement, then discharged the weapon. Without pause, she traded the piece for the one the servant held out to her and repeated the process, felling a second bird.

"Well done, Lady Hatton," said Lord Richmond with a grin. "I have never known a woman who could shoot, but you have proven yourself proficient with that round."

Once the birds were retrieved, Lord Richmond had felled two to add to Fiona's two birds, Nicholas one, and one of the neighbours had managed one as well.

As they continued down the side of the river, Nicholas nudged her with his elbow, his lips curved more to one side of his lips than the other. "Well done indeed, Wife."

"Did you doubt my abilities?"

"No, I know better than to doubt any claim your father makes of you, and he told me himself you were proficient."

After their next flush of birds, two men approached with their fowling pieces and servants. She did not miss Nicholas's sudden stiff bearing at the sight of the younger of the two men.

"Who are they?"

Nicholas started and began to fidget with his gun. "The older gentleman is the Earl of Leicester and the younger of the two is the Duke of Clarence."

Fiona's gaze jolted back to the two men. "The Duke of—"

"Yes." Nicholas turned to follow after his servant as they began to walk down the edge of the river once more.

When it became too dark to shoot, they returned to the house, the afternoon proving to be a great success. Once they had walked a distance down one side of the river, they crossed at a footbridge and made their way down the opposite bank. By the time they had returned to the castle, Fiona had killed six brace of pheasants[3], Nicholas had five brace, and Lord Richmond had four brace plus two males, Sir Anthony and Mr. Darcy both had a respectable four brace, and their neighbours boasted of fewer, though each had birds upon their return to the castle so all should have been content with the result of today's shooting party.

She entered the house on Nicholas's arm. He brought her to her rooms, then kissed her cheek. "I shall leave you to your maid."

Taylor had Fiona undressed and in a hot tub of water with her usual efficiency. The sting of the bath was welcomed after the chill of the evening that had set in by the end of their shooting.

"Would you like to wash your hair, my lady?"

"Not now. It would be impossible to have it dry before dinner."

---

[3] A brace is a pair. In *Mansfield Park,* Tom is mentioned as returning with six brace of pheasants—6 males and 6 females.

"Then I shall prepare your gown while you soak. Call if you need me."

Fiona relaxed back into the tub and closed her eyes, letting the warmth seep back into her body. At the door squeaking, she opened her eyes to find Nicholas approaching in his dressing gown. He dropped it from his shoulders with a grin. "Shift forward."

"I beg your pardon?"

"I want to share your bath."

"Do you not have your own?"

His low laugh lit a fire within her. "I could if I wished it."

As soon as he sat behind her, he moved his legs to her sides and pulled her between them, her back to his chest. His fingers began kneading at her shoulders and she moaned. "If this is why you decided to join me, you may do so more often."

"I thought your shoulder would be sore. You managed your piece well. I think most ladies would have problems adjusting for the recoil."

She tilted her head to give him better access. "I am always a little sore after shooting, are you not?"

"No, not really."

Before long, his lips had replaced his fingers. "During one instance when you took aim, I watched you instead of shooting my piece. The confidence you displayed was appealing."

He found the sight of her shooting alluring? "I had not noticed you do so. You enjoyed my accompanying the gentlemen?"

"Yes, very much so." His lips claimed his favoured place under her ear, and she melted. How could he do that with such ease?

Fiona's hand rested on Nicholas's arm as they descended the stairs for dinner. Tonight's meal was to be more extravagant than those she had experienced at Richmond Castle thus far. Lady Richmond had included her in the final preparations and had accepted two of her suggestions, which was gratifying. Even though she had been managing Larchfield for some time, she had learnt a number of things from Lady Richmond already.

When they entered the drawing room, her eyes wandered through the guests. Lord Richmond spoke to two gentlemen near the fire with Lady Richmond standing at his side, speaking to two ladies who were, no doubt, the men's wives. Miss Montford was beside her grandmother.

Nicholas steered her to where the Darcys and the Greenes stood together.

Amelia immediately leaned towards her with a grin. "I heard you killed more pheasants than any of the men. Well done."

Nicholas nudged her with his elbow. "She had spectacular aim." Thankfully, he behaved more boastful over her achievement than resentful. In the moment, she had not thought to ensure he shot more than her, but he had never seemed insecure so as to require it. Shooting with a husband and not her father would require different considerations it seemed.

"As did you; you shot almost as many pheasants as I did." Despite her quick response, her cheeks burned a little at his compliment, and she could not hold Nicholas's eye since it reminded her of his confession in the bath that he found her confidence attractive. Poor Taylor was likely in her dressing room mopping up the water that had overflowed onto the floor when Nicholas had turned her around soon after and loved her. Her cheeks heated a bit more.

When her gaze turned to the Darcy's, Lizzy had one eyebrow arched upward while she watched them. Why was she regarding them in such a manner?

Amelia took Fiona's free arm and tugged. "Come."

"Where are we going?"

"Since you were not here this afternoon, Grandmamma insisted I introduce you to the ladies before dinner. As it is, you have met most of the gentleman, have you not?"

Fiona shrugged. "Some did not request an introduction, so I made the acquaintance of a mere handful."

"Nevertheless, would you not prefer to have a knowledge of who is at the table?"

The idea had merit, even though she had no desire to leave Nicholas's side. As Amelia steered her from group to group, requests were made for introductions with almost every lady in the room. When they reached the last party, a lady with flaxen hair and a willowy figure turned her brown eyes upon Fiona. "Lady Greene, I do not believe I am acquainted with your friend. Would you introduce us?"

"Her Grace, Rebecca Lancaster, Duchess of Clarence, may I present, Lady Fiona Montford, Viscountess Hatton."

The lady's eyes flared for but a second. "I was informed this afternoon that Lord Hatton had wed. I wish you joy."

"I thank you, Your Grace." Fiona returned the duchess's curtsey. So, this was Nicholas's first love. The duchess was not what Fiona had expected. But what had she imagined when he spoke of Her Grace? If Nicholas had not wed Fiona, he would have likely departed Ireland without a second thought for her and wed a lady more like the duchess. Would she have made him happy? He appeared and behaved contented now, and she could not imagine him being more so.

No chance for conversation was to be had with the duchess since Lady Richmond called them to dinner a moment later. Before she could excuse herself to find her husband, the duchess glanced up and down Fiona from her head to her toe. What was that about? Was Her Grace critiquing her gown? The cut and fabric of her ivory evening gown was as fine as any Fiona had seen in the drawing room thus far, and Nicholas had given her the emeralds after their bath. Surely, the necklace, bracelet, and matching ear drops were as costly as any the duchess owned. She touched the bracelet as Amelia returned her to Nicholas, who was quick to offer his arm to take their place in the walk to the dining room.

Since Fiona had been present when Lady Richmond had spoken of the seating arrangement, she had been aware she would sit by Sir Anthony, but her stomach tightened when the Duke of Clarence took the seat to her left. Nicholas was seated on the opposite side of the table.

"So, I am to sit by the lady who shoots like a man," said the duke with no trace of humour to his expression.

"I doubt she is the first nor that she will be the last," said Sir Anthony.

"She is the first I have seen. Not many gentlemen would allow their wives such a, dare I say, accomplishment. I also thought Lady Richmond would pay more attention to rank when arranging the seating."

Sir Anthony shrugged as the first course was served. "I would not object to my wife shooting if she had the inclination."

"My father taught me," said Fiona. "He took me on his rides of the estate, he taught me to shoot, and he allowed me to join the hunt.

Since I will inherit his title and Larchfield, he thought it prudent to educate me on the workings of the estate, so I need not rely solely on my steward."

"You inherit your father's title?" The duke was now almost turned to face her. He had obviously not been told of her situation.

"His earldom. Yes, I do."

"Would that not be the providence of your husband to run the estate?"

"The estate will be mine, not my husbands. My father ensured I was protected with the marriage settlement. After all, my husband acquired my fortune of thirty thousand pounds when we wed, and he will benefit from Larchfield's profits. He also has my charming company for the rest of his days—or the rest of mine. I believe he considers himself fortunate."

"Fortunate indeed." Sir Anthony glared at the duke. "Lady Hatton, your husband mentioned the stallion you have been riding since your arrival. I am impressed. I took him out on my last visit. He is an excellent mount, though he can be a handful."

Thank goodness for Sir Anthony! "Nicholas chose well. Adesius is a joy to ride. His gait reminds me of the horse my husband rode in Ireland. The stablemaster at Moydrum calls him Kelpie."

"Kelpie? What sort of name is that?" The duke was grating on her nerves and the incredulous tone of his question made her spine stiffen. How had the duchess chosen this boor over Nicholas?

"A kelpie is an evil water spirit of Irish mythology that takes the form of a horse to lure people to their deaths."

The duke sniffed and turned to speak to the person on his opposite side. She glanced at Nicholas, who sat between Amelia and Miss Jane Montford. At least he had not been placed beside the duchess!

"I have never been to Ireland, but my friends, who have gone, tell me it is a beautiful place." Sir Anthony watched her with an open and friendly countenance. She could have hugged him for his kindness!

"I know no place more enchanting, but I am hardly impartial. There is a place on the northern coast where the rocks look like huge steps called the Giant's Causeway. 'Tis one of my favourite places to visit and has a wonderful legend associated with it. According to the tale, an Irish giant by the name of Finn McCool was not best pleased when a Scottish giant named Benandonnar made claim to Ireland. Finn believed Ireland was his island, and Bennandonnar had no claim as far as Finn was concerned. In his anger, Finn began throwing boulders into the sea off the northern coast. When he saw how the boulders could form a path, he continued, building a causeway to the Isle of Staffa in Scotland, with the intention of challenging Bennandonnar to a duel over who had claim to Ireland."

Sir Anthony's eyebrows drew down a little in the middle. "How did the fight end? Who won?"

Fiona grinned and took a sip of her wine. "Well, that depends on who is telling the story. I have heard versions where Finn defeats Benandonner soundly. But an old man once told me that when Finn first saw Benandonner, he ran back to Ireland and hid because Benandonner was so much grander than Finn. When he arrived home, his wife helped him disguise himself as a baby. Benandonner, of course, finds the causeway and goes searching for Finn, but finds a child instead and assumes the child is that of the giant he is to battle. Believing that if the child is so huge that Finn must be enormous,

Benandonner flees back to Scotland destroying the causeway so Finn cannot follow.[4]

Sir Anthony chuckled and shook his head. "So, either way, Finn is the victor."

"An interesting tale," said Amelia.

"How quaint," said the duchess. Her tone was anything but complimentary while she sat watching them, her wine glass poised near her lips. Amelia's eyes widened while she stared at the duchess, her jaw parted a bit. By her expression, her new sister had not expected the duchess to be so openly rude.

"My wife taught me a great deal about Ireland while I was there. I must say I have never seen a place that is such a verdant green. It is a beautiful country." The set of Nicholas's shoulders was tense. Was he angry with her or the duchess?

Fiona fidgeted with her wedding ring. She would not give the duchess the satisfaction of showing any disquiet at her impolite behaviour.

The conversation continued around her with Sir Anthony including her more often than not since the duke continued to converse with those to his opposite side. When Lady Richmond called for the ladies to depart to the withdrawing room, Fiona tensed even further than during the dinner. She would need to situate herself with Amelia and Lizzy. Mayhap if she remained in the company of family, she could escape any further censure for the time being.

---

[4] https://www.wildernessireland.com/blog/build-bridge-myths-legends-giants-causeway/

Chapter 25

Lizzy linked arms with Fiona before they left the dining room. "Can you believe the audacity of the duchess?" Lizzy spoke in a soft voice while leaning close to Fiona's ear.

"I knew before I married Nicholas that I would have difficulties because I am Irish. I am not surprised by her disdain." She was not either. Due to the lady's past with Nicholas, Fiona had expected it from the moment the duke joined them shooting. However, while Nicholas had indicated Amelia knew of what had occurred between him and Rebecca, he had said naught of Lizzy.

"Yet, from what I heard you tell the duke, you have excellent connections, and your fortune is likely similar to the duchess's."

"Better," said Lizzy. "The duchess does not inherit an estate nor a title, does she?"

"No," said Amelia from her other side. When had Amelia joined them?

"Yes, well, I cannot prevent or change their prejudices."

Amelia huffed. "You should not be subjected to them at all. If you need a respite, give me a signal, and I shall say I need to look in on Isabella. You can offer to do so in my stead and cuddle with her in the nursery. In case you did not know, babies are remedies for every ill—sadness, anxiety, fear. The moment they are in your arms, that all goes away."

"Except for the worry for their future," said Lizzy.

Amelia sighed. "You are correct, of course, Cousin. I shall say that I could never envision Nicholas as a father, but he has been different of late, would you not say, Lizzy?"

"I agree. He is more settled, although he still called me 'Busy Lizzy' yesterday."

With a grin, Amelia shook her head. "I am simply pleased he has not played some terrible prank as yet."

Fiona bit her cheek. One of Nicholas's older tricks would likely require him to sneak into his sister's or cousins' rooms at some point, and since he was with Fiona more often than not, it was unlikely without her involvement or knowledge.

When they reached the withdrawing room, Amelia and Lizzy steered Fiona to the sofa and sat on either side of her as though her protectors. "I do appreciate your company. While I can manage the venom aimed in my direction, I imagine it will be lessened by your presence."

"The point is you should not have to manage, and we shall protect one of our own," said Amelia. "I am still appalled at Rebecca's behaviour this evening. We were friends as children. She was always a genial lady. Grandmamma heard but is certain she misunderstood the slight. She is determined to give the duchess a second chance."

"I am sure it is difficult," said Lizzy. "Grandmamma has known her since she was a little girl. Of course, she would want to give her the benefit of the doubt."

Fiona nodded. "I agree. Childhood friendships change as we grow and become who we are meant to be. Some of our most intimate acquaintances remain so, but other relationships alter. I do not believe it surprising. From what I understand of the association between your families, I have no doubt Lady Richmond views the duchess as a member of the family." Said lady was across the room with two other ladies, staring at Fiona while they chatted. They possessed the tell-tale appearance of those who were gossiping: heads tilted together, a sly curve to their lips.

"They are speaking of one of us," said Lizzy. "Oh, Grandmamma is waving me over. I shall return when I am able."

As soon as Lizzy bustled off, Amelia leaned closer. "I also believe Rebecca is jealous."

Fiona stiffened. "Jealous?" The possibility had not escaped her consideration, of course, yet would that not mean the lady did hold some depth of feeling for Nicholas?

Amelia regarded her with her eyebrows raised. "She spent a prodigious amount of time with my brother when they were younger. Perhaps the duchess regrets her choice."

The lady across the room smirked at Fiona before turning her back on her. By the duchess's demeanour since she arrived, she could not credit Lady Richmond's and Amelia's assertions of her kindness. Would a genial lady bed a gentleman she cared about and who professed to love her when she intended to wed another? The act seemed selfish.

"I require a bit of air." Fiona rose and Amelia followed suit.

"I shall accompany you."

"The solitude will do me some good. I assure you I shall be well."

Her new sister watched her with her eyebrows drawn as she departed the room. Fiona crossed the hall and entered the library, departing through the doors to a terrace. Lady Richmond's gardens were beautiful and filled the space within what remained of the castle walls as though they had been there since the castle was built in the 12th century.

"Why are you not with the ladies?"

She spun on her heel to Nicholas standing behind her. When had he joined her? "I needed air."

He stepped impossibly close and took her hand, drawing her into his arms. "I am sorry for what the duchess said to you. It was deplorable."

"Your sister believes her jealous."

"Amelia told you that?"

"She did not elaborate, other than to say that the two of you spent a prodigious amount of time together when you were younger." Fiona shook her head. "I came out here to escape the tension of that room. Can we pretend it does not exist for the moment?"

Her husband gave a wicked grin and guided her back into the library where he pressed her against the shelves. "This reminds me of the morning after we wed. Do you remember? You wore naught but that dressing gown covering your thin nightgown, and I pressed you against the bookshelves..." His hands wandered over her while his lips attacked the curve of her neck, making her knees weaken. He needed to do so little to garner such a response from her.

"Anyone could walk in?"

"I locked the doors."

"You will wrinkle my gown." Her voice was so weak. She pushed him around, so his back was against the shelves and began to work at the fastenings of his fall and plunging her hand inside.

She had not used such initiative before, but her body lit aflame when he ceased his attentions to her and gripped the shelf behind him with one hand. When she bit his earlobe, he groaned.

"Fiona."

The breathlessness of his tone gave her the courage she required to drop to her knees. "You are mine." Then she left no doubt that she was claiming every last bit of him.

Nicholas stamped into the hall and came to a halt. Where was his wife? He would have thought she would be shooting with them again today, but she had not come to the stables where their party awaited them.

"Where is Lady Hatton?" he asked a passing maid.

"I believe she is in the drawing room with Lady Richmond and her guests."

He gave a small jump. What would she be doing with the ladies? Without pause, he strode to the drawing room and opened the door. True to the maid's word, Fiona sat in a prim manner with her hands in her lap, a barely perceptible curve upon her lips.

"Is aught amiss?" His grandmother lifted her eyebrows.

"I should like to speak with Lady Hatton for a moment."

Fiona said something to the lady she was speaking to, then followed him to the library. This was a poor choice of location. How would he have a coherent conversation after what his wife did to him the night before in this very room? He had heard men speak of such things before, but he had never...well, he had to admit the reality of it exceeded any expectation!

"Are you not shooting with us today?"

She scraped her teeth along her bottom lip. "I thought I should spend the day with the ladies."

"Should?"

"Yes, I do have certain responsibilities as your wife. As much as I would wish to avoid some of them, I know I should not."

"You need not do this, you know. My grandmother still runs the house, and to tell the truth, I could care less if the ladies and gentlemen of the *ton* take issue with your shooting."

She smiled and pressed her hand against his chest. "I am well and can manage a drawing room of ladies for the day. We can ride tomorrow. If you should like to join me."

"Grandfather has grouse shooting planned for the morning. If you should like to ride, we can do so when I return."

"I shall look forward to it."

He frowned and drew Fiona into his arms. "I cannot persuade you to change your mind and join me this afternoon?"

His heart sank when she shook her head. "No, not today, but you should go. Your grandfather will be waiting for you." He inhaled when her lips pressed against his. "I shall rub your shoulder when you return...and any place else you desire." One side of her lip curved in a way that made him groan.

"I shall never leave if you say such things."

She turned him by the shoulders. "You cannot sit with the ladies for the afternoon, so go."

"I believe I could do well in a room full of ladies. Do you disagree?" He spoke over his shoulder with an eager grin.

"Oh, I am certain you could charm them if you made the attempt."

He planted his feet so she could not push him further. "How shall you manage the duchess?"

"I have your sister, Lizzy, and Jane. They have noticed the duchess's rudeness and taken to acting as my protectors—not that I require it."

When he relented and walked with her to the door of the drawing room, his entire being revolted at leaving her. At least with him, his wife would not be a target for the foil of Rebecca—no, the duchess. The men hunting would not treat her poorly with him at her side.

As soon as he stepped out of the castle and was walking to the stables, he glanced back over his shoulder. His gaze was drawn to a lone figure standing in the drawing room window. Fiona! He smiled, and she kissed her fingers before pressing them to the glass. His pace slowed.

He despised leaving her thus! She did not belong in his grandmother's drawing room, she belonged with him. How odd the accomplishments he once considered shocking when they were first acquainted were now the ones he favoured the most. He wanted her company shooting, hunting, riding, or whatever gentleman's diversion she would partake of with him. He would miss her today.

His feet stopped, and he stared at the ground. He would miss her. When had that begun? After dinner last night, he had noticed her depart the drawing room through the open door and followed her as though she were a siren singing just for him.

He took two steps and peered back once more, and his shoulders dropped. She was gone. These feelings were familiar yet as different as could be. He had missed the duchess after her marriage, but not like he longed for Fiona when she was not with him. When had that happened? One moment, he was going on pleasantly, and the next, his heart was full of his wife. God help him, but he loved her! He had never intended to give his heart over to another, yet somehow, his wife had stolen every part of it, and without him even knowing. What was he to do about it? She had never professed to love him, so what if he were the only person in their marriage experiencing such depth of feeling?

He would have to watch her with care—scrutinise. Mayhap, if he looked close enough, he would discover those hints of her regard for him. How odd that now he desired her to love him as he did her!

Fiona left the window and resumed her seat by the countess.

"Is aught amiss?" asked Lady Richmond.

"No, my husband thought I would be shooting with him today. He had not expected me to stay behind." She had needed to remain rooted to where she stood when he looked back at the castle. Everything in her screamed to run after him, to ride somewhere just the two of them. While she could not object to her husband's family, she had grown weary of the other guests—the duchess in particular. Fiona had no need of a lady reminding her of why she was not the best choice for Nicholas. She knew that quite well on her own. He had need of a more traditional sort of wife, one who sewed and played pianoforte. Fiona possessed no sort of accomplishments.

"I remember when Hugh and I first wed. He turned down every invitation for shooting parties for the first year. He had no wish to leave me, you see. His father teased him mercilessly, but Hugh had no care for the talk. We were happy."

"You are still happy, are you not?" They appeared the very portrait of a contented couple.

"Oh, yes." Lady Richmond covered Fiona's hand with her own. "I am merely telling you this, so you know that ache at his leaving is nothing more than an illustration of the depths of your attachment. If you did not love him, you would not care. He also would likely not seek you out as he did if he was not in love with you."

Fiona only nodded and smiled. In love with her? Despite his attraction to her, he had never professed any such attachment. He treated her with care and affection, so she could not complain, could she? Yet, why at the notion of his never loving her did a hole open up where her heart should be?

Chapter 26

Fiona could not credit her current predicament. She had gone riding with Nicholas this morning. He had taken her to a secluded glen where he liked to think. The place was one he held dear and was beautiful with a small stream trickling over rocks hewn from the current over the years.

He had removed saddlebags from his horse and a blanket he had tucked under him, which he placed on the ground. She had never dined upon a rug spread upon the grass, but since Nicholas had no desire to share his private hideaway, nor her it seemed, he had kept his plans simple.

They dined by the edge of the stream, partaking of crusty bread, cold beef, as well as apples and pears they had picked from the orchard before their departure. When they were finished eating, her husband had claimed her lips and loved her in a manner she had never experienced. The way he held her gaze, and his demeanour was so different—more languid and heartfelt. It had been all she could do not to cry from the intensity of what was in her heart. Then, he held her for long after while they talked. He had been more than she could have hoped!

Due to the intimacy of it all, upon their return, Fiona had taken a walk while Nicholas returned to the house to refresh himself, only to find herself sitting upon a bench looking out over the gardens, her cheeks damp with tears. How had she ended up thus? She so rarely cried. Why was she crying now?

"Fiona?"

She startled at the soft voice of Jane Montford, who stood a few feet away. "Jane, you should not creep up on a lady in such a way."

"Forgive me, but I hardly crept, as you put it. Two twigs snapped as I approached, but you seemed to be elsewhere. Are you well?"

With a nod of her head, Fiona attempted a smile. "I am quite well, I thank you."

"May I sit?"

Fiona glanced at the bench beside her, then back at Nicholas's beloved cousin. "Yes, of course. Forgive me for not offering sooner."

"I suspect you have a great deal upon your shoulders and had not considered it. Pray, do not think me offended." Jane's bright blue eyes watched Fiona in a penetrating way that she could not hold. "I am prodigiously good at listening and offering advice, should you wish it, and I vow never to speak of what you tell me."

Fiona clenched her eyes closed. "While I appreciate your offer, I am not certain you have the perspective I require. Who would you suggest?" She had not wanted to offend Jane, but she would surely shock a maiden with her confessions.

Nicholas's cousin turned and tilted her head. "Perhaps Amelia or Lizzy? Grandmamma is in possession of a good shoulder to lean on and wise advice without censure. If you need to talk about whatever is making you so sad, do not hesitate to request it of one of us. None of us would deny you."

Lady Richmond? No, she could not speak to the countess! While the lady had been genial since Fiona's arrival, she still hoped for the approval of Nicholas's grandmother. "I shall keep your recommendations in mind. Thank you for ensuring I was well."

As soon as Jane gave a tight smile and departed, Fiona used the back of her hand to wipe another tear from her cheek as they began to flow anew. This was ridiculous! Why could she not cease this infernal crying? She covered her face and stifled a sob.

"Fiona?" When she straightened with a jerk, Lizzy stood before her. How long had she been standing there? Was every Montford in the county to pass while she sat here? In the future, she would need to locate a more private location if she was to partake in a bit of maudlin behaviour.

"I should return to the house." Fiona rose, but Lizzy's hand on her arm made her pause.

"Jane knew I was walking with Fitzwilliam and told me to come find you." Lizzy took Fiona's hands and held them between them. "What has you at sixes and sevens? Jane thought perhaps you were not comfortable speaking with an unwed lady, but I promise you may tell me anything."

Fiona sank back onto the bench. "I doubt that. You would see me differently if I told you."

"I doubt that. Have you harmed someone?"

She lifted her eyebrows. "Of course not."

"Then how bad can it be?"

After a great exhale, Fiona let it all loose: how she met Nicholas, her overwhelming attraction to him, the thoughts she had of her future before marrying her husband—all of it. When she was finished, she sank back and pressed her palms to her cheeks. "I was so stupid and naïve."

"Most of us are when we are younger. I was no different before I wed Fitzwilliam."

"You?"

"The first time I met Fitzwilliam, he insulted me, and I let him wound my vanity and pride. When he happened upon me with my grandparents in London, I desired nothing more than to be far away from him, but he insisted I become better acquainted with the man who was so dreadfully uncomfortable in public."

"Forgive me, but your situation bears no resemblance to mine. You did not propose marriage to your husband to escape an arranged match. I am also certain you managed to maintain propriety in your courtship." Unlike what she had allowed Nicholas at the ruins.

Lizzy smiled and lifted one eyebrow. "No, I was not escaping an arrangement, but Fitzwilliam and I had a...horrible time behaving within the bounds of propriety. I turned my head to catch his lips under the kissing bough, I pulled him behind some draperies during a game of hide and seek, and on one occasion, when we happened to find ourselves alone at his London home, we came close to anticipating our vows. I had to right myself in his bedchamber."

"But you intended to wed him." Had Nicholas already planned to say yes when they behaved as they did?

"And Nicholas had more or less proposed to you at that point, but I believe somewhere deep in your heart, you recognised Nicholas as the man you were meant to be with for a lifetime. Otherwise, you would not have been so overwhelmed by him from the beginning."

"Do you truly believe in couples who are meant to be together?" How many claimed to be so when they first wed, but eventually, the bloom faded, and they found themselves wishing to be with another.

"I believe I was meant to be with Fitzwilliam. No one could complement me as he does, and I know no one could complement him as I do.

Fiona smothered her amusement. "You have no improper pride."

Lizzy shrugged one shoulder. "I am aware of how many have been offended by my husband's manner before we wed. People have commented how much more genial he is now and how he smiles."

"He did not smile before?"

A bubbling laugh burst from Lizzy. "He possessed a countenance more like this."

Fiona had to clamp a hand over her mouth when Lizzy drew her eyebrows down and gave a fearsome scowl. "Oh, my."

Lizzy's arm wrapped around Fiona's shoulders. "Are you unhappy in your marriage? You can be honest. Amelia was quite morose when she was made to marry Sir Anthony. They were forced by a rumour that spread throughout London, claiming they had an assignation on the terrace of the Marquess of Ormonde's ball, which they had not."

"No, I am not exactly unhappy, but I do believe I was not meant to be a wife. What accomplishments do I possess? What do I bring to my marriage besides the ability to beget an heir?"

"Shooting, fox hunting, and riding from what I have been told. Oh, and Grandmamma has said you are exceedingly knowledgeable on how to run a house." Lizzy ticked each off on her fingers as she listed them.

"Other than your grandmother's praise, which she has not told me, those are all gentlemen's pursuits. I am not blind to the stares and the comments that were made when I returned from shooting with the men. The gentlemen gave me side-long glances and were not best pleased that I shot more pheasants than them." Since when was this a problem? She had never given one whit before to how people viewed her. Marriage had altered so much!

"Does Nicholas care?"

Fiona sighed. "He seems to enjoy my successes. I am certain the gentlemen give him no quarter, but yesterday, he sought me out because I was in the drawing room with your grandmother. He wanted to know why I was not joining them."

"See. As long as Nicholas does not object, why fret about what others think? From what Nicholas has told me, you never cared before."

"That was different." She flinched. She had responded without thought. Where had that response come from?

"Because you were not in love with Nicholas?"

Was that the reason? "I suppose it could be. Before we wed, my actions affected no one but myself and my father, but he cared not about marrying again or so he claimed. Now, my differences not only reflect upon him, but also your grandparents, Nicholas, and eventually, any children we may have. I never had to consider so many people before. You must realise that my scandalous diversions could reflect upon you and your husband as well."

Lizzy laughed. "I assure you that Fitzwilliam was impressed by your skill with a piece. He even spoke of it after the hunt. You must understand. I have witnessed his disdain when he abhors the behaviour of someone, but he has shown no hint of it when speaking of you."

"Still—"

"Fiona, no one in the family has spoken of you poorly. If it makes you feel better, we have all commented on how you and Nicholas watch each other, how he is obviously in love with you, and you with him."

Fiona's insides jumped at Lizzy's words, but she tamped them down with haste. "I doubt that."

"Ah, he has not spoken of his feelings." Lizzy tilted her head forward to ensure she caught Fiona's gaze. "Have you spoken of yours?"

"I only realised I was in love with him recently. He has never spoken of any deeper attachment than friendship for me. What if I tell him and he cannot return the sentiment?" She would be heartbroken. Her chest hurt just speaking of it. While affectionate, he had never given any hint of feelings that went beyond what their relationship was: companionship of more than one variety. They shared similar interests and their attraction had not seemed to wane. On the contrary, what occurred between them became more intense and gratifying the longer they were together. Perhaps it was that way for her because she loved him, but he may not have the same experience. That notion stung as well. When had she become so sentimental?

Lizzy's eyebrows drew down a little. "I do not believe that would happen. He may have deceived himself, but Nicholas has not been so open in a long time. His recent demeanour must be a result of his contentment. What else could it be?"

"Satisfaction?" She lifted her eyebrows.

After a moment or two, her friend burst into laughter. "I shall listen if required, but I would prefer not to know specifics of what occurs in your bedchamber or maybe outside of it, considering what you confessed about the ruins."

Fiona's cheeks heated. "I could not speak of particulars anyhow."

"That is a relief," said Lizzy.

"What am I to do if he never loves me?" Gah! She sounded so fragile!

"You need to speak to him. I believe you will discover his feelings match yours. He may be just as afraid to admit it as you are."

She could bear no more. Fiona rose and smoothed her skirts. "I suppose I should return and refresh myself for tea. If I do not appear soon, Nicholas will come looking for me."

"Do consider what I have said."

She nodded, and when they entered the house, Lizzy went in search of her husband, who the footman claimed was in the nursery with their son.

As Fiona made her way to their suite of rooms, she took in the portraits of the Montford ancestors along the walls. Before her marriage, she had considered Larchfield a responsibility as well as a sort of curse rather than the legacy it was. Richmond Castle had brought more of the long-term consequences of her opinions before marriage to the fore. By never marrying or having children, she would have ended the earldom and Larchfield would have reverted to the crown. Her father had mentioned it more than once, but she never let the repercussions take hold. She would have let down her father and those who depended upon them. What a spoilt child she had been!

"There you are!"

She started and halted in the open door of her bedchamber. Nicholas stood in the middle of the room, a box in his hand.

"Forgive me for startling you, but your maid claimed you had yet to return." He paused then frowned as he stepped forward to pull her inside. After he closed the door, he drew her close. "Have you been crying?"

"What are you holding?" She had no wish to explain why she likely appeared blotchy and boasting of red-rimmed eyes.

"Oh, I wanted to give this to you." He opened the lid, and she gasped at what was nestled within the fine velvet.

"How beautiful." She fingered the large broach with its blue stones and pearls. A matching necklace, ear drops, and a small cluster of pearls to one side that she pointed to. "What are these?"

"When I asked my grandmother, she said your maid can sew them to your gown for the ball. One goes between your breasts and one here and one here." He brushed his finger along her bodice, pausing at each place he mentioned. "Your gown is blue, is it not?"

"The underdress is a shade of blue resembling that in the stones with a white overlay. They will look very well with it, I daresay."

"Excellent!" He took the box and placed it upon the bed. "Now, what has your eyes so red?"

Should she tell him? What if he could not return her feelings and matters between them became awkward? "A great deal has occurred since we wed. I think I am overtired." Lizzy would be disappointed in her for the deception.

"Then I shall remain with you while you rest."

"Will I truly rest?"

One side of his lips curved in a wicked grin. "That is entirely dependent upon you, my dear."

She was in trouble, indeed!

Chapter 27

The sky was clear and the moon was full and bright on the evening of the harvest ball. Nicholas had readied himself, but from what Fiona's maid had claimed, his wife required more time, so he had sought out a glass of brandy and stood on the back terrace while he watched the stars twinkle in the sky above. The full moon meant they were not as bright as the new moon, but they were still a sight to see.

He swallowed another sip of the strong liquor in an attempt to quell the uneasiness in his gut. Tonight, he would confess his love for Fiona. After the final dance, he would spirit her away to the gardens and beg her forgiveness for taking so long to understand his feelings. He could only pray she felt the same for him. He had been an addle-pate. Something inside him surely recognised her as his perfect match, but his mind had fought tooth and nail that he required a lady with the usual accomplishments as well as other considerations. Fiona was capable of standing up to him, not to mention putting him in his place if the situation warranted. She had been what he had needed all along.

"Nicholas?"

His grandmother stepped up to his side and leaned against the stone railing. "I had thought you would be with Fiona, not out here."

"Fiona was not ready, so I was enjoying the peace before the tempest arrives."

Gran stiffened. "You are likening my ball to a tempest? I should hope my guests behave with more decorum than that portends."

"Are the Duke and Duchess of Clarence to attend?"

"Well, yes. Why would I exclude them given they are staying nearby with the duchess's family? I would not be so rude."

With a sigh, he faced her. "We all witnessed the duchess's ridicule of my wife at every dinner they attended, and Amelia told me what has occurred when the ladies gather. That alone should exclude her from being invited." He had rather expected the duchess to shun Fiona, but he would not countenance the snub.

"As much as I saw the former Lady Rebecca behave with such malice, I could not credit it with the young lady we spent the summers with but a few years ago. I do not understand how she could alter in so drastic a fashion." Her disdain stemmed from jealousy and nothing more. Her behaviour was inexcusable. Despite the disappointment he once felt, he never disparaged her husband to others.

"She is envious, Gran," he said in a firm tone. "I made her the offer of my hand before she wed the duke, and she chose to be a duchess, but now she seems to regret her choice."

His grandmother's brow furrowed. "How do you know she regrets her marriage?"

"Because she followed me to the library at the Marquess of Ormonde's ball and suggested we could be lovers." He had never thought to speak to his grandmother so plainly, but how else was he to justify why he wanted to slight a duchess?

"Is that why you departed for Ireland? I do remember you left the Ormonde's ball with haste that evening?"

"Yes, I was not best pleased and told her I would never agree to such a scheme. Departing before the Season had begun seemed the best way to avoid her. At one time, I thought she loved me, but if she had truly cared for me, she would be pleased to see me happy instead of belittling my wife in company. I am beginning to believe Fiona's assessment of her is correct."

"You spoke to Fiona of your feelings for another lady?" The incredulity in his grandmother's voice was obvious by the pitch of her voice.

"I thought I loved Rebecca as I ought, but since marrying Fiona, I know my feelings were not as strong as a deep abiding love can be. Perhaps I suffered a boyish infatuation with her. I do not know. All I know is that what I feel for Fiona is far beyond what I ever held dear for the duchess."

Gran tilted her head. "What does Fiona believe?"

"That the duchess wants to have her cake and eat it too—that Rebecca never loved me, or she would have chosen me over the duke." He scraped the bottom of his shoe against the floor, back and forth. "I do not trust the duchess as I once did, and I will not allow her to abuse my wife, even if that means cutting her in a ballroom full of people."

Grandmamma's eyes widened. "I see. I do wish you would have spoken to me of this earlier."

"By the time I had thought to, you had sent out the invitations. Besides, you could not exclude her without excluding her father. I also confess that I was not comfortable with confessing the attachment we once held."

His grandmother crossed her arms over her chest and exhaled. "I do understand. I suppose you are correct to censure the duchess so, though I hope such discord does not unfold for the entirety of the ball to witness."

"If it makes you feel better, I shall not cut her unless she has done something to warrant such an irrevocable breach."

"I suppose that should give me some relief." Gran stood and placed her hand upon his sleeve. "As much as it pains me to say it, Fiona will struggle with acceptance in London. The girls and I shall do all we can to be of aid to her, but some will look down upon her accent and her Irish heritage."

"She has lived with a certain contempt in her own neighbourhood due to her penchant for riding astride and shooting. Her reception by those who have come for the hunting is not surprising to her. 'Tis why she had once been opposed to marriage."

Grandmamma gave a slight twitch. "When did she change her mind?"

His cheeks heated, and he watched the toe of his shoe as he traced it along the wood of the floor. He had not meant to be so unguarded. "Our courtship was not traditional, but I do believe we would have found our way to each other regardless of her wishes and mine. At the time, neither of us were seeking to be wed.

She narrowed her eyes ever-so-slightly. "I suppose I shall have to gather pieces of what you and your wife reveal inadvertently."

He would never survive Fiona's wrath should he somehow give away that she proposed to him to avoid the arranged marriage her father desired. That little morsel of information would never cross his lips!

"When do you expect the first guests to arrive?"

"I should have known you would change the subject. As for the guests, I expect them at any moment, so you should see if your wife is ready and come to the hall so we may greet them as they arrive. Your marriage will be announced this evening to those who were not at the shooting party, so the two of you should be present in the receiving line."

He nodded. "I shall bring her down for you."

"No need."

His head jolted to Fiona who stood framed in the door, the dark azure blue and white of her gown were striking, but nothing to the woman who wore it. Her red locks were swept up and piled atop her head with curls framing her face and pearl-tipped pins scattered throughout, the broach and pearls had been added to her gown with great effect, and the necklace fit her graceful neck as though they had been made for her. The manner in which she stood, straight and tall with an air of grace and elegance she likely did not know she possessed gave her a brilliancy others lacked—she was every bit his viscountess.

"I hope I have not kept you waiting."

"No, my dear," said Grandmamma. "You have just a moment for my grandson to compliment your gown before we need the two of you in the hall."

As soon as his grandmother bustled out, Nicholas ran his hand through his hair. "Good God, Fee. You look magnificent."

She brushed her hand down the front of her gown. Was that a hint of a tremble in her fingers? "Thank you. Your grandmother insisted the gown was not too much for a ball in the country. It is far grander than what I would wear at home."

"You are splendid." He caught her hand before she could clasp it with her other and drew her closer.

"The jewels—"

"No, the gown and the jewels would do naught if the lady wearing them was not the most handsome of my acquaintance. I am

the most fortunate man here tonight because I have you on my arm."
Now was the perfect opportunity to tell her how he felt.

Her cheeks pinked, and her eyes darted to the side. "I do not know what to say."

He brought his cheek to hers. "The only sight more beautiful is when I love you. Your hair tumbling over your shoulders and the expression you wear...I have never seen anything that captivates me more."

She drew back and cupped his cheek in her palm. "Nicholas—"

"I beg your pardon, sir," said the butler in the doorway. "Lady Richmond requests your presence in the hall. The first of the guests has arrived."

His shoulders dropped. "I love you" had been on the tip of his tongue when Fiona cupped his cheek. The last thing he wished to do was rush the declaration.

"We should go." Fiona's lips pressed together and with her hand holding his, began to step towards the door.

"You will dance the first with me, yes?"

She turned her head back. "Of course."

"And the supper set?"

Her lips curved to one side. "Two sets, sir?"

"And the last."

She gave a wide grin. "Next, you will request an assignation on the terrace."

"How did you know?"

Her laugh filled the room and lifted his spirits. "You are incorrigible. Come, before your grandmother fetches us herself."

With a groan, he begrudgingly followed and joined his grandparents in the hall where they greeted each and every guest as they arrived for the ball. When the Duke and Duchess of Clarence entered, Fiona stiffened beside him as they greeted his grandmother and grandfather. The duke bowed and his wife curtseyed, both giving a cursory glance to Fiona before they entered the ballroom.

"You will tell me if she is rude to you."

"I can manage. I see no need to make a fuss over her pettiness."

His grandparents passed them and entered the ballroom. He and Fiona needed to accompany them, but first... "Whether she is jealous or not does not matter, you are my wife, and I shall not allow her to treat you as anything less. Do you understand?"

"I do. Thank you."

The musicians tuned their instruments and created a cacophony of sound while the guests milled about the ballroom awaiting the first dance. Not long after, the room grew quiet, and his grandfather raised his arm.

"Lady Richmond joins me in welcoming you to this year's harvest ball. We have a great deal to celebrate this year. Two great-grandchildren have joined our family, and our grandson, Lord Hatton, has wed and brought his bride home to Richmond Castle. I hope you will welcome Lady Hatton to Yorkshire as we have welcomed her into our family." He nodded at Nicholas, who steered Fiona to the line.

"Relax, my dear." When he glanced to each side, his sister and her husband were to their left and Lizzy and Darcy were to their right with Janey and her partner on their other side. His family was doing their best to shield his wife while they danced.

Fiona smiled and when she took Darcy's hand to turn with him, laughed at something he said.

She appeared happy and carefree during their dance, and before they could leave the floor, Darcy requested Fiona's second set while Lizzy took Nicholas's arm. "I should prefer a glass of punch to dancing the next if you do not object."

"Why should I object?"

"By the way you are watching your wife, I am certain you are ensuring no one so much as peers at her with any sort of contempt."

"She should not be forced to endure the spiteful comments some will, no doubt, make."

"From what she has told me, she has lived with censure for some time. As long as you love her and support her, she requires little else." Lizzy watched him in a way that made him flinch back.

"What are you asking me?"

"Well, you do love her, do you not?"

"I shall not speak of this with you." Fiona would be the first to hear his feelings.

Lizzy grinned and lifted that one infuriating eyebrow that implied she knew all. "Good. *You* should tell her."

"Lizzy, leave us be."

She waved dismissively with her free hand while she took a sip of the punch he had handed her. "Amelia and I have gotten to know Fiona, and we want to see the two of you happy."

"You have reason to believe we are not content in our situation?"

"I am not saying that." She pressed a hand to her upper stomach and grimaced.

"Are you well?"

She shrugged one shoulder. "If my suspicions are correct, I am perfectly well."

He stared at her for a moment until what she was not saying hit him. "You are with child again?"

"If I am, it is still very early."

He glanced out to Darcy who just started the second half of the set with Fiona. "Does Darcy know?"

"Of course he does. After his dance with your wife, he will stand by my side and give his haughty glare to any gentleman who attempts to request a dance. We shall likely sneak away after supper. He was ecstatic when I suggested it."

"I can imagine." He watched Fiona until the dance was over. Would they be so blessed one day? Thus far, Fiona's courses had come at a regular interval—at least according to her, they had. Their intimate encounters were frequent enough. One would think Fiona would fall with child sooner rather than later.

"Do not worry yet," said Lizzy.

"Who says I am worried?"

"Fiona will fret if she does not notice signs of a babe soon. If you are already worried, you will make her upset at the situation much worse."

"I..." He huffed and started towards his wife who was honouring Darcy at the end of the music. Mayhap they could sneak away before supper instead of after.

Chapter 28

The dancers wove and turned with each other as they stepped through the pattern of the quadrille. The ball was a tremendous success. In the receiving line, Fiona had marvelled at how many had travelled to attend Lady Richmond's grand fete. Nicholas had explained that Lord and Lady Ormonde had come from Wiltshire and were staying with friends to attend. Such a long journey for one evening!

Lady Richmond introduced her to a great many of her friends, so many that Fiona feared calling many of the guests by the wrong names. How was she to remember so many people?

"I am pleased to see that Lord Hatton is married and settled," said Lady Ormonde with a slight curve to her lips. "I was friends with his mother, and I am certain she would have liked you, my dear. She would be happy to see her son settled and content."

Fiona glanced over her shoulder where her husband stood beside his grandfather, who was speaking to a couple of gentlemen. As had been his wont thus far this evening, when she was not on his arm, she oft times caught him watching her. He would give her a soft smile when their eyes met that never failed to set her stomach aflutter.

She returned her attention to the genial lady before her. "I am gratified you think so. I would love to know more about his mother. He has spoken a little of his parents, but I do not believe he remembers much of them."

"He was so young when they died." The lady shook her head, a shadow falling over her eyes. "It grieves me they could not see the matches their children made. Bella would have been beside herself over her granddaughter, and so flattered they named the babe for her. We spoke of our hopes and dreams for our children. Lord and Lady Richmond encouraged Bella to marry for love, and she was determined her children would do the same. She would be overjoyed by both of her children's marriages."

"Thank you, my lady."

"Lady Ormonde," said Nicholas as he approached. He held his arm out to Fiona, who fit her hand in the crook of his elbow, his hand covering hers. "I hope my wife has been behaving herself." Fiona might have been offended if her husband had not chuckled after his surprising statement.

She lifted her eyebrow. "You know I am capable of decorous behaviour, sir. Did you wish me to do or say something shocking?"

"Why not? I believe the gossips are awaiting a vulgar display. Why not indulge them?"

"Lord Hatton!" Lady Ormonde laughed. "I believe you are the one behaving in a shocking manner."

Fiona pinched his arm. "Do not mind him. He enjoys teasing me, and since I do tend to take people aback by riding astride and preferring shooting to needlework, he is having a bit of fun at my expense."

The lady's head tilted while she looked between Fiona and Nicholas. "I believe that makes you quite fascinating. I have known a lady who shoots but not one who rides astride. Your mother must have been beside herself when you were young."

"I was raised by my father. He saw no harm in the diversion until I was older, but by then, it was too late."

"I beg your pardon, ladies," said Lord Richmond. "I require my grandson for a short time. Forgive me, Lady Hatton, I know he just rejoined your charming company. I hope you do not mind."

Lady Ormonde's head perked up. "Oh, I see my husband gesturing for me to join him. Excuse me."

As soon as the lady bustled away, Fiona squeezed her husband's arm. "I shall join Lady Richmond until you return."

Before she could leave, Nicholas drew her back by her hand and brushed a kiss to her knuckles. "I shall not be long."

Fiona sighed and watched the dancers. Where had Nicholas gone with his grandfather? Lord Richmond said he had only required her husband for a short time. That had been at least twenty minutes ago. As much as she had planned on spending the evening with Nicholas, he had been pulled away from her more than once. She should not be so selfish since she would retire with him after the ball, but before they had greeted the guests, he had spoken as though he would not leave her side. Her heart had beat a little quicker at the promise.

She stood beside Lady Richmond while she and the assembled ladies spoke of the upcoming London Season. Fiona had little to offer on the current conversation—she had never attended a Season, so she did her best to maintain a pleasing countenance instead of displaying her true feelings on some of the opinions being shared. She could have groaned when the lady across from her brought up some scandal from the Season prior with a shock so practised, she appeared comical. Why did some ladies take such pleasure in shaming others? Fiona had never enjoyed the practise herself. Good Lord, she needed air!

She held up a hand towards the doorway of the room. "Pray, pardon me, but I believe my husband waving for me to join him."

Lady Richmond peered over her shoulder, but before she could put a stop to Fiona's ruse, Fiona hastened away and ducked around another grouping in an attempt to conceal her escape. Thank heavens! One more moment of gossip and insufferable discourse on a subject she had never experienced for herself was not to be borne! Lady Richmond managed the encounter well. Grandmamma never engaged in the gossip or spoke of it herself, only speaking to the particulars and which events might prove to be worthwhile. She was adept at re-directing those distasteful discussions for more productive ones, a task that was sure to be exhausting!

From the ballroom, Fiona took the corridor that led to the library and slipped inside. Thank heavens, the room was blessedly empty! After a sizeable exhale, she made her way to the window to stare at the gardens and wrapped her arms around herself. The paths amongst the different beds were lit by torches for guests to mill about and relieve themselves of the warm, stale air of the public rooms. The scene was lovely.

As much as she missed Ireland, Richmond Castle was not the frightening place it was when she first arrived. How she had shaken when she had alighted from the carriage to meet Nicholas's family! He had been correct that she need not be scared. His family was wonderful. His sister and cousins had each, in their own way, become like sisters to her, and their husbands were equally welcoming. They ensured they treated her like family. As much as she had jumped headlong into this marriage, she had assumed Nicholas's family would be kind. Thankfully, she had been right.

Voices from outside the room made her turn her ear in that direction. Was that Nicholas? She paused for a moment and closed her eyes. The lower tone was indeed her husband's, but he was not best pleased; his tone was hard and not his usual genial manner. A lady's voice countered whatever her husband said. The argument drew louder as the voices approached the library.

Fiona glanced about her. Should she stay? Should she go? Oh, blast it! She ran on her tiptoes through a door to her left. The room was dark, but a hearty fire burned in the grate. A grand dark oak desk stood against the far wall with a row of shelves behind it, laden with books and an occasional cluster of miniatures of various family members. From her previous visit to this room, the grouping of portraits behind Lord Richmond's desk were the miniatures painted of his wife since she came out as well as tiny likenesses of each of his grandchildren.

She leaned against the wall by the entrance with the door cracked.

"Nicholas, you must listen to me."

"I told you not to address me so informally, madam. When I departed the card rooms, I also requested you not follow me. The request was simple. Why do you insist on ignoring my wishes?"

"Because I do not believe you feel nothing for me—that you could dismiss your love for me so easily." Fiona stiffened. The only woman who would be so bold was the Duchess of Clarence. "I care not if you are married," said the lady. "You needed to wed to sire an heir, so it would make sense for you to do so. It is not as though you could love one such as her. Fiona's stomach twisted mercilessly, and her eyes stung, making her squeeze them closed.

"Watch yourself, Your Grace."

"Do you not see? Now that you are married, we can be together again."

Fiona swallowed a gasp. The duchess was audacious, to say the least!

"I beg your pardon?" Nicholas's pitch was higher than was his wont. "What would make you think that I would betray my vows to my wife? I have given you no encouragement or reason to believe that I have any interest in furthering our intimacy. In fact, I informed you before the last Season that I have no intention of ever involving myself with you again. Naught has changed since the Marquess of Ormonde's ball."

"You surely wed that hoyden for her fortune and connexions. From what my husband has said, she is not only set to inherit her father's estate, but also his title. It makes it understandable why you would marry an Irish. Why else would you choose her?" Fiona propped her forehead against the edge of the door. She should not be listening. She trusted her husband, but it was nigh on impossible for her to tear herself away.

"I married her because I am in love with her! An emotion you do not seem to possess."

Fiona's head shot up. He loved her? He would not speak so if he did not mean it, but could he merely be attempting to rid himself of the duchess forever?

"I have loved you—"

"No! If you had loved me when I made the offer of my hand, you would not have departed as you did, while I slept and without a goodbye, and wed another. If you had loved me, you would not have approached me at the marquess's ball in the hopes of us becoming lovers. If you had loved me, you would not have proposed this harebrained scheme. After you left, you would have wanted me to find my own happiness instead of having me cling to an impossible relationship that would provide nothing but grief. Instead, I chose a lady who challenged me and who enjoys the same diversions I do. She is kind and thoughtful and her insight into your true nature was accurate. You want to have your life, but you want me tied to you for the rest of mine. Well, I shall never do what you intend for the simple reason that I love my wife, and I would never, ever betray her or injure her in such a way. So, once and for all, I would have you remove yourself from my sight for I want none of you."

"Nicholas, you cannot mean—"

Fiona straightened, took a fortifying breath, and opened the door. The duchess's eyes widened when they lit upon her, the woman's hand outstretched towards Nicholas, who jumped back as though the duchess's touch scalded him and rushed to Fiona's side. He took her hand and levelled a glare upon the duchess.

"Do not speak to me so informally, madam. You will depart this ball, or I shall tell my grandparents of this entire exchange—of the past as well. Would you prefer they make the request of your husband? Would you like him to know your actions have made the both of you unwelcome at the home of the Richmond Earldom? My grandfather may not be a duke, but he *is* influential in the House of Lords."

When Nicholas's fingers entwined with hers, Fiona drew herself as straight as possible. "My husband has spoken his piece. I believe it is time for you to leave, Your Grace."

Chapter 29

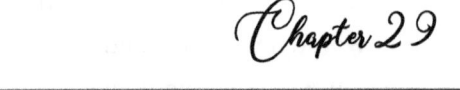

Nicholas's heart dropped into his stomach when Fiona appeared in the doorway to his father's study. How long had she been in there? How much had she heard? No matter what Fiona now knew, the problem before him remained. He needed to get rid of the interloper.

He levelled the duchess with as hard a glare as he could manage. "You are no longer welcome here, Your Grace. Leave." He ensured his voice was harder than it had been thus far. His wife had to know he did not want her here regardless of how this situation appeared.

"You would take her part over me." The duchess's eyes held no sign of tears, no sadness in their depths. Instead, her chin lifted, and the rancour in her gaze was unmistakable. "Do not think your wife will be welcomed by the *ton*. I will see to it those of quality shun her. You will see. No one will invite you to their parties or balls. You will be snubbed by all of London."

"Perhaps," said Fiona with a curve to one side of her lips. "But as the wife of Viscount Hatton, I have such extraordinary sources of happiness attached to my situation. My husband loves me—he said so himself—he is attentive, and we take pleasure in each other's company. If those in London choose to exclude us, I believe we could be content in the country or at Moydrum. So, you see, I have no cause to repine."

Nicholas squeezed his wife's hand. "I would be content to spend my life at Moydrum with you by my side. Besides, those of consequence to me will accept you, regardless of what the duchess says or does."

"Since your family has been so welcoming, I would not think to doubt your friends." Fiona's countenance gave no hint of disquiet.

"I am relieved you have such faith in my ability to choose my friends."

"Why should I doubt you?" The tilt of her head implied a challenge that made him smile. Since his response about Moydrum, they had both faced each other and ignored the duchess. She deserved no such attention, but were they to continue on as they were until the woman realised she was not welcome?

Nicholas turned his body towards the lady who owned his heart. "I cannot imagine. I am the most trustworthy of souls."

"Trustworthy? I was merely commenting on your amiability and loyalty. Most gentlemen of character would be more inclined to seek those traits in a trusted friend. Would they not?"

"You think me amiable then?"

She followed his lead and faced him head-on, perching her free hand on her hip. "When you wish to be, yes. You can also be recalcitrant—"

They both startled at the slam of the door.

He wasted no time and drew Fiona into his arms. "She is gone...finally."

"I was not certain I could continue such random nonsense for much longer."

"Random nonsense? So you do not find me amiable or loyal?"

She shoved at his shoulder with a scoff. "You are confident enough without further compliments. I do have a question about what happened before I entered."

He blew out an exhale. She would want to know if he truly loved her. "Of course. Whatever you wish to know, I shall tell you. I have naught to hide. The duchess approached me as I departed the cardrooms to return to you. She refused to let me pass when I attempted to enter the ballroom, so I came here in the hopes of persuading her to leave me be."

Fiona placed the tips of her fingers over his lips before he could explain further. "I was here before you entered with her, and I heard the argument as you came down the corridor. You freely gave your opinion on her presence for anyone to hear. The tone of your voice I shall not forget. I have only heard it so unforgiving when you addressed Sir Malcolm after his comment to me."

"Well, he deserved the utmost censure for what he said."

"Yet you did not know his insult at that time."

"You brought your riding crop down upon his face. I was sure it must have been serious indeed for you to have responded so."

His wife bit her lip, but with his finger, he freed the tempting bit of flesh. "You can ask me anything, Fee."

Her eyes widened. "You called me Fee."

"I have called you thus in my head more than once, and I did call you Fee once before, although I had not done so on purpose."

She nodded. "I remember."

"Do you object?"

"No, you surprised me—both times." Her hand slid up to his shoulder as though she was anchoring herself. "Did you mean it...when you said you love me?" Her gaze held his. Of course, his wife would not shrink from what she wanted to know. She was braver than most.

"I had wondered how long it would take you to ask." He drew her a little closer. "I do—I do love you with all my heart. I think I loved you from the moment you unseated me from my horse. I shall never forget how you stood before me, bold as brass, and demanded to know who dared trespass on Moydrum lands. When you ripped your hood from your head, I had the wind knocked out of me a second time that morning. I had never met a lady such as you, and to confess the ungentlemanly part of myself: God, I wanted you."

She burst into laughter but wiped a tear from one eye. "I realised I wanted you the first time you kissed me."

"I am not worried if you do not carry the same depth of attachment that I do since I am certain—" She covered his mouth with her fingers once again. Why would she just not let him speak?

"Hush now. You should know that I have loved you for some time now, although I would not say it was from when I knocked you from your horse. I never understood why you stoked my ire so, but I believe now that I was fighting whatever feelings were blooming within my heart. I was such a silly goose and so determined to be ridiculous. How you fell in love with an immature, naïve girl like me I cannot understand."

He cradled her cheeks in his palms and kissed her. "I could not get you out of my mind. Often, I dreamt of you berating me, your eyes upbraiding me, and I could think of naught but stopping your mouth, much as I often did. It was no wonder that whenever you were angry, I would kiss you."

Her eyebrows lifted. "Since you mentioned it, did these dreams of me end with a kiss?"

His cheeks burned as he chuckled and shrugged.

"I do not fault you for it," she said. "I thought of you in indecent ways as well."

He straightened a bit. "You did? You must tell me. How did you think of me?"

She pushed at his chest and tried to pull away. "No, I shall do no such thing."

His arm wrapped around her waist and brought her flush to his body. When he pressed his lips to that place under her ear, her breathing hitched just as it always did. "Let us retire."

"The ball is not over. Besides, as much as I would prefer to hide away with you, we should ensure the duchess departs."

He groaned and dropped his head to her shoulder. "I want her gone from our lives."

"Perhaps she will leave of her own accord, and we shall not be forced to embarrass her or ourselves."

After one last sweet kiss to her lips, he held out his elbow, so she would be on his arm when they entered the ballroom. By keeping her close, he would ensure the duchess knew Fiona was protected. "Promise me that as soon as she is gone, we shall retire."

"If you wish."

He forced one foot in front of the other as they returned to the ballroom. More than anything, he wanted to be alone with his wife. They had confessed they loved each other. He had no desire to return to the ballroom much less ensure Her Grace had departed the ball.

When they approached the entrance, a footman stepped from a nearby servants' corridor and opened the door for them. "Sir."

"Thank you, Ian," said Fiona.

His grandmother bustled up to them. "The Duchess of Clarence entered appearing furious and marched over to her husband. A few people around him gasped as she began to speak. Your grandfather has approached in an effort to quell any scene, but you must hasten to tell me what has happened."

Nicholas pinched the bridge of his nose. Fiona had been correct that they needed to return. "She cornered me outside the ballroom and insisted we talk. I told her I am not interested in any information she may have, but she insisted. She has insulted me and my wife and has threatened to have us both shunned for the Season. I have moved to protect Fiona and myself from her vitriol and told her to leave."

His grandmother glanced between them and pursed her lips. "Very well." She straightened and motioned for them to follow her into the melee. When she reached his grandfather's side, she placed her hand in the crook of his elbow.

"What is the meaning of this Hatton?" said the duke in a booming voice.

"I am not best pleased by your wife's treatment of mine, and I will not tolerate her disrespect a moment longer. She has made her distaste for Lady Hatton's company quite obvious over the past fortnight, so I would think the disdain she feels would behove her to depart without delay and not return. One would believe she would have declined my grandmother's invitations after their first time in company, yet Her Grace has attended every luncheon and dinner and has come to this ball. I am simply relieving her of any obligation to remain."

The duchess's eyes shifted between her husband and Nicholas while he explained, a noticeable release of her shoulders evident when he did not mention her propositions. He may not hold any feelings of affection for the lady anymore, but he would not reveal her true intentions unless he had no choice in the matter.

"As I explained," said his grandfather, "my grandson would never make such a demand without good reason—unless your wife wishes to apologise for any slights she has made towards Lady Hatton. If your wife were to show true remorse, I am certain Lord Hatton would be gracious enough to forgive her.

The duchess scoffed. "I would never—"

"The Duchess of Clarence does not belittle herself so in public. She has done naught that requires an apology. Richmond, I am insulted at the accusation that my wife has behaved inappropriately. We shall not stay where we are to be maligned. We take no leave of you nor your wife."

The duke turned without acknowledging Nicholas or Fiona, although he could not be upset at being snubbed. He had never enjoyed the Duke of Clarence's company.

His grandfather wore a dark expression. "I would see you in private. I will know what has occurred to cause such drastic measures. Dearest, pray, see to our guests." Gran bustled away, waving Lizzy and Amelia to join her.

No sooner had those around them returned to their conversations than Grandpapa led them to the library and closed the door behind them. "I know the duchess has been rude to Fiona during her time in this house, but your grandmother had determined to leave matters be and never invite her to one of our events in the future so long as the duchess held on to her vitriol. We hoped to maintain alliances."

Nicholas took in a deep breath and released it. "Just before the duchess accepted the duke's hand, I had asked her to marry me, and she had accepted. She was not aware of the contract being spoken of by her parents and the duke, and when she discovered their plans, she was overwrought but wed him anyway."

His grandfather's eyes widened for a moment. "Your grandmother and I thought the two of you to be friends and that perhaps you both held tendres for each other at different times, but we never knew your friendship had become more. I now understand why you changed some around that time. I suppose it also explains her dislike of Fiona, although why she would not want to see you happy— if she cared, why would she not wish you joy?"

"After the birth of her son, she approached me at the Ormonde ball. She desired a more intimate relationship since she had birthed the duke's heir. I suppose you could say she renewed her addresses this evening. 'Tis why I wished to depart for Ireland without delay." His grandfather would be shocked, yet he would not keep any portion of this from him. If their reputations or standing were called into question, as earl, his grandfather needed to know.

Grandpapa paled and glanced at Fiona. "You have told your wife?"

"She had known of the duchess since before we wed. I have kept nothing from her."

"In fact, I overheard their argument this evening," said Fiona. "I have been aware of the duchess's reasonings for her visible dislike. Her response to my existence will have no effect on me. She made her choice, and she must live with the consequences of her decisions. We are not responsible for her unhappiness nor her disappointment." She was correct. At one time, he could not imagine being free of the duchess's influence, but after tonight, he could only claim the influence of one lady—his wife's.

His grandfather nodded. "Well said."

"I am aware this rift could cause problems—"

"Do not worry. I agree Her Grace has behaved in a manner ill-suited to her status as well as in a manner meant to insult Lady Hatton, who will become Lady Richmond one day. I hope you will forgive us, Fiona, for allowing her to remain unchecked for so long, but we knew her as a young girl. It has been exceedingly difficult to witness her behaviour towards you."

Fiona hastened forward and grasped Grandpapa's hands. "Pray, do not take yourself to task for it. I have understood your position, and I know you hoped she would accept me. I am not upset with you. In the end, I do not know if I am truly angry with the duchess. I believe what I feel is no more than pity for her."

"You are too good," said Grandpapa.

His wife laughed. "No, I would never claim to be too good. Perhaps I see my good fortune where she cannot find hers. I would pray she seeks some contentment in being a mother to her child. Not everyone is so blessed."

"We should not leave your grandmother fending for herself."

"We are retiring," said Nicholas.

"No, you must return to the ballroom lest people believe I am displeased. After a quarter hour, you may sneak away if you so choose."

Nicholas let his shoulders drop. "Very well."

His grandfather chuckled. "I expected more of an argument."

"As long as I have my wife on my arm, I can bear it."

Fiona smiled and set her hand upon his forearm where it belonged. "That is good since I would not seek to be anywhere else."

Chapter 30

Nicholas took in the ballroom before him. Little had changed since the altercation with the duke. The same glowing candles, the same glittering crystal and silver, and the same finely dressed peers and gentlemen accompanied by their wives and daughters milled about the room. A number of couples had come after the scene earlier and ensured he and Fiona were well. The guests' questions and well-wishes never lasted long before they continued their evenings. No doubt a few desired tittle tattle to take back to their friends.

"Come," Nicholas whispered near Fiona's ear. He could not help but grin at the gooseflesh that prickled along the back of his wife's neck, disappearing under the silk of her gown. She was as susceptible to him as he was to her. How could he not take pleasure in that knowledge?

At her slight shift towards him, he then took her hand to lead her through the throng, nodding to gentlemen here and there, until they reached the doors. More guests milled in the hall, so he ducked into the servants' passage and up the stairs until they reached the family wing, startling one maid they happened upon on. He placed a finger over his lips as they passed to which the maid giggled and continued on her way.

At the end of a corridor, Nicholas steered Fiona into his dressing room. "I told my valet I would not require him tonight. Will your maid be waiting for you?"

"No, I saw no reason for her to spend the entire night awaiting my call."

Fiona stepped ahead of him, entered his bedchamber, and stopped beside his bed. One by one, she pulled each of the pins from her long red tresses and allowed them to fall about her shoulders. His breath caught in his chest. Lord, but she was beautiful and the more unkempt she was, the more attractive he found her.

As soon as her hair was about her shoulders, she turned and drew it over her shoulders. "Will you unfasten the back?"

He had no need to be asked more than once! His eager fingers fumbled with each button until the bodice was loosened, and he turned her around to bring her into his arms. Their remaining clothing was removed between kisses as they helped each other undress, laughing at a few particularly difficult moments. Their amusement never lasted long. He was too impatient to hold her close and demonstrate how much he loved her. He had done so before, of course, but this time, his wife not only shared his feelings, but knew of his love for her. They would have a freedom they had never had before.

When Fiona stood naked before him wearing nothing but her necklace, Nicholas hastened to rid himself of his trousers. As he gazed at her, he was struck a bit dumb. How had he been so fortunate as to marry this lady? He had hoped to wed a worthy woman, which was unfair. He needed to be worthy of her as well.

He slid his hand around her side, relishing the soft velvet of her flesh as he pulled her to him. The sensation of her pressed against him was too much for him to ignore. He had no desire to release her, so while he sought out her lips, he steered her the remaining few steps to the bed where he sat and pulled her astride him.

His fingers combed through her hair as he enjoyed the pleasures of her kiss. With her position upon his lap, her chest was too tempting and too close to ignore. His lips trailed along her collarbone, bestowing tiny nips and peppering kisses, before venturing further and drawing her nipple into his mouth. When he suckled hard, she gasped and entwined her fingers into his hair, grinding down upon his already painful erection. As her passion mounted, she held his head so tightly to her breast, he would have had difficulty moving if he wished—not that he wanted to. Those little noises in the back of her throat and the digging of her fingernails into his shoulders only served to increase his own ardour.

He nipped the side of her other breast, and Fiona moaned and drew his head back to claim his lips once again. Her small hands pushed at his shoulders until his back met the coolness of the sheets, then she sat up baring herself to him.

She was the most stunning creature he had ever beheld. Her flaming tresses fell about her shoulders and her emerald eyes gazed upon him with such longing he could barely draw breath.

"I love you, Nicholas."

He gasped and closed his eyes when she took him and guided him home. His hands came to rest on her hips as he let her move as she would. He could do no more than watch as she rode him, her palms on his chest, and her lips parted. In his imaginings, he had dreamt of her being so uninhibited, but the reality was far better. Yet, he wanted her in his embrace.

When he sat up, he wrapped one arm around her waist. "I love you, too."

The sensation of her against him was too much. His heart was so full of her. How would he not expire from it all?

He aided her in her movements as they rocked and relished the difference their love made upon their coupling. Despite how their marriage came about, the revelation had levelled the last barriers that existed between them, which had to be why this was so much more intimate than before. Their gazes held and the love in Fiona's heart was evident upon her countenance, or maybe it had been there from the day they wed. He had been so convinced she felt no more than friendship, perhaps he had been blind to what was before him.

"Fiona, I—" He could not force the words from his mouth.

The arm wrapped around her quickened their rhythm, while the fingers of his other hand sought out what would ensure her completion. When he brushed over it, the fire that lit in her eyes and the gasping cry urged him to increase his efforts.

"Nicholas, I cannot. 'Tis too much."

She whimpered as he continued, the sound increasing his need for release. Two more flicks of his finger was all it took for her to curl around him and bury her face against his shoulder while the room filled with the cries of her satisfaction.

Nicholas gritted his teeth to ensure she reached that pinnacle before he succumbed and let his wash over him, dragging him under the wave. He could not draw breath as he lost himself in the sweetness—in the rightness of his wife. She was more than he had ever hoped for, and she was his. Nothing could be more perfect.

Fiona's lips brushed against his temple, his eyelid, then his nose as she unfurled herself from him. Tears rolled down her cheeks, and he cradled her face in his palms.

"Did I hurt you?"

She shook her head. "No, I am just so relieved and happy. I feel so silly. I used to never cry. I do not know why I seem to be in tears so often now."

With a gentle touch, he brushed the damp from her jawline. "You are not silly. I could not speak my heart was so full. When I realised I was in love with you, it was so stupid to keep my feelings from you. Even if you did not reciprocate my feelings, I know you would never tease or laugh at me."

"But I did the same. I have always had a difficult time trusting people. While I do not remember my mother leaving, I have always believed myself a curse to those I love. Maybe my mother would not have left if I had not been born. My father would have his wife, and I would not have caused him so much disquiet—"

This time, Nicholas covered her mouth with his fingers. "Your father loves you, and I doubt he would change a thing. You are certainly no curse. Knowing you love me is my greatest blessing. I would have never thought being knocked from my horse would be a circumstance I would be thankful for, but in this instance, I can only be so. Otherwise, we would not have met."

"We would have met," she said. "My father would have called upon you, and we would have been introduced at Lord Meath's ball."

"But would our story have taken a similar course? Without our singular meeting, would we have reached this same point?"

She bit her lip, then shrugged one shoulder. "I do not know, but I prefer to think we would. I do not want to consider my life without you in it."

He toyed with a curl that had fallen over her breast. Her curls were like silk through his fingers. "I would not want to think of my days without you either." He laid back upon the coverlet and pressed his palm to her stomach. "One day, I know you will grow round with our child, and while I anticipate the day, I must confess that I am relieved he has not come yet. For now, I am enjoying having you to myself."

"And the rest of your family," she said with a laugh.

"And the rest of my family." He had almost forgotten about them.

Fiona glanced about them and burst into chuckles. "Your legs are hanging off the bed."

"I wanted you close, which would have been almost impossible while trying to manoeuvre to the centre." He grabbed her with a swift movement and rolled them while Fiona shrieked at the abruptness of the motion to shift them to the middle. "Is that better? Now you have the pillow to lay your head upon." He yanked the coverlet from behind him to cover them both.

"You are so considerate." That glint in her eye made him dig his fingers into her ribs.

"Always with the cheeky responses."

"You like my cheeky responses," she gasped out between giggles.

He sighed and ceased his onslaught. "Yes, I must confess I do. I love your cheeky responses, I love your ability to soothe my niece with tenderness, I love that you do not let your sex keep you from taking part in a diversion—"

"Though you did claim otherwise for a time."

"Yes, well I was a numbskull."

"A numbskull?" Her voice was tinged with laughter.

"I heard it on the ship when I was sailing to Ireland. From the way the sailor used it, it means 'stupid.'"

She smiled widely. "Can I tell your sister and your cousins you confessed to that?"

"To being an idiot?" He scoffed. "No, you may not. But lastly, I love so many things about you, I could go on for entirely too long, and I must confess I am distracted by the sight of you beside me at this moment. You undo me, Fee, and it is terrifying. You hold my heart in your hands."

Her palm cradled his cheek. "When I drew my pistol on you and you glared up at me, I lost my breath at the handsome man upbraiding me with his eyes. I am just as undone by you. Do not believe for one moment that I shall not protect your heart as if it were my own; for if you hurt, I shall as well. I could have never loved another as I love you."

Nicholas rolled his wife under him. "We are quite the pair, are we not?"

"Disgustingly besotted?" Her one eyebrow winged up.

"I could not have described our situation better myself."

The End

265

Acknowledgements

What a crazy roller coaster! I started this book and had some idea where it was going, but Nicholas and Fiona had minds of their own. The first time, they got a bit friskier than I'd planned before marriage and took it in a direction I didn't want to go, so I backpedalled and tried again. The second was bland. Nicholas and Fiona are anything but bland. Then, came incarnation number three, which is what you have just read. I owe a huge thanks to Carol S. Bowes, my friend and editor on most of my books, who video chatted the three versions and agreed that this was the direction Nicholas and Fiona should take.

I also am very appreciative to Marie who proofreads every word and sends me a list of corrections just for the fun of doing it. She's a gem to have on my team. I can't thank her enough for her contribution.

Next, to my friends and family who are always supportive. My husband who can make me crazy but is always on my side—even when I'm not sure it's my side.

And lastly, to my fans and readers, who I am always thankful for. You allow me to get these stories out of my head so a new one can take over. Thank you for keeping me from boredom and for your unwavering support.

Hugs and love to all!

About the Author

L.L. Diamond is more commonly known as Leslie to her friends and Mom to her three kids. A native of Louisiana, she spent the majority of her life living within an hour of New Orleans before following her husband all over as a military wife. Louisiana, Mississippi, California, Texas, New Mexico, Nebraska, England, Missouri, and now Maryland have all been called home along the way.

Aside from mother and writer, Leslie considers herself a perpetual student. She has degrees in biology and studio art but will devour any subject of interest simply for the knowledge. Her most recent endeavors have included certifications to coach swimming and a number of fitness certifications. As an artist, her concentration is in graphic design, but watercolor is her medium of choice with one of her watercolors featured on the cover of her second book, *A Matter of Chance*. She is also a member of the Jane Austen Society of North America. Leslie also plays flute and piano, but much like *Pride and Prejudice's* Elizabeth Bennet, she is always in need of practice!

Author's works:

Rain and Retribution
A Matter of Chance
An Unwavering Trust
The Earl's Conquest
Particular Intentions
Particular Attachments
Unwrapping Mr. Darcy

The Wedding Planners Series:
Book 1: *It's Always Been You*
Book 2: *It's Always Been Us*
Book 3: *It's Always Been You and Me*
Book 4: *He's Always Been the One*

Undoing
Confined with Mr. Darcy
Agony and Hope
His Perfect Gift
That Perfect Someone
The Peculiarity of Mr. Darcy's Mirror

The Montford Cousins:
Book 1: *An Endeavour to be Worthy*
Book 2: *A Gentleman of Worth*
Book 3: *A Worthy Woman*
Coming Soon: Book 4: *Jane's story (Untitled)*

www.ingramcontent.com/pod-product-compliance
Lightning Source LLC
Chambersburg PA
CBHW060406180626
46817CB00007B/2537